3 8043 27027952 0

KU-072-451

Knowsley L......... Ser...

Knowsley Council

Please return this book
before the date sho...

Maher HU3
Gallagher "
DAVIES
Boland
?

W'

COUNTRY LOVING

For Ruby Grant and her husband Oliver, life slows down alarmingly from the moment they move to the country and set foot in Troy Cottage. At least Ruby can finally start writing her novel in peace – until her daughter Poppy turns up with boyfriend and dog in tow, and announces she's pregnant! Then son Josh needs somewhere to do his washing and her father wants to stay for Christmas... Despite this, Ruby finds village life surprisingly seductive, especially Hamish, a handsome journalist. Surely there's no harm in a little crush – but can Ruby avoid the hazards of country loving?

COUNTRY LOVING

COUNTRY LOVING

by

Julie Highmore

Magna Large Print Books
Long Preston, North Yorkshire,
BD23 4ND, England.

British Library Cataloguing in Publication Data.

Highmore, Julie
    Country loving.

    A catalogue record of this book is
    available from the British Library

    ISBN   0-7505-1975-4

First published in Great Britain in 2002 by Review
An imprint of Headline Book Publishing

Copyright © 2002 Julie Highmore

Cover illustration by arrangement with
Headline Book Publishing Ltd.

The moral right of Julie Highmore to be identified as the author
of this work has been asserted by her in accordance with the
Copyright, Designs and Patents Act, 1988

Published in Large Print 2003 by arrangement with
Headline Book Publishing Ltd.

All Rights reserved. No part of this publication may be
reproduced, stored in a retrieval system, or transmitted in any
form or by any means, electronic, mechanical, photocopying,
recording or otherwise without the prior permission of the
Copyright owner.

Magna Large Print is an imprint of Library Magna Books Ltd.

Printed and bound in Great Britain by
T.J. (International) Ltd., Cornwall, PL28 8RW

All characters in this publication
are fictitious and any resemblance
to real persons, living or dead,
is purely coincidental.

For Pam and George

Thank you, David, for all your support and encouragement. Thanks to Louise, Philip, Andy, Carol, Sophie and Kate for the helpful feedback. And a big thank you to Flora and Caroline, and everyone involved at Headline.

PART ONE

JUNE

'Oh yes, and a nice bottle of wine,' I tell Oliver.

'Right,' he says, jotting it down. 'OK, that's pitta bread, humous, Earl Grey, *Guardian*, olives and a bottle of wine. Australian Cabernet?'

'Definitely.'

He folds the list and tucks it in his shirt pocket. 'Ready?' Our first Upper Muckhill outing. Very exciting.

'Settled in to old Bert's place then?' asks a petite, grey-haired passer-by, who looks as though she might weigh less than her two bags of food. She stops and puts her shopping down. 'Jean,' she says with several puffs and a quick nod of the head. 'Jean Crowbar.' (Or something.)

Friendly locals, hooray. 'I'm Ruby Grant,' I tell her with a big smile. She nods and puffs again and I can't help thinking she'd be better off without that cable-knit cardigan on such a day. 'And this is Oliver Jeff–'

'Jeffries,' she says. 'Yes, I know. Second

17

husband. Architect. You work from home.'

Oliver's jaw drops. 'And my shoe size?'

She looks down at his feet. 'Meg – that's Ted's wife – thought you'd be a ten or eleven. Only we was sorting through Bert's things, God rest his soul, and wondered if you could make use of his shoes. Big like you, he was.'

Oliver stares wide-eyed at the woman and I hook my arm through his. 'We'd better get to the shop,' I say, steering us away. 'Nice meeting you, Jean.'

'Ted's out of lard, if you was wanting any,' she calls out. 'Had a bit of a run on it, he says.'

'Right.'

'Got a lovely bit of tongue in today, though.'

'Oh, good.'

We're outside the shop and Oliver shakes the hand that's been thrust at him. 'Veronica Weatherall, parish councillor,' announces its owner – late fifties, rigid blonde hair, all done up in Tory blue. 'You must be Oliver.'

She turns to me. 'And Ruby, I believe. I hear you've got two grown-up children. You barely look old enough, my dear.' For some reason this doesn't feel like a compliment.

'Joshua and Polly, isn't it?'

'It's Poppy, actually.'

'Mm, unusual name. And what do they do, your children?' Well, mostly they mind their own business, I'm thinking, as I scratch around for a better word than 'unemployed'.

'They're both in the leisure industry,' chips in Oliver.

'Ah yes, very worthwhile. We're hoping to get a little sports centre going in the infants' school annexe. Volleyball for the seventy plus, that sort of thing.' She opens a large clip-top handbag and pulls out a spiral notepad. 'While I've got you here, can I put you both down for bus-shelter litter duty? You'll find we all tend to muck in in Muckhill.' She unscrews her fountain pen top and looks up at our horrified faces. 'Shall we say every other Tuesday?'

In the dark and chilly village shop, Oliver and I try not to quietly weep. After scouring the shelves in vain we eventually take a bottle of Liebfraumilch, two cod-in-butter-sauces and a tabloid to the till, where Ted introduces himself but we feel we needn't bother.

'Got yourselves a bargain there,' he says,

huge bushy eyebrows bobbing up and down below a completely bald head. It's as though all his hair one day decided to relocate. We look quizzically at our purchases. 'Old Bert Roberts' place,' he adds.

'Ah right, Troy Cottage,' I say with what I hope isn't too smug an expression. It certainly was a good price. We are, however, beginning to find out why.

'Wanted to buy it myself, but what with business being a bit slow...' he says as he scans our items.

I look around the shop and wonder why that could be.

'That's eight pound forty-three, if you please.'

'You what?' exclaims Oliver, raking the items back out of their carrier bag. 'Look, two tiny portions of endangered fish, a bottle of undrinkable plonk and a fascist rag. Let's face it, Ted, you should be paying us.'

Ted, momentarily stunned, then bursts into a hearty laugh. 'Bit of a wit, are we?'

Back home, after Oliver and I have stoically worked our way through dinner, I take my new journal upstairs and sit on the bed, pen in mouth, first snow-white empty page propped on my thighs.

Nice thing about the village, I write, *is average age roughly sixty-eight. So much better than living next to second-year university students, who look as though someone should still be crossing them over the road, and who make you feel old and boring when you ask them to clear front garden rubbish due to rat sighting. I'm guessing no one in Upper Muckhill will play hip-hop till the police hammer on their door either.*

One quiet, bordering-on-dull evening I have an urge to contact people. I start with Josh.

'Hi, it's Mum.'

'Alright?' he says through a yawn.

'How are you, then?'

'Good, yeah. Haven't seen you for ages. I came round your house the other day, only the key wasn't under the stone. So I couldn't get in.'

'That's because Oliver and I have moved.'

'Uh? Oh yeah ... Christ, I forgot.'

'I put our new address and phone number through your door. Didn't you find it?'

'Wait up,' he says, and I hear small mountains of mail being kicked around, then the noise of ripping envelope.

'Upper Muckhill?' he says eventually,

drawing on a cigarette. 'Where's that then?'

'Actually, they pronounce it "Muckle" round here. You should come and stay. It's lovely. Bit of a trek, though.' I explain about the two bus journeys it takes to get here, and that some of those only run on Wednesdays and Fridays.

'You mean it's in the countryside?'

'Well, yes.'

He begins opening more letters, says, 'Shit, the bastards are cutting off the electric tomorrow,' and generally forgets I'm there.

'Josh?'

'Mm?'

'If you want to visit I could always come and pick you up.'

'Oh right, yeah, that'd be cool,' he says, suddenly enthusiastic. 'Got fuckin loads of clothes to wash.'

Next I ring my brother and talk about our fabulous new rural life: the tranquillity, the lack of stress, how much healthier we both feel. 'It was such a good move,' I say. Oliver's guffawing behind me. I don't tell Tim we're plagued with mice and passing miserable evenings on two deck chairs in the living room – both sofas refusing to fit through any Troy Cottage door. Nor do I mention that the old kitchen range I bragged endlessly about is now The Enemy, and every hot meal so far has come from the microwave in a bag you have to cut open. 'We wish we'd done it years ago,' I add doggedly.

Tim says he'll call me back tomorrow as he's expecting five dinner guests any minute. Picturing his pristine candlelit flat and bevy of witty, if somewhere to the right of Augusto Pinochet, guests, I feel a pang of envy. The sole exchange in Troy Cottage this evening having been:

Me: 'What's that smell?'

Oliver: 'Search me.'

On Sunday the bell ringers strike up and I wake startled and palpitating while Oliver rolls around the bed saying, 'What the...' I put my pillow over his head, then make my way towards the kettle, clambering over un-opened crates, then squeezing past forests of pot plants and those old shelving units I was sure we'd find use for. When I whine about the lack of space, Oliver says not to forget that the house was built for folk who required only a couple of oil lamps and a spinet to make their lives complete.

'So much for quiet country life,' he grumbles when finally emerging from bed. He's determined to hate everything about it.

Reckons the average IQ is a single figure, says his body isn't getting the recommended daily amount of carbon dioxide, that he can't sleep at night for the deafening silence. I must admit he's not looking his best; the crisp country light showing up lots of grey in his once-lovely fair locks, and the tiny doorways forcing his six-foot-one frame into a semipermanent stoop. ('Oh how quaint,' we'd cried on first seeing those doors four months ago.)

I hurry to the hall mirror to see if I too am changing. No, still the same longish, thick-ish, dirty-blonde hair of indeterminate style and texture. Bit of a mess, really. I think of a plait, pull my hair back and start weaving. Uh-uh, too *Little House on the Prairie*.

Back in the kitchen, Oliver continues to grumble about this and that. It took a huge effort to get him to leave the city, but after months of pressure he suddenly caved in when I pointed our that if we lived some-where remote we'd no longer have student neighbours, or my children and their friends letting themselves in at two a.m. to drink the last of the milk.

After breakfast I'm nominated hunter-gatherer and set off for provisions in the new Range Rover I've yet to get the hang of.

I feel like King Kong on a tightrope as I slowly tackle the narrow country lanes, burying myself in hedgerow each time a car approaches. At one point a cyclist overtakes me with a friendly wave.

The supermarket brings welcome relief from the chaos of Troy Cottage: the smell of freshly baked bread (rather than the aroma of Bert Roberts' elderly dog); acres of things in their proper places; clean floors. It's heaven and I don't want to leave, so I take my time buying enough to feed a small town, have a cup of coffee and a Danish pastry, read a Sunday newspaper – then remember Oliver's at home with only tap water and one of Ted's stale pies.

I return to lovely, peaceful Troy Cottage to find him standing on a chair in the kitchen. 'Behind the fridge. Quick. Do something.'

I decide to make the most of this. 'OK. Tell me I can have the nice office chair and not the crap one that gives you backache.'

'Yes, yes.'

'And that you'll never again wear that hideous maroon jumper Paula made you.'

'Oh really, Roo...'

I make out I'm going to leave the room.

'OK, OK,' he says, and I move the fridge-freezer a couple of inches, plonk a cup over our fourth mouse this weekend and slide a piece of cardboard underneath. I see Oliver's knees buckle at this point, so dash to the door before he collapses on to the flagstones.

Slotting in, I write in my journal. *Upper Muckhill feeling very much like spiritual home already. Have assimilated so speedily, in fact, that am already growling at weekend day-trippers who surround village green with parked vehicles and go off in search of circular walk with map in see-through plastic pocket hung from neck – some, I note, with the word 'Map' on. Just in case one thinks it's for putting the dog in, presumably. After a five-mile, or eight-and-a-half if they take the long circle, walk they heave themselves up the last small incline to the green – desperate for refreshment and a sit-down – only to find that Ted flips his Open sign to Closed at one o'clock precisely every Saturday, and that the Dog and Gun keeps 1950s' opening hours and would rather have the receivers called in than serve food on a Sunday evening. In a small surge of pity last weekend made one young couple tea for their flask and enthused about walker-friendliness of Great Piddington, nine miles away.*

It's Saturday afternoon and I'm back in my old urban street, ringing Ali's doorbell and glancing anxiously over a shoulder at my mighty Range Rover squeezed between a skip and a recently torched Mondeo. When I ring the bell again I see movement through the frosted glass of the door and hear the dulcet tones of Ali telling me to shut the hell up.

'Well, if you're going to be like that...' I say when she appears, paint-splattered and scowling.

'Hey, Ruby.' She bends and air kisses my cheeks. 'Sorry. Thought you were the Mormons again.'

We squeeze past the lodgers' mountain bikes parked in the narrow hall, step over coats that have fallen from the newel post and arrive at the familiar demolition site, fondly referred to in the house as the kitchen – farmhouse table with just the odd speck of pine visible through the permanent debris, old squashy sofa stacked with newspapers and dozing cats, permanent smell of something slightly gone off.

'This is great timing,' she says, picking up a corkscrew and surveying the clutter for a bottle to attach it to. 'I need someone's opinion on my latest piece.'

I'm not sure if she's talking about a painting, a man or a gun, but as she's waving towards her studio I guess it's the first. Which is a shame as I have almost nothing to say about Ali's unfathomable artwork, but am now expert at telling her that whichever Mick, Rick or total Dick she's seeing is obviously insecure, afraid of intimacy, etc.

'No booze for me, Ali. I'm driving, remember.'

I watch while a large penny drops.

'Oh Christ,' she says, rolling her eyes. 'How's it going in the back of beyond?'

'Great, great. Only Oliver never stops sneezing, due to Upper Muckhill being surrounded by fields of oil seed rape, and we can't walk barefoot round the house because of all the mousetraps.'

'Traps? Bloody hell, Ruby, how barbaric. You'll be chanting in fields and sacrificing young humans before you know it. I always said the country was an uncivilised place.'

'You might be right.' I tell her about our shop. How Ted only stocks the *Sun* and the *Daily Mail*, and how all the bread comes with green spots. 'It's beautifully peaceful, though,' I add. 'Especially at night. Just the occasional sheep bleating. The odd owl.'

'Uh, creepy,' she says with a shudder,

28

wiping paint from her hands on to a tea towel. 'Hey, come and tell me what you think.'

She leads me through to her studio where I find myself standing in front of a colossal creation – part oil paint, part cloth and then anything that came to hand it seems – twigs, polystyrene trays, lengths of rope and what might be a dead animal at its centre. This is a bit of a departure from the Lucian Freud-meets-Munch portraits she usually does of her lodgers and other unsuspecting models. I put my hand to my chin and tilt my head this way and that, trying to come up with a comment that doesn't include the word crap. I say, 'Well, this is new.'

'Thought I might pebble-dash the whole thing when it's finished.'

'Good idea.'

'Apparently corporations can't get enough of this sort of thing. God, imagine never having to teach again. Cup of coffee?'

'Lovely.'

As I follow her back to the kitchen, I take in the platinum-blonde crew cut, studded ears and bare midriff. I still have problems relating this Ali to the one I knew fifteen years ago – she was Alison then – when we would natter while waiting in the playground and occasionally take tea together amid typhoons of children. In those days she had flawless Princess Di hair, was the size of a pipe cleaner, always firmly belted into a sensible mac and never without a hint of aquamarine eye-shadow. Her house was made up of acres of shiny surfaces and loos you could let your child paddle in.

'Shit,' she says now, rummaging through a wall cupboard. 'No coffee. Let's go to the Karma. I need to get out the house.'

Alison would never have run out of coffee. This was thanks in part to ex-husband, Kenneth, who left her a daily 'To do...' list on the cork board – 'Collect suits. Trim forsythia. Jif behind cooker'... A quantity surveyor, I think.

The windows of the Karma Café greet us with the usual clutter of postcard ads: 'Room to let in Buddhist, mobile-phone-free, lesbian household for non-smoking, anticapitalist, vegan single parent' being fairly typical.

Inside, I peruse the posters: 'Working with Angels for Joy and Abundance (Bring a crystal if you have one)', 'Experiencing the Wisdom of Trees', 'Feng Shui Consultant'... Hey, feng shui. Just what Troy Cottage needs. I find a pen and jot down the number. For all we know, Oliver and I have our deck chairs in hopelessly ill-omened places.

Not much has changed in the years I've been coming to the Karma. Early thirties couples with rosy-cheeked offspring still wander in, remove four cycle helmets of assorted sizes, then patiently encourage little Beatrice or Jacob to eat a plate of serious salad. 'No, darling, they don't have Monster Munch. Come on, one more broccoli floret and we'll buy you something nice at Mr Kahn's shop.'

'Anyway,' says Ali, after we've joined a long communal table. She's telling me about her latest, a fibreglass sculptor. 'He's exactly my type. Artistic, sensitive. It's going really well.'

'That's great. So, are you saying he answers his phone, lets you spend entire weekends at his place, introduces you to his friends and makes plans he sticks to?'

She flicks back her nonexistent hair, and chews the inside of her mouth. 'Well, not exactly.'

I sigh and shake my head at her.

'OK, OK,' she says, stirring her tea energetically. 'But as selfish, up-their-own-arse commitmentphobics go, he's really quite nice.'

'Oh good.'

'Please, Ruby,' says someone behind. I automatically turn round, but see one of the earnest parents trying to wrestle a salt cellar from his two-year-old's rigid fingers. 'Give it to Daddy and eat your aduki beans,' he asks calmly, 'or you'll be late for your t'ai chi.'

Back home again I pick up a pen.

Fear this journal is substitute for much-announced book I should get going on. 'Good luck with the novel!' they wrote on my farewell card at the language school. 'See you on the Booker Prize programme!' Oh dear. How was I to know they'd take me so seriously when I said reason for giving up job was to move to the country and write? Actual reason for giving up job – accommodation officer for shabby, under-funded EEL establishment above a sandwich bar – was that it was crap. Although qualified to teach after a whirlwind four-week course, I knew the moment I was shown the teachers' resources room – half a shelf of course books, a photocopier with 'OUT OF ORDER' on it, and a note on the table saying, 'I've got the cassette player. Pete' – that it wasn't for me. 'Any other jobs going?' I asked, and for several years after regretted those four words.

It soon became evident that the world of the average student, whose parents were forking out thousands for 'A three-week intensive English course at a highly regarded and well-equipped school in the heart of this beautiful city', and the world of the average host family willing to accept the pitiful amount the Academy of English Excellence gave them to house, feed, water and wash the clothes of said students, were very different.

'Why they no have shower?' the students would complain. 'Why they have two taps not one? I burn myself, I freeze myself. In my country we have one tap for mix water. Why they eat boil-led potato every evening and use filty cloth for wipe plate? In my country everyone have dishwasher. Kyrgyzstan is very modern country.'

Then of course there were complaints from the other side. 'Sometimes he doesn't get in till nearly midnight. '('But Marco is thirty-eight, Mrs Butcher.')

'She refused to eat her faggots, so the kids wouldn't neither.' (Monique: 'En France we do not eat large animals' droppings.')

I had my favourite landladies, Brenda being one of them. Don't get me wrong,' she said over the phone one day, 'Vladislav's a lovely boy.

Only he will keep stealing Derek's Delta card and getting cash back on it, bless him.'

The good schools in town paid well and got host families who served croissants for breakfast and didn't use double negatives at the dinner table. I had only one of those, Mr and Mrs Beauchamps-Jones, who weren't really in it for the money. Students who stayed there were sworn to secrecy about their en-suite bathroom and the pepper-and-aubergine-tartlets-with-basil-pastry starters.

JULY

It's early evening, and Oliver and I are outside with a bottle of wine, reading Anthony and Joanna Trollope respectively.

'What's that racket?' asks Oliver, placing a finger on the page.

'Wood pigeons,' I tell him. 'They only know one song and it's not that catchy.'

'No, something else. Listen.'

Then I hear it. A kind of throaty, rumbling noise, gradually getting louder. It's coming our way and after an eternity an old Transit van pulls to a halt by our gate. We both stand to see a familiar mass of Pre-Raphaelite hair emerge from the passenger side.

'Hey, it's Poppy,' I say, and hurry down what will one day be a meandering terracotta path.

Poppy gives me a hug, then points to her six-foot-four friend, who's slowly unfurling himself from the driver's seat.

'This is Dan. Dan, Mum.'

'Hello, Dan.'

'Easy.' He nods his shorn head then goes to the back of the van and lets a dog out.

'Come on, Ganja. Come on, girl,' he says, clapping his hands and heading for the house. 'Time for munchies.'

I turn to Oliver but he's disappeared. Hiding the milk, I expect.

After drinks all round, I give them a guided tour of the cottage while Oliver rustles up a pasta dish. As we pass through the kitchen on our way to the garden Poppy mentions that Dan's an organic-only veggie, is that a problem? Oliver tells her you wouldn't find a more organic house than this one. I think he's referring to the strange fungi ballooning in the downstairs loo.

'Cool,' says Dan.

At the bottom of the garden I heave open the door of the large brick-built shed and lead us in through the cobwebs.

'God, it's enormous,' echoes Poppy's voice.

While I fumble around for the light switch, Ganja runs in and sniffs at various unrecognisable items left by Mr Roberts. A forty-watt bulb comes on and Dan goes into raptures. 'Hey, electricity,' he's saying just as Oliver joins us. 'This would make a great home. You know, for like a couple or something.' He points at our two stacked sofas.

'Even got furniture. Wicked.'

'Actually, it's going to be a light and airy study with a Scandinavian ambience,' I say, but I'm not sure they're listening. Poppy's carrying out some sort of measurements with the aid of spread arms, Dan's checking that the old metal windows work and Ganja's cocking a territorial leg in one corner. I turn to Oliver and watch the colour drain from his cheeks.

Journal entry (one a.m.). *Stepparenthood. Have often wondered how I'd have fared if Oliver, and not myself had had a fourteen-year-old daughter and a son of almost sixteen when we got together. We met at my neighbour's 'street party'. 'Well, you know...' Charlotte the ceramicist whispered outside our houses when she invited me, '...all the* interesting *people in the street.' I guessed that precluded Bill and Pauline with the cartwheel on the front of their house, Terry and Michele (Tel and Chel) with four under-fives and no volume control on their TV, and Strange Anthony with trains in his loft. And I was right.*

'Hi,' said a nice-looking, fair-haired man as he let me in through Charlotte's basement door. 'I'm Oliver. Bit of an interloper.' We shook hands, got me a drink and chatted in a corner

for most of the evening. He was from the other side of town and had been talked into coming to the party by Jeff at number four. He said there'd be lots of desperate women here. I laughed and looked over at where eight or so females were hanging on every word of Adam, the nutritional therapist: patchy beard, softly spoken, collarless shirt and undoubtedly gay. Cath and Ali were bravely dancing to some Andean music, and Charlotte was once again trying the phone of the all-male, shared postgrad-student house opposite.

Oliver and I saw quite a bit of each other after that – always meeting in town because I'd told him my children were four and six and cute as buttons. After a fortnight or so I came clean in a big way, spewing out my despair at having to get not one, but both of them out of police cells in the past week – 'Josh for loitering with intent and Poppy for lifting her top and flashing a police-man after a night on the cider.' Oliver then seemed keen to meet them, especially Poppy, so I invited him round for dinner one evening. Not a roaring success. None of us could eat much, due to Poppy's nose being septic from a recent pierc-ing and bearing too much resemblance to my five-hours-in-the-preparing vegetable lasagne. And despite jolly attempts by Oliver and me to get GCSE/current music/changing fashions *conversations going, Josh's only utterance was, 'Can I go now?'*

'Have you thought of boarding school?' Oliver asked as he and I washed up.

'I'm not sure they'd take me,' I said.

Wednesday is mobile library day. A large green vehicle discreetly situates itself by the village green with a take-me-or-leave-me air, while various retired folk and mums with toddlers pay it a visit. I decide to investigate. Oliver, the readaholic, has run out of books and resorted to perusing the *Parish Newsletter* in idle moments, so I go upstairs to try to entice him away from his drawing board. He's on the phone and says he'll join me out there in a tick. But I know he won't. I'd guess visiting a mobile library is one of those things he'd never really see himself doing – like taking to a moped.

I'm back a dispiriting twenty minutes later with a pile of books Oliver can't help deriding over lunch.

'Well, a lot of people like her,' I tell him as he pushes four Catherine Cookson novels to one side and reaches over the Brie for the *Parish Newsletter.*

'Anyway,' he says gruffly, 'you should be writing or something, not loafing around

41

reading these. Or there's your old job. They're always offering it to you.'

'But then I'd have to give the bread-making machine they bought me back.' I look over at the unopened box in the corner, wondering why they thought moving to the country would suddenly make me domesticated. 'Anyway,' I add, 'I *would* write if I had a surface to put the computer on.'

He raises a disapproving eyebrow at me as we both know I shouldn't be complaining. Before moving in we'd tossed a coin to see who would get the tiny boxroom upstairs and who'd have the spacious, converted outhouse to work in. Despite the fact that Paul Duffy ('Building Contractor. Large or small, just call Paul') still hasn't been round to quote for doing up the shed, I'll definitely have got the best deal. Oliver's office is so cramped he has to move his chair on to the landing before he can leave the room.

'Just call Paul' does turn up one evening with a short pencil balanced on his ear and begins to attack the shed with his chubby fingers, saying, 'Dear, dear, dear,' and 'Strewth, would you look at that?' as he wiggles bits of window frames, and stamps hard on the floorboards. I'm clutching a picture I tore out of *House & Garden* as a guide to what I'd like, but by the time he's half dismantled the place and quoted a high four-figure sum, I'm crumpling it in my pocket, perilously close to tears.

That evening I make one of my regular calls to Poppy and she asks what's up, so I tell her about the quote for the shed.

'No prob,' she says. 'Dan did a woodwork course at the tech. Well, he would have done if he hadn't dropped out. He'll do it for you. Won't you, Dan? Mum wants her shed done up.'

I hear a background, 'Cool.'

'No, no. I don't think–' I begin.

'He made his mum a really nice spice rack.'

I tell her I'll sleep on it, but the next day the familiar sound of the old Transit van grinds to a halt outside and Dan emerges with the dog and a big blue toolbox.

'Alright?' he says.

We strike a deal over coffee. Fifty pounds a day plus materials plus lunch.

Dan says, 'That'll top up the Jobseeker's Allowance nicely,' and bends down and takes a hammer from his toolbox. 'Windows first, yeah?'

I wonder how I'm going to break all this to

Oliver when he gets back from his day in London. He arrives around nine thirty, says, 'Sodding M25,' and falls into a deck chair looking exhausted, and somewhat incongruous, in his Armani suit. I hand him a large G and T and get the impression he's pleased to be home.

Query, I write later. *Can living in a village turn you religious? Found myself at a church service the other evening, when in fact had only intended to pop in and take a look at the building's Norman bits. Ted, looking odd without his grey polyester shop coat, whispered a welcome and handed over the Order of Service and a hymn book, and before I knew it I was in a congregation of fifteen, singing 'Who would true valour see' next to a small, suited man whose tumultuous voice regularly held notes three seconds longer than everyone else's. Although slightly worried about the Mediterranean vegetables left roasting in the oven, soon began experiencing mild religious fervour and the feeling that a large emotional gap was being filled. Can only put this down to context and fact that I no longer have altars of art-house cinema and Tesco to worship at, and now regret having promised vicar, who shook one of my hands with two of his and seemed inordinately pleased to see me, that I'd bring my husband along on Sunday.*

After discovering one Saturday that the village fête is upon us, I try to talk Oliver into an afternoon of hedonism on the school playing field.

'Oh, come on,' I say, tugging at him. 'They'll be crowning Miss Upper Muckhill, you know.'

'Really? Perhaps I'll see you down there, then.'

I go alone and within ten minutes I've frittered away all my money buying geraniums and guessing the number of marbles in the bottle. Rather than go home, I join the crowds gathered behind a two-foot-high rope to enjoy the daredevil motorcyclists – how vulnerable we'd feel without that rope – where I'm accosted by Veronica, the parish councillor.

'I hate to bring this up,' she says after a certain amount of small talk, 'but some of the villagers are a little concerned about the noise levels.'

A motorbike roars by, a man standing on the saddle and no one steering. 'Pardon?'

'The young gentleman working on your shed, dear.'

'Oh.' She's talking about Dan's suitcase-sized portable stereo and off-key singing. I nod with what I hope is a concerned and I'll-get-on-to-that-right-away expression.

'It was brought up at Thursday's meeting,' she tells me, and I feel myself blushing. 'Apparently they're even having to close their windows in Little Crompton.'

After apologising more times than is really necessary, I start to make my way towards the exit.

'So,' I hear Oliver saying to Miss Upper Muckhill – crowned, sashed, off-the-shoulder puff-sleeved dress, just done her GCSEs – 'what time are you marching with the majorettes, then?'

'Oliver?'

'Roo!' he says with a jump, turning his back on the beauty queen. 'Hi, hi. Um, thought I'd have a go on the...' his eyes rapidly scan the field, '...bouncy pirate ship.'

'Really?' I say, looking over to where large youths he'd normally hide behind a tree to avoid are jumping randomly and careering into one another. 'I'll come and watch.'

'Right.'

Oliver, who two weeks ago thought white spirit was a Body Shop perfume, is rapidly

46

becoming a DIY expert, throwing himself into the decorating with gusto. Things like 'grout' and 'duck tape' have now entered his vocabulary, and the retractable ruler that follows him everywhere manages to slash one of my limbs on a daily basis. When he asked one day what I thought about 'a bit of tongue and groove over the washing machine, I got quite excited for a while.

'Matt or sheen?' he asks before setting off for Do-It-All again.

'Um, whatever,' I say, and within a couple of hours he's back turning the nicotine-shade living room to Hawaiian Sunset. The change in the room is great, but the change in my spouse is unsettling. I think he's probably mining decades of stored-up energy. It's exhausting to watch and I'm beginning to miss the Oliver who found it an effort to put his toothbrush back in the rack.

One evening I catch him jotting down notes as he watches one of those, 'Sue us, see if we care' programmes, where an unwitting couple has their perfectly nice home transformed into a lilac nightmare.

'Just promise me you won't stencil any-thing,' I say, looking over his shoulder. I see him cross it off his list.

After three weeks, the newly furnished house (armchairs, yippee) looks so good – no friezes, mock four-poster bed, or handy ceiling-height cupboard to hide the TV away in – that we feel we should have some of the locals round.

'Do we know any?' asks Oliver. I say I think nor, so we wander down to the Dog and Gun in an attempt to widen our social circle – or just get one, really.

AUGUST

'Ali just rang,' I tell Oliver one Saturday morning. 'She's coming over this afternoon. Probably needs to, you know, chat.'

'Oh yes?' His eyes bob up to the ceiling and back. 'Subtext: find something to do this afternoon, Oliver, so Ali and I can character assassinate some poor guy whose only crime is not to want to shack up with her, her ghastly daughter and assorted crusty lodgers.'

'That fence needs mending.'

'How about I do it when Ali's here?'

'Good idea.'

She eventually arrives at five forty-five with what can only be described as perfection in tow. A man with a flawless, olive complexion, thick dark hair with a slight auburn hue, Andre Agassi's smile... I could go on.

'Jesus, Ruby,' she says. 'This place is barely on the map. We went to – what was it, Hamish, Upper Muddleton or something?'

'Isn't that in the next county?' asks Oliver, putting his hammer and nails to one side then shaking the stranger's hand. 'Oliver.'

'Hamish,' says a deep rich voice. 'Hamish Roselli. Actually I think we came via Wales.'

They then go into one of those conversations men seem to enjoy so. 'We turned on to the B3374 when we should have waited for the...'/ 'Ah no, you have to stay on the A97 as far as...'

I take Ali into the house and leave Oliver marking our a road map with a stick in the soil.

'Christ, Ali, where did you find him?' I whisper inside the door.

'Lovely, isn't he? Half-Scottish, half-Italian.'

'He's gor–'

'Right!' says Oliver, rubbing his hands together and beaming. I've never seen anyone so happy not to have to repair a fence. 'What'll you have?'

Apparently Hamish and a friend have just opened a café/bookshop two streets away from Ali.

'That's where we met last weekend,' she tells us. 'Hamish came over and said if I was going to read the entire works of Doris Lessing could I at least stop helping myself to the sugar lumps.'

'Lucky it was my day on, not Pete's,' says

Hamish. He smiles and deep laughter creases splay out around his chestnut eyes. Oh my. 'He'd have made a citizen's arrest when you turned down that page corner.'

'Well, I needed to go to the loo.'

Hamish attempts to ruffle her cropped hair. 'Isn't she adorable?'

No, but you are. 'So what do you do when you're not in the shop, Hamish?'

'Oh, a bit of journalism.' His eyes dart around the room. 'Investigative mostly.'

Ali turns to me. 'You know that exposé on St Mungo's school dinners?'

Hamish squirms and clears his throat. 'It hardly made the broadsheets, Ali.'

'Ah yes, wasn't it in the *Liddleton Echo?*' says Oliver, frowning. 'Something about dinner ladies skimping on portions, then feeding their families on the surplus?'

Hamish nods reluctantly and Oliver ploughs on. 'Jolly enterprising of them, I thought. I mean, what are they on? Minimum wage, I bet. And kids are all overweight these days, anyway.'

I throw him a shut-up-or-I'll-break-your-legs look and offer everyone more tea.

'Got anything stronger?' asks Ali.

I glance at my watch. 'Dog and Gun?'

53

'OK, so that's three steak and chips,' Oliver tells Betty, landlady since 1843. 'How about you, Ali?'

'Have you got anything vegetarian?'

'Oh yes, my dear.' Betty runs a shaky pencil down the menu open before us on the bar. It stops at roast chicken. 'There you are.'

'Right.'

'Served with leg of carrot and potato breasts, I believe,' says Oliver.

Ali orders salad and chips, and as we make our way to a table she grimaces at an enormous Dog and Gun mural, complete with dangling rabbits, all glassy-eyed and dripping blood. I think I hear her hyper-ventilating and put my hand on her shoulder. 'We don't have to stay long.'

'But I want to,' she says, now transfixed by the large polished snare hung above the fireplace. 'I mean, I'd hate to miss the cock-fighting.'

'No, no, my dear,' rasps a weather-beaten man from a corner table. 'Thass on Toos-days.'

His friend slowly lays a domino on the table and looks up. 'It'll be the bear-baiting tonight.'

They go back to their game, breaking into

a duet of chesty laughs, and I see Hamish throw them a quizzical look, his journalistic nostrils flaring slightly at the scent of a story. Pleasing images of Hamish paying regular investigative trips to Upper Muckhill dance through my head.

'I've often wondered what those dreadful noises were,' I say quietly to him.

A week later Dan's finishing off my study, plugged into the Walkman I gave him. A Velux window and new pine floorboards have transformed Mr Roberts' old potting shed into, well, just what I wanted. Between us we dust down and arrange the old sofas, then install desk, kettle, cushions and blinds, and I'm feeling pretty chirpy as I hand him his final week's wages.

'And here you are. A little extra for getting the new Aga going.'

'Thanks.' He packs up his tools and heads for the door, where he stops and points at the large green sofa. 'Does that one like turn into a bed?' he asks.

'Yes, it does. It's quite comfy, actually.'

'Cool,' he says, nodding. 'Cool.'

That evening, Oliver and I go down to the Dog and Gun to celebrate, accepting all kind offers of drinks from Betty and the regulars, and consequently downing way too much.

'You were right, Roo,' Oliver says, as we cling to each other and stumble home past silent stone cottages. 'It's good here. Just you, me and the pood wigeons.'

I'm dragged from sleep late next morning by the sound of a barking dog. With foggy eyes and some queasiness I go to the window, from where I believe I see strange clothes hanging haphazardly on the washing line. With a craning of the neck I also think I spot the back of a van. I guess I'm hallucinating, and through a headache the size of Birmingham, wonder if tea might be the answer. Down in the kitchen I'm on automatic pilot – filling the kettle, opening the curtains – before sporting the note under an empty milk carton. 'Mum, hope you don't mind,' it says. 'Had a bit of hassle with the landlord.'

Poppy, it seems, is pregnant.

'So's Ganja,' she tells me over our cups of black tea. 'Which is great, cos I feel we're going through this like major event together.'

I want to point out to her that Ganja will

have given birth, weaned her babies and be taking Saga holidays before Poppy's having her first contraction.

'Anyway, we told the landlord and he went berserk, right? Going on about the terms of the lease and stuff. Oh yeah, and the rent arrears ... and that mural Dan did. Anyway, if we could just stay in the shed for a few days, or like a week...'

Ganja joins us at this point, sniffing around for food and Poppy hands her the empty milk carton to chew. 'We're both having these weird cravings,' she explains. 'Me, I can't get enough of Dan's Swarfega.'

I'm convinced I'm going to be woken up any minute by Oliver with a breakfast tray and a quality newspaper, a peck on the cheek and a 'Fancy a stroll down to the pub for lunch?' But the strange dream goes on, so I try to get my head round the situation, i.e. Oliver's upstairs in a blissful world of me, him and wood pigeons, while I'm downstairs with three new tenants, plus six or seven embryonic ones, and still nowhere to write.

Later, I creep up the stairs with coffee, bracing myself for Oliver's reaction to the news – 'I can't be married to a grand-mother!' – but on the landing I hover for a while, then place the mug on the floor. Taking the key from the inside of our bedroom door I quietly lock it from the outside with a gentle click, pocket the key and retrace my steps. Downstairs the phone rings and I hurriedly grab it.

'Alright?' says Josh.

'Hi, how are you?' My head's thumping. Must find the paracetamol.

'I'm good, yeah. Listen, I was thinking of coming to visit. Only there's no buses today.'

'Oh OK, we'll come and pick you up.' What am I saying? 'About an hour?'

'Sounds good.'

I dress in some odd bits of clothing I manage to find downstairs – a sleeveless top, Oliver's shorts, which, when secured with a leather belt are faintly ridiculous but do make my legs look slim – then make my way to Poppy and Dan's new home and ask if they'd mind collecting Josh.

Five minutes later I'm backing the Range Rover through the gate to set off down the now familiar country lanes. It's the height of summer and the scenery is breathtaking, as mile after mile of colourful hedgerow brushes by. An old U2 tape of Oliver's blasts out of the cassette player and I sing along at the top of my voice. It hurts my head, but what the hell.

After a few miles I pull off the road, get out and sit for a while in a field, listening to birdsong and taking in the picturesque valley before me. It's the perfect spot to set up an easel, write a sonnet or ruminate on existential issues – as opposed, that is, to idly wondering where you can buy milk round here on a Sunday.

Having driven past dozens of closed village shops I eventually find myself on the city's outskirts in a conveyor belt of cars, careering into a superstore car park.

'Just milk, just milk,' I say over and over, but blindly grab a trolley and proceed to fill it to the point where I'm having to carry a bottle of wine under each arm while I queue at the checkout. I arrive home mid-afternoon to find Josh on his knees and looking perplexed in front of the washing machine, a can of lager in one hand and a roll-up in the other.

'Alright?'

'I'm nor sure, to be honest.' I go over and kiss the top of his head. 'Just turn the dial till C's at the top.'

'C,' he says. 'C.'

'Comes after B?'

'Got it.'

I collect the remaining bags from the car and plonk them on the table. Josh spots the Jammy Dodgers I bought especially for him and chomps his way through them while I squash packets and tins into cupboards, ram peas into a full freezer drawer and stand for a full minute holding a litre bottle of Coke, wondering where on earth to put it. Josh kindly takes it off my hands, unscrews it with a loud 'ffft' and takes a couple of swigs.

'How's it going then?' I ask. 'Found any work?'

'Well...' He's back on the biscuits and munching energetically. 'The DSS keep trying to get me jobs in telesales, customer services, that sort of crap. But I've got dead good at fucking up the interviews.'

I look over at his cigarette-burned T-shirt, threadbare trainers and scrappy goatee. 'How do you manage that then?'

'Oh, you know, make out I've got a stutter.'

'You could give it a go, Josh. They probably make quite good money in those call centres.'

'Yeah, well, I didn't get an English degree

to listen to abuse all day and have to put my fuckin hand up when I want the toilet.' He fills the kitchen with a resounding belch. 'You know Dominic, yeah? Got a First in Environmental Studies?'

'Did he? That's good.'

'He's planting fuckin fuchsias in the municipal gardens now.'

'Mm. Well, I suppose it's a foot in the door.'

Oliver joins us at this point, chin thrust forward, fury in his eyes and shirt buttoned up wrongly. 'You do realise I had to pee out of the bedroom window?'

'Alright, Oliver?'

'Oh, hello, Josh. How are you?'

'Pretty good, yeah.'

I go over to Oliver and try to give him an apologetic squeeze. He tells me Poppy and Dan eventually heard his cries for help.

'I'm sorry,' I say. It's a bit like hugging an ironing board. 'I was just trying to protect you from bad news. Only then I forgot and–'

'Well, next time you decide to lock me in the bedroom, perhaps you'd slip a chamber pot in first?'

Josh is tipping crumbs into his mouth. 'Our landlord fitted these rope ladders. You know, you just sort of unroll them when the house is on fire and you're stuck on the fourth floor?'

'Perfect,' says Oliver. He picks up a pen and makes a note.

'I keep mine hanging down all the time,' continues Josh, 'cos of all the fuckin keys I lose.' He screws up the biscuit packet and head-butts it towards the bin. 'Fell off it once when I was pissed out my head.' He laughs to himself at the memory, while I gasp.

'Nah, it was alright. I landed on Emily.'

'Oh, good.'

Later, when Josh is fast asleep on the sofa with the remote control in his hand, I sneak upstairs with my journal – no key in the bedroom door, I notice – and settle on the bed.

I once read, I write, *that some life-altering astrological thing happens to everyone round about the age of 28. Something to do with Jupiter. For me it was the Open University (well it didn't say earth-shattering) but for my husband, Jeremy, until then a perfectly sane college lecturer and father of two, with a keen interest in cigarettes, booze and sex, it was Buddhism, which he found in a big way. So big, in fact, that the list of things he felt he should abstain from soon got in the way of normal married life, and before long I found myself a single mother, trying to get maintenance from an ex-husband who was seeking enlightenment in the Himalayas. Which was tricky.*

After a while he moved the search to Somerset, and Josh and Poppy would spend the odd weekend in their father's double-decker bus home, playing with the unfettered children of his new friends, staying up until three and eating locally gathered food, mostly dandelions by the sound of it. All of which, of course, they thought great fun and far preferable to life with a mother who made them wear clothes and eat off plates. When I drove them down to Somerset one Friday evening to find the bus gone, we cried all the way home. Tears of joy, in my case. Poppy occasionally hears from her father – now a travelling poet – and either writes back to say, 'Sorry, no can do,' or slips a tenner in the envelope for him.

I return from a fruitless hour in the mobile library to find no one at home and myself locked out – Oliver having confiscated every key in the house. I swear and plonk myself on a patio chair, then realise I'm not completely alone as Ganja ambles over to me, dragging the thirty feet of rope that attaches her to the washing line post. She collapses on her side, and while stroking her half-spaniel ears I notice small lumpy movements in her distended tummy.

'Poor old girl,' I say. 'It's not much of a life, is it? Come on. Let's go for a little stroll. Nothing strenuous, I promise.'

After I've undone the rope around her neck she waddles to the gate with me, her doe eyes flickering up to mine with a 'Do I really have to do this?' expression. However, as I turn to close the gate behind me she's suddenly off like a whippet from its stall. Up the lane she hurtles, her ears flying parallel to the ground as she bounds scissor-fashion in a straight line towards the stile at the end.

'Please don't try and jump it,' I say under my breath, eyes half closed. But she's not that stupid, and instead burrows through a gap in the hedge she's obviously already discovered. By the time I've clambered over the stile Ganja is nowhere in sight.

'Damn.'

I lean against the wooden post and survey the large ascending field before me, wondering which of the one hundred and eighty degrees would be the best way to go. There's a footpath of sorts leading to a wooded area, so I take that in the hope that

Ganja knows to keep to the country code.

'Ganja?' I call weakly as I reach the trees. 'You can come out now.' I stand perfectly still for a while, just listening. Nothing.

It's two thirty, it's August, and the sun is giving me ash-blonde highlights I'd pay sixty pounds for at Choice Cuts. As I trek along the winding footpath I begin to tire and lose patience.

'GanJA!' I eventually yell. 'GanJA! Where ARE you, you STUPID BITCH?'

I hear twigs snapping nearby and sigh with relief as I approach a sharp bend in the path, but from behind the cluster of greenery in front of me appears, not the dog, but Veronica and what could only be Mister (matching lightweight cotton jackets, his and her walking sticks). They're travelling at quite a pace in single file, ruddy of face and breathing noisily.

'Afternoon,' they bark in turn and I quickly step aside to let them pass. When Veronica thinks I'm out of earshot I hear her say, 'What did I tell you?'

I spend hours zigzagging across fields, circling copses and clambering up hills, until eventually I've lost Upper Muckhill as well as the dog. My heart weighs a ton and tears sting my eyes as I heave myself over yet another stile on to a narrow country lane. Left or right, I wonder, but then in the distance I spot the low bridge that always makes me duck when I drive under it in the Range Rover. I'm only half a mile from home, but am far too distressed to go there. Instead, when I reach the village I see it's ten past six, so fall into the pub.

'Water,' I gasp at Betty. My arms are ablaze with nettle stings, hair sticks to my damp cheeks. 'Please.'

'You look a bit out of sorts, my dear,' says Jean Crowbar's husband, Lenny. Lenny would be listed under *Fixtures and Fittings* should the pub ever be sold.

I gulp down the drink and shake my head. 'I just can't find Gan– the dog anywhere.' I tell him what happened.

'Oh, she won've gone far,' he reassures me, lifting his pewter tankard to his face. 'Not with her being in the family way. Reckon you'll find her back at home already.'

'Really?' I let out a sigh of relief while Lenny wipes froth from his upper lip with a sleeve.

'Unless she's gone into labour in a ditch or summat.'

'Right.'

Back at Troy Cottage, Dan's preparing dinner for everyone. The dog's beside him, blast her, chin on the table, salivating over the numerous packets of dried pulses – ranging in colour from pale to dark brown – being removed from a rucksack.

'We found Ganja in Little Crompton,' says Poppy. 'Just sitting by the bus stop, yeah? Like she'd been waiting for us for hours. Dan couldn't've tied her up properly.'

'Fuckin did. Oops, sorry Mrs ... er...'

'Ruby,' I tell him for the hundredth time. 'I'm sure you did, Dan. I expect some kids came and let her loose.'

Oliver saunters into the kitchen at this point, wearing a smirk. 'Oh, there you are.' He pecks my cheek and hands me a set of door keys. 'I think we're quits now. Don't you?'

'Very funny, Oliver. Listen, Dan's cooking for us tonight.'

'Oh, jolly good.'

I see him glance over to where Dan's soaking mung beans and chopping small dark crinkly mushrooms, one of which he's now holding up to the light and sniffing.

'Do you think this one's alright, Pops?' He hands it to Poppy.

'We picked them on our walk,' she tells us.

Oliver turns to me with panic in his eyes. He doesn't have the most robust stomach in the world. Even frozen peas have been known to give him indigestion.

The next day I leave Oliver writhing around in bed and set off for Ted's in search of Milk of Magnesia. As I open the shop door a small, hand-written postcard in the window catches my eye.

'Are you a frustrated thespian?' it says (only someone has crossed out the 'th' and put an 'l'). 'Then why not come along to the Village Hall on Tuesday, 20th September when the Upper Muckhill Players will be auditioning for their Christmas production. No acting experience necessary. Bring warm clothes.'

This sounds too good to miss so I scribble a note on the back of my hand, then hurry home to tell Oliver, who often talks about his highly acclaimed performance as Hamlet in the sixth form.

'I hardly think *Puss in Boots* is in my league,' he says, then stretches out an open palm to me.

'What?'

'Rennies? Settlers?'

'Ah. Right. Won't be long.'

As I hurry back to the shop, I imagine myself taking curtain calls, clutching bouquets and getting rave reviews in the *Parish Newsletter*. At the age of fourteen I'd desperately wanted the role of Juliet in our school's Shakespeare production, but had the misfortune of catching the heaviest cold of my life the day before auditions – my fanatically rehearsed lines then emerging at the crucial moment as 'Robeo, Robeo...' All for the best it turned out, as Juliet had to be kissed by the revolting Anthea Pritchard in the death scene. (Single-sex school – although we had our doubts about Anthea.)

SEPTEMBER

Poppy's beginning to show, making her plight and my guilt all the more real. September rolls in, bringing a definite nip to the air and, no matter how many fan heaters Oliver gives Poppy and Dan, I can't help feeling my pregnant daughter shouldn't be living in a shed.

'Oh, go on,' I plead, as Oliver hides behind *Architect Monthly*. 'They use the kitchen and bathroom as it is.'

'Really? I hadn't noticed.'

'It would just be a temporary arrangement until they find their own place. And I'm sure they'll be really quiet if they know you're working in the next room.'

Oliver cups a hand to his ear and we both listen to the distant sound of Dan practising his guitar. Oliver shakes his head and there's a long silence between us.

'I'll wear that gymslip you bought me last Christmas,' I say in desperation.

He arches an interested eyebrow. I sometimes wonder if Oliver has Japanese blood in him, so unashamedly drawn is he to things pubescent and female.

'And I'll absolutely never play *The Best of Kenny Rogers* again.'

He puts down his magazine and takes my hand. 'OK, my little sex slave, tell them they can move in.' He leads me to the stairs and pats my bottom. 'I think you know where you hid it.'

As I slip into my ludicrous ensemble – including one of Oliver's ties – I can't help wishing I hadn't thrown in the Kenny Rogers bit.

'The thing is, right?' says Dan the next day. 'We like really value our independence.' He's frying up the two pork chops I bought Oliver and me, having recently decided organic vegetarian food has become a corporate rip-off and also that he and Poppy should eat for three. 'It's really nice of you to offer, Mrs ... er...'

'Ruby.'

'But it's dead cosy in Troy Shed, isn't is, Pops?'

Poppy's sneezing into her hands. 'Yeah, we like it. But...' She sneezes again.

'But what? It's too cold? Damp?'

'It's just that we can't get a good picture on the telly you gave us. Can we, Dan?'

Dan's got his head in the freezer. 'Oh,

gutted,' he says, rummaging around. 'No oven chips.'

'Sorry,' I hear myself saying.

Puzzle. If many of my parents' generation were in full-time work by fourteen, choosing engagement rings at sixteen and fighting for their country at eighteen, why then do today twenty-somethings require a parent to slice an uncut loaf for them? What has happened in the past sixty years to delay the growing up process? Fear I and many like me are to blame. Or maybe we were right and our parents expected far-too-adult behaviour from us? I remember Mum telling me that now I was seven I could make her and Dad a nice pot of tea and bring it to them in bed on Sundays. Seven! Josh still had his food cut up and a top on his beaker at seven. But think perhaps we were too protective. If Poppy had learned the hazards of electricity at seven, maybe I wouldn't have caught her sticking an all-metal knife in a plugged-in toaster last week, trying to retrieve Dan's plectrum.

One morning Veronica comes to our door in a large floppy hat and a bit of a fluster.

'I have to stay neutral, of course, being a parish councillor,' she says apropos of nothing.

75

'Hello, Vero—'

'Only if you'd like to write to me condemning the proposed Upper Muckhill Flying Club, please do so.' She thrusts a leaflet in my hand. 'I haven't been here, OK?'

With that, she hurries back down the path, collar turned up and chin buried in chest. (As if anyone wouldn't recognise that strident rambler gait.)

The leaflet informs me that Mr Potts, whose farmland houses an old USAF runway – now grassed over and used only by Mr Potts' son, Trevor, for private landings and take-offs – has applied for planning permission to open a flying club/school, his former business having been decimated by foot-and-mouth.

'YOU MUST TAKE ACTION NOW!' it says, rather bossily. 'Before the peace of our beautiful village is shattered, and learner-flyers begin crashing into our marrow patches every five minutes.' Or words to that effect.

'Can't see what all the fuss is about,' protests Oliver over dinner that evening. 'I rather enjoy the thrum of a light aircraft on a lazy Sunday afternoon.'

Dan picks up the leaflet and reads it, lips moving. 'Hey, an airport. Cool. That means we won't have to go all the way to Heathrow when we need to get to Greece or America or something.'

Poppy sighs and explains things to him in words of one syllable. 'And, no, you can't have flying lessons. We've still got to pay for the stroller, remember.'

'That thing,' mutters Oliver, who agreed to lend them the money, not realising pushchairs these days do everything except give birth, and cost around the same as a small Fiat. It sits in our hallway, all hi-tech and cumbersome, as a constant reminder of his generosity.

At seven forty-five one evening I throw a half-baked jacket potato at Oliver, brush my teeth and hurry off to the village hall auditions, where I discover – wouldn't you know it – Veronica sitting halfway along a table of panellists with a gavel in her hand. A few other hopefuls shuffle in, while around the table members of the committee are discussing the agenda.

'OK, sweeties?' a man with greying, cor-rugated hair eventually says to the others. 'Shall we get this painful business over with?' They all laugh and he turns to the ten or so of us gathered by the Edam, baguette and Mrs Allsop's Chunky Pickle buffet. 'Did you all bring something to read and something to sing?'

Shit.

'Yes,' everyone else calls back, some of them then unravelling wads of A4 paper and sheet music. One man pulls an accordion from its case and a young woman is slipping into her tap shoes. I'm considering going home, but convince myself that by the time it's my turn I'll have come up with something.

After a couple of minutes Veronica bashes the table with unwarranted brutality – more to shut up her colleagues than the silent, shaking candidates – and the evening's business begins. We're all allocated a number – mine's eight – and a woman in Fair Isle settles her ample bottom on the buttoned piano stool.

An hour or so later, after, among other acts, a densely freckled youth named Julian has gangster-rapped to a background tape, a middle-aged man with ponytail and guitar has read some Dylan Thomas and sung a Pete Seeger number with gusto, and Jean Crowbar has been Celine Dion, it's my turn.

'What are you going to read for us, Ruby?' asks Veronica.

'It's a poem. Actually I know it off by heart.' The only one I do. This is thanks to the truculent seventeen-year-old Poppy who studied Larkin for A level English and took great pleasure in reciting it ad infinitum. I clear my throat and launch into 'This Be the Verse', blushing slightly at having used the 'F' word in Upper Muckhill. Young Julian shouts, 'Right!' and punches the air, and Veronica raises her eyes to God but I plough on, giving it as much expression as Poppy used to, which was rather a lot.

'And your song, sweetie?' calls the man with crinkly hair when I've finished and people are politely clapping.

Oh well, here goes. I take a deep breath and throw myself into 'Ruby Don't Take Your Love to Town', my wildly thumping heart providing the rhythm.

It's not long, however, before I'm being accompanied by the odd guitar chord. One or two people then begin humming. Towards the climax of the song, the entire ensemble, with the exception of young Julian, who's looking bewildered and embarrassed, seems to be joining in. We sing with feeling about Ruby's final departure,

Veronica an octave above the rest of us. It's all rather jolly actually, but during the last chorus a nose is blown loudly, a chair gets scraped back and a short, ruddy-faced man leaves the panellists and exits through a back door.

Veronica breaks the ensuing silence with, 'Oh dear, poor Norman,' and a smattering of applause accompanies my exit from the temporary stage.

'Norman?' I ask the other contestants, but my question just hangs in the air.

When everyone's had a turn the committee huddles around the table for a while before announcing that it will spend a few days deliberating and inform us by post. Veronica dismisses us with a 'Thank you *so* much for coming,' but as we gather our coats, sheet music and so on – just a coat in my case, of course – she calls out, 'Ruby, could we have a quick word?' My pulse quickens. The laws of karma are making up for Juliet.

'We hear you're a writer,' somebody says as I seat myself at the table.

'Well, no, not really...'

'I don't know if you've seen the *Parish Newsletter?*' asks Veronica.

'Ye-ess.'

'One bloody yawn from beginning to end,' comes a gruff distant voice.

The man with corrugated hair offers me a cold pale hand and tells me he's Toby, writer in residence.

'Oh?'

'Well, you know, a little poetry, the Christmas Panto–'

Veronica interrupts. 'The thing is, we're looking to launch an alternative, much brighter, punchier village magazine.' She toys with her gavel, then gazes thoughtfully at nothing in particular. 'We like to think of ourselves as an innovative, cutting-edge little community here in Upper Muckhill.'

I look around and count two quilted jerkins, three pairs of bifocals and a cravat. 'Uh-huh.'

Toby, easily the hippest guy in town in his collarless shirt, places his chilly hand on my arm. 'We'd like to see features on local arts events, interesting characters.' He gives a little cough. 'Poets, perhaps.

'Politics,' chips in Veronica, the local councillor.

'A problem page,' suggests a woman with furrowed brow and tightly clenched hands. 'Anonymous, of course,' she adds in a whisper.

'And you want me to write it?' I ask.

'Well, write and edit. You and Toby,' Veronica tells me. 'We thought it would be good to get an incomer involved.' I think she's referring to me. (Oliver believes you have to spawn three generations of farm workers before losing this title.) 'Of course, Toby's going to be rather busy on the pantomime, but we could ask the folk of Upper Muckhill to contribute. Letters, recipes.'

I glance around at their expectant faces, all of a sudden wishing I had a busy job at Price Waterhouse. 'I was hoping to get going on a novel,' I tell the group rather limply. They're all staring pleadingly at me, heads tilted, eyebrows raised.

Veronica gallops on. 'My husband, Frank, will be our advertising exec, so there'll be some remuneration. Shall we say twenty per cent of advertising revenue?'

I rack my brain to think of who but Ted would place an ad.

'Can I let you know?'

Toby grasps my shoulder. 'Of course you can, sweetie. Why not pop round to Rose Cottage next week and we'll chew the fat.' He fishes a card from a pocket and hands it to me.

'OK.' I suppose that gives me a few days to

come up with a debilitating disease. I get up and put on my coat. 'So have I got a part?' I ask.

At this they all suddenly find the table very interesting, except for Veronica, who manages to smile and purse her lips simultaneously. Her way of apologising, I think.

Dan bursts into the kitchen on Saturday evening, just as Oliver and I are clinking our glasses over a lovingly prepared leg of lamb. He's obviously excited about something and stops to catch his breath.

'Poppy says it's moving.' More panting. 'You gotta come and see.'

'Now calm down, Dan,' says Oliver, fork poised over his plate. 'What's moving? The shed? A large panther-like creature in the shrubbery?'

'Our baby. Come on.' He flies out the door and leaves it open.

Oliver groans, picks up our two plates and sticks them in the oven, and we troop over to Troy Shed, where we find a dreadful picture fading in and out on the television and Dan with his ear against Poppy's exposed middle. He sits up when he sees us.

'This is *so* cool.'

'Are you sure, Poppy?' I ask. 'I mean, you

are only four months.'

'Thing is, I've never been good at like keeping a record of dates.' She gets up and covers herself. 'It's been happening a lot, only I thought it was indigestion and just sort of ignored it.'

Oliver's on his haunches, trying to tune the TV in. 'There's always the radio, you know,' he's saying. 'You get some quite decent plays on Four.'

'So what did they say at the ante-natal clinic today?'

'They reckon I'm six months' gone, right? Only, what do they know?'

'Actually, I think they have this equipment.'

'Yeah, they wanted to tell us what sex it was, only Dan said that would take all the fun out of it.'

Fun? I can't say I remember it being fun. But at least Poppy's got an enthusiastic partner. I have a quick flashback to pre-Buddhist Jeremy not being able to stand the sight of my voluminous tummy. He turned up for Josh's birth but brought some marking with him.

'Have you got a coathanger?' Oliver asks Poppy and Dan. After they've looked at him blankly for a while he goes off to get one of ours and within minutes of his return has constructed an indoor aerial.

'Oh, brilliant, it's *Casualty*,' says Dan, settling cross-legged in front of a still-grainy picture.

'I think we'll have to perform an emergency Caesarean,' a spotty doctor in a spotty white coat is telling a spotty nurse. 'She's obviously in terrific pain.'

'Well done,' I tell Oliver out the side of my mouth and we head back home.

'To Poppy,' I say, when we re-clink glasses.

We're halfway through our meal when Dan bursts in again, panting. 'Quick. She's in labour and we don't know what to do.'

My heart misses a beat. 'But we've just seen her and she was fine.'

Oliver slowly draws breath. 'May I suggest you avoid all hospital dramas, Dan.'

'Oh, please, Mrs ... er...' he says, now tugging at my arm. 'She's like yelping and whining and her fur's all sweaty, right?'

Ah yes, I remember that feeling. 'OK, Dan. Make sure she's got a big bowl of water. I'll be over in a minute.'

'Cool.'

I expect Oliver to fume at the prospect of puppies, but instead he calmly helps himself to more potatoes. 'What I don't understand,' he says, resting his elbows on the table and clasping fingers beneath his chin, like someone considering the complexities of chaos theory, 'is what they do with their clothes. I mean, I've never *not* had a coat-hanger in my entire life.'

Re village magazine editing, I write, five puppies later. *Think perhaps I'm being punished for giving up stable and, more importantly, paid employment. What to do? Can think of no better way of becoming most detested person in parish than taking on role of one who has to reject A's rhyming couplets on her lively spaniel in favour of B's letter about the number of potholes in the village.*

OCTOBER

On a thirty-mile round trip for Oliver's ink cartridge – wish Ted would stock them – I come across two elderly women in big quilted coats, green boots and billowing headscarves standing at the entrance to Potts Farm. 'Stop Potts!' says a placard. I wonder if the three people who've driven past today would know or care what that was about. I pull over and trudge through mud and manure to where one is passing a flask to the other.

'Hello, I'm Ruby Grant.'

'Yes, we know.'

'How...? Oh, never mind. Is this about the flying school?'

'Yes, dear.' They introduce themselves as Maureen and Peggy. Maureen, the plumper of the two, pulls a petition from a deep pocket. 'Have you signed one of these?'

Only about a dozen times. I wonder if anyone actually checks for repetition? I take it from her and change my handwriting yet again. As I hand it back she's shielding her eyes from a nonexistent sun and peering at the horizon. 'Uh oh. Here he comes.'

An ancient Land Rover takes an age to wind its way up the hill, then stops with a shudder beside us. The petition gets thrust back into a pocket as a short, florid man in tweeds and checks jumps down with a squelch and wishes us good afternoon. When he holds a podgy hand out to me I recognise him as the person who walked out on my audition piece.

'Norman Potts.'

'Ruby Grant.'

'Yes, I know. Awful nippy today, isn't it?' He turns to Peggy who's swaying hither and thither as the breeze catches her placard. 'That looks jolly heavy, Peg.' He takes it from her, jams it in the ground and cradles it with his arm. 'So how's your Brian now? Back on his feet?'

'Doctors say it won't be long.' She's still swaying slightly.

'And you, Maureen? That knitting business of yours doing nicely?'

'Oh, not so bad, thanks.'

'How long have you ladies been here, then?'

Just the four hours, they tell him.

'Stone the crows,' he says, handing the placard to me. 'You can't be standing around like this all day.' He heads towards his vehicle. 'I'll get young Trevor to fetch you three chairs.'

'Oh, that's very kind, Norman.'

'Very kind.'

As we part to let him drive through, Norman slows to a halt and stretches his head out of the window until his bulbous, weather-beaten nose almost touches mine.

'About this magazine you're writing for us...'

Jesus. 'Well, I don't know if–'

'Just make sure it's good clean family reading.'

'Of course.' He obviously didn't approve of the Larkin poem.

'Anything that poofter's involved in needs a blinkin X certificate.'

'Pardon?'

'Hear, hear!' cries Peggy above the din of the engine. 'Maureen and I thought we might have to picket Toby's panto this year. You know,' she continues behind her gloved hand, but still at full volume, 'after last year's *Cinderella.*'

'Sorry?'

'The glass slipper fitting Buttons? And he and Prince Charming having a gay wedding?' Maureen reminds me, as though the world has talked of nothing else since.

'Smutty, homo rubbish,' shouts Norman, before revving his engine, winking at me and pulling away in a shower of mud.

Back at home, ink cartridge plonked on Oliver's desk, I sit down with my journal.

Think I am not a real woman, I write, *for mere twenty minutes today spent hunting in shops for various items of clothing left me deeply depressed. As in fact shopping always does. I see real women, all dreamy and pre-orgasmic, gliding around department stores, fingering scarves and leather gloves, spraying on perfumes and enquiring about little trolley suitcases, and wonder if I have a chromosome too many, or something. I really don't get it. In fact, to be ordered to 'Shop till you drop!' could be a fitting sentence for any serial murders I may commit. Heard recently that shopping malls might create creches for men, which of course begs the question, 'Why do they have to go along in the first place?' Oliver would no doubt say it's because somebody has to be able to find the car in the multistorey afterwards.*

Rose Cottage turns out to be as pink as the shirt Toby's wearing, with lots of clematis but not a rose in sight.

'Welcome to my humble...' he says with a

theatrical wave of the arm. 'Shoes off, if you don't mind, sweetie.'

I look him in the eye. 'I prefer Ruby.'

'Ah ... as you like, s– Ruby.'

We walk through to the dining room, which sounds easy – and in most people's homes would involve merely placing one foot in front of the other – but here I'm forced to perform something between a flamenco and a belly dance in order to avoid breaking the antique artefacts and *objets d'art* that make up his home. Toby, who's obviously spent years mincing through the cornucopia, is seated and glancing at his watch when I arrive at the dining table.

'Nice things,' I say, surveying the room.

'I do dabble a little. It helps support my poetry.'

I think he wants me to ask about his writing, but common sense tells me not to. I ease myself into a stripped church pew, still slightly sticky with beeswax.

'OK,' I say, 'why don't you tell me exactly what you've got in mind?'

'*Vis-à-vis* the magazine?'

I sigh, wishing I was at home watching *Watercolour Challenge*. 'No. Climbing Everest together.'

Toby looks temporarily puzzled. 'Ah yes,'

he says. 'Very droll. I can see our magazine's going to have a nice satirical edge to it.'

I stumble back into Troy Cottage at seven – literally stumble – as there's a mountain of items, from ironing board to ancient chipped crockery, stacked in the hall and completely blocking my path.

'Back door,' calls a muffled voice.

I circle the house and Oliver greets me in the kitchen, looking dishevelled and moist but nevertheless awfully pleased with himself. 'OK, close your eyes.'

I look around for the expected food, Toby having produced only one cup of camomile tea in three hours. Nothing. Ah well. I do as I'm told and am led by the hand into the hall.

'Da-dah!' sings Oliver.

There, in the large walk-in larder, a.k.a. junk cupboard, is a neat, freshly painted little office; my trusty old computer nestling under the slope of the stairs on a small table, my yellow anglepoise lamp beside it and a Habitat blind at a window I didn't know existed.

'Um...'

'Great, isn't it?'

'Yeah...'

'Everything works. It's all plugged into the hall socket.' He switches on the lamp as proof.

I look at the stuff piled in the hall and point. 'What about–'

'Oxfam.'

I give a small gasp.

'Oh, come on, Roo, when are you ever going to use those Rollerblades?' He goes over and picks up the unopened macramé hanging-basket-making set I was given in 1979 and waves it at me. 'I mean, honestly.'

'I suppose you're right.' I look back at the mini office. 'I don't know what to say. It's brilliant.' I stand inside and stretch out my arms to either wall. 'Amazing.'

Oliver spends half an hour chucking things into the Range Rover while I throw together a meal, stopping occasionally to go and swivel on my office chair. I try not to notice he's given me the crap one.

I'm still undecided about the magazine job, so discuss it with Oliver over our food.

'What do you mean, no money?'

'Well, hardly anything, really. A percentage of the advertising.'

Oliver looks crestfallen. 'You mean I went to all that trouble...' He nods towards my new office.

'Well, I have got a novel to write as well.'

'So you keep saying.'

Later, I give Toby a ring. 'OK, I'll do it,' I shout above his background Wagner.

'Splendid.'

'Only I think we'll have to charge for the magazine. Pay me a fixed salary plus a percentage of profits.' Oliver's nodding his approval behind an upside-down *Country Living*.

'We thought as there's nothing much else to do,' Poppy's saying, 'you know, what with me being like huge and us living in a cultural desert...'

We're all gathered by Troy Shed, arms akimbo, looking up at the new satellite dish.

'You can get old *Dallas* episodes and everything on it.'

Dan's nodding. '*Buck Rogers*. It's wicked.'

'Did it absolutely have to go on the front?' asks Oliver.

Dan gives him a puzzled look. 'You got it, flaunt it, right?' He looks at his watch. 'Hey, Italian football. Come on.'

'Football?' Oliver pulls a face. 'I don't think so.'

'I'll tie the puppies up.'

Oliver sighs. 'Just a quick look then.'

After two hours I wander over to the shed to tell Oliver his dinner's ready. As I walk through the door, he and Dan leap from the sofa like synchronised swimmers, all four fists punching the air. 'YEE-ESS!' Three puppies are chewing Oliver's trouser bottoms but he seems oblivious.

'Dinner time, Oliver.'

'Aahh,' he says, flopping back into the sofa, his eyes not leaving the action replay while a hand works its way back to his can of Stella. 'Look at that. Beau ... di ... ful.'

Poppy's reading at the table. 'Hungry?' I ask her, beckoning with my head. She nods and follows.

'Anyway, I was walking past that Toby's house,' Poppy says over her third helping of lasagne, 'and he comes running out, right?'

'Oh, yes?'

'Says would I like to come in for a cup of coffee.'

'Really?'

'Only, I couldn't get in, yeah?' She's scraping the last of the crusty bits off the lasagne dish. 'Not past the hall, anyway, cos his house is full of all this junk.'

'What did he want?'

'Mm, that was good.' She puts her fork down and strokes her tummy. 'Well, he gives me this stuff to read.'

'What, his poetry?' I get up and start transferring everything to the dishwasher.

'Uh-uh. Says he's writing a Robin Hood panto and would I like to play the part of, um ... now what is it? Hang on, I'll go and get it.'

She returns a couple of minutes later with the script and shows me the list of characters.

'That's me. Maid Marion Pregnant.'

I'm speechless as I look down the *Dramatis Personae*.

Friar Tuck (audience to shout, 'Careful how you say that!' every time mentioned)
Not-So-Little John (large aubergine to be placed in tights)
Will (do it for) Silver
...and so on.

'But, Poppy, this is—'

'Brilliant, isn't it? Toby says he's got to OK it with the moral majority. So it's not like definite.'

The door suddenly flies open with a blast

of cold air.

'Where did they find that ref, eh?' Oliver's saying to Dan. 'An optician's waiting room?' He stops and rubs his hands together. 'Hey, something smells good.'

I direct them to the bread bin, and retire to the living room with a fibre tip.

Easy living, I write. *Have I burned my bridges? When in town last week became seriously anxious, not to say unhinged, when almost run over by mountain bike. 'You stupid bloody wanker,' I (and others) heard myself shouting with raised fist. After stepping back on to the pavement, realised I was actually on very busy road and that the object of my ire had in fact been merely peddling at normal speed in authorised cycle lane. Does dropping out of urban hubbub and enjoying a place with no need for cycle lanes mean one can never go back, I wonder. In same way that selling up and moving down market 'for a while' might lead to a protracted old age in a one-bedroomed Northumbrian starter home.*

Word of the new, interactive, *contributions welcome,* village-and-surrounding-area magazine gets around like the wildest of wild fires and within days I find myself the recipient of more information than I could possibly use. 'Happy 60th on the 24th, Dad. Love Karen, Darren and baby Lee', being a typical contribution. I find 'Coffee morning in aid of Sudan' rather touching, but 'Would the retards who encourage their scabby dogs to crap copiously in Troy Lane kindly seek psychiatric help' went straight into the bin when I suspected it came from Oliver.

I hear him now, plodding down the stairs for the third time this morning. 'For you, I believe,' he says. 'It seems Mrs Allsop won last night's curry cooking competition with her unusual duck tikka masala.' He hands me Veronica's fax. 'Shall I alert Reuters, or will you?'

'Shit,' I say, taking it from him. It's just taken me an hour to write a piece on the duck that appears to have gone missing from the village pond. I show Oliver the story on screen.

'Mm,' he says, reading it over my shoulder, 'this calls for one of those difficult editorial decisions.' He scratches his un-shaved chin by my ear, bringing to mind the gravel I must sweep back on to the drive. 'Why not give *Private Eye* a call? See what they'd do.'

The phone rings and he shoots off to take it in the hall.

'Oliver Jeffries,' he says in crisp, business mode. 'Yep, hang on. I'll just get her out the cupboard.'

It's Veronica. 'Did you receive my fax?' She does this every time.

'Yes, thanks.'

'Frank's just fixing us up with a modem. Have to keep up. Half the village is on-line now.'

This we know – Oliver having thrilled to the news one morning that he'd received eleven messages overnight, only to discover three identical recipes for plum duff from Mrs Allsop ('You'd better nip round and give her an e-mailing lesson'), plus assorted complaints, including one about cows in the infants' playground again.

'I don't know why they don't just put an electric fence around the school. That should sort the buggers out,' said Oliver, who's never been overly fond of small children.

Venturing into Troy Shed at the moment is like visiting the Globe Theatre and Old Trafford rolled into one, as Poppy rehearses her lines with little regard for Dan's TV football.

'Oh, Robin,' she projects, one evening over the top of Inter Milan, 'I SherWood like you to make a decent woman of me,' then mumbles a few of the other characters' lines. I sit and watch, quietly wondering how I can avoid the spectacle of *Robin Hood* when the time comes, but I suppose being Upper Muckhill's chief and only arts critic, that might be tricky.

'Oh, look, it's a girl, and I'm going to call her Robina.' (Mumble, mumble.) 'No, it's not a blackcurrant drink, it's your *daughter*, Robin.'

'YE-ESS!' we hear from the sofa. 'Two nil!'

The puppies turn their attention to Dan, who suddenly disappears under a mass of wriggling flesh and high-speed tails.

Feeling this is way too much excitement for one day, I return to Troy Cottage where I find a crumpled hand-delivered envelope on the floor. 'RUBY GRUNT' it says on the front, making me sound somewhere between an *Archers* character and a porn star. I open it, thinking, here we go again – a bring-and-buy sale for the playgroup, a 'Knitathon' in aid of the church spire. Oliver rifled through the pile beside my computer the other day and wondered at the lack of enticing charity events. 'I'm sure if we organised a Shagathon in aid of distressed architects, I'd never have to work again.'

Inside is a single sheet with more capital letters – large and irregular. 'IF YOU WANT A STORY FOR YOUR MAGAZINE,' it says, 'ASK NORMAN POTTS WHAT HAPPENED TO HIS SECOND WIFE.'

I sit myself down on the stairs and examine the wobbly handwriting. Either it was written by a four-year-old, or somebody has cunningly used their left hand. It could have come from the village idiot, I suppose, but I'm not too sure we've got one.

I hear Oliver scraping his chair on to the landing.

'Hi,' I say breezily as he then plonks down the stairs behind me. I get up and tuck the letter into the nearest pocket. 'Don't suppose you saw someone delivering a note just now?'

'Nope.' Oliver's office overlooks hills and dales and grazing sheep, nor the busy little lane in front that leads up to the council houses. He squeezes between me and the pushchair. 'Thought I heard Veronica's court shoes coming up the path though. You know how the house shakes.' He disappears around the corner and I take out the note and re-read it. Veronica? I don't think so.

103

Feeling restless now, I return to Poppy and borrow Ganja, who practically attaches the lead herself in her hurry to get away from the rumbustious offspring, but then casts concerned glances back at Troy Shed when we head down the path.

It's one of those delicious damp grey days when the sky's so low you can almost touch it, and the smell of rotting leaves and wood smoke makes you want to rush home and take up weaving. The only sound to be heard, apart from the odd bird or bustling rodent, is the pad of Ganja's paws on Troy Lane tarmac. Until, that is, the drone of a light aircraft, now emerging above the misty hedgerow, intrudes into the silence. Trevor Potts, I suppose. Ganja and I stop in our tracks and look up as the plane buzzes overhead. I try multiplying the noise by three or four, then imagine it as a constant factor in our lives. It really wouldn't be pleasant.

'Oh, sod off and crash into a distant forest,' I shout, just as the engine gives a little splutter and cuts out. Oh dear. I hold my breath, cross all my fingers and promise God I'll tell Ted he didn't charge me for that *Radio Times* if He'll only make the engine start up again. The nose of the plane is definitely lower than its tail now and I'm frantically chewing my bottom lip as it starts heading groundward in utter silence. Just when I'm thinking I ought to breathe out, there's a splutter or two, the engine comes to life and Trevor Potts ascends into the murky sky with a high-pitched, throaty roar. What a delightful sound it is.

'Come on, Ganja,' I say, once my heart's stopped racing and I've checked for my purse. 'Got to go and see Ted, damn it.'

Question. Can too much fresh air addle your brain? Where three months ago I was capable of whizzing through the Guardian *cryptic crossword in no time, now find myself rather stretched by* Take a Break *wordsearches. Was also disconcerted last week when Oliver correctly answered every third question on* University Challenge, *while my one point was for 'Phil Collins!' The sole difference I can see in our lifestyles is that Oliver leaves Troy Cottage only to step into the car and drive to polluted cities, whereas I'm often out gardening or strolling around the village and therefore inhaling far more clean air. Put this to Oliver, who plucked* Take a Break *from my hand, saying the brain needs exercise to keep functioning, you know, in the same way that the libido peters out if you only shag once a decade, so why not try reading an article a little longer than a nursery rhyme for a change? Of course I knew all this, but it's so easy to wind down when one's longest conversation of the week took place in the shop with Jean Crowbar, and revolved around Rosemary Driscoll's daughter husband's new job with the cable company. Had never met, nor previously heard of the Driscoll family. Am now determinedly feeding my mind with a Richard Dawkins book, which has a rather nice photo of 'the thinking woman's crumpet' on the sleeve to turn to at times of incomprehension or drowsiness.*

Every day has become a bad hair day and I feel compelled by growing lankness and the inability to see the television through my fringe to get it into shape. I sit at the kitchen table considering the alternatives – a gruelling, traffic-jammed trip into the city, then handing over the equivalent of a week's food bill plus car-parking fees, or nipping over the road for a seven-pound-fifty trim at Tina's Hair Affair (Unisex).

I give Tina a ring. 'Could you fit me in today?' I ask. It's Saturday, so I'm not too hopeful.

'I'll just check my appointments book,' she

says. 'Bear with me.' I hear children's TV in the background. 'Now let me see ... um ... I can do you in ten minutes?'

'Great.'

A child of around seven is sitting in the front garden with his back to me, bundled up in coat and balaclava and happily digging in a sandpit. Tina's son, I presume.

'Hello there,' I call out, at which he leaps up, grabs a Kalashnikov, and aims it at my knees.

'Freethe, muvverfugger!' he tells me through missing teeth, and I suddenly recall the endearing little lisp Josh had at that age.

'Is Mummy in the house?' I ask.

'Who wantth to know?'

I give him a friendly smile and squiggle my nose at him. 'I'll just knock, shall I?'

Tina – thirty-five, hair in a topknot, leggings, moccasin slippers – leads me through to the salon, a room that cleverly doubles as a kitchen, I discover. Coiffed models of the Tom Selleck and early Kylie Minogue variety smoulder at me above toaster and mug tree. One punky, blue-haired girl with a wacky, startled look is slightly the worse for wear due to the deep fat fryer to her bottom left. Tina lifts the lid of a simmering saucepan, has a quick sniff and turns the ring down.

'May I take your coat?' she asks, pulling a chair out from the kitchen table and carrying it over to where a decorative mirror rests against the wall beside a tub of combs and scissors.

'Thanks.' It's all I can do to slip my arms our of their sleeves. I just want Scottie to beam me over to Choice Cuts and erase Tina's short-term memory.

'So what did you want done then?' she asks, gradually imprisoning me in a neck-to-toe nylon affair, then politely holding the chair out for me.

'Nothing. I mean, just a teeny, teeny trim.'

'Shampoo?'

I glance at the overflowing washing-up bowl in the sink. A plastic shower attachment dangles from a nearby hook.

'A dry cut's fine,' I whisper.

She nevertheless gives me a quick dampening spray from a 'Sainsbury's Bathroom Cleaner' bottle.

'How much do you want off? Couple of inches?'

'Oh no. Half an inch. Quarter even.'

I want to go home so desperately, but once she starts work I begin to feel I'm in safe hands. She methodically divides sections of hair, slowly teases out the knots, then swiftly cuts off three times as much as I said, in much the same way all hairdressers do. I relax and we make polite at-the-hairdressers conversation. Busy? Staying at home for Christmas? Thought of using mousse?

I notice a big shiny book with 'Clients Comments' written on the front. 'May I?' I ask, leaning over for it and placing it on my nylon-covered lap. It's a struggle not to whip a pen out of my bag and put an apostrophe in the title.

'A really proffesional cut,' writes one punter. 'I'll definately come again.'

'Great beans on toast,' says another. I laugh and point at it.

'Oh yeah. It was Maximilian's tea time, so I done a bit extra. Talk of the devil,' she says as the back door bursts open and Mad Max announces he's hungry. Tina slips the scissors in her mouth and continues combing through my hair while her free hand seamlessly pulls a Twix from a pocket, unwraps the end and hands it to her son.

I flick back towards the front of the book and read through the comments, amazed at the number of ways you can spell professional. 'Watch out Nicky Clarke!' catches my eye. Written by Jessica Potts, I see.

'Jessica Potts?' I ask. 'Is she related to Norman, the farmer?'

'His wife. Well, *was*, more like.'

'Oh?'

'Dead weird if you ask me, just disappearing like that.'

'Really?'

'He says she run off with a cattle-feed salesman from– 'Ere, Maximilian, git your hands away from her neck. I've told you about that.' I turn to see a docile-looking cat on the worktop, her eyes bulging from the throttling she's receiving. Tina returns to her snipping.

'Only I don't reckon so.'

'No?'

'Never met no one so fussy about her hair. She come here twice a week, you know.'

'Really?'

Tina points at a photograph beside the mirror of someone not unlike Claudia Schiffer on a good day.

'Modelled for me even, when I done the county hairdressing finals.'

'That's Jessica?'

'Yeah. Pretty, in't she?'

'Mm.' I try to picture the Pottses doing things conjugal, but it's not easy.

'She don't look forty-eight, does she?'

'You're kidding.'

'No, really. But, you know,' she lowers her voice. 'You name it, she'd had it done. Norman's son, Trevor, used to say she was GM.'

'GM?'

'Yeah, geriatrically modified.' Tina goes into convulsions. 'Geddit?'

She slowly recovers, scrunches up my still-damp hair with her fingers and lets it fall into place, then shows me the back with the aid of a small shaving mirror.

'Anyway, there's no way she would've run off with a bloke without having her split ends sorted out first. That's for sure.' She rips the Velcro apart behind me and shakes locks on to the floor. 'There you are then.'

I look in the mirror, tilting my head to avoid the weeping clown printed on the glass. It's possibly the best haircut I've ever had. I hand over ten pounds and tell her to keep the change.

'Oh, ta very much,' she says. 'Now show the customer to the gate, Maximilian. Like what I taught you.' She hands him a semi-automatic and tweaks his cheek. 'Mummy's little helper, aren't you?'

'They're called After History, did you say?' I'm talking to Poppy about the band Dan's been playing with for years. 'Great name. It really conjures up the end of the world, doesn't it? No more history. A kind of post-Armageddon nothingness.'

'Actually, it's cos when they were at school that's when they always practised. After history. Just sort of stuck.'

'Oh, I see.'

'So d'you think it'll be alright then?'

'What, a band practice in Troy Shed?' I'm filled with horror at the prospect but apparently they've been barred from every-one else's house. 'We'd better ask Oliver when he gets back from London this evening.'

'Trouble is, I think they're on their way over.' She's got that apologetic, *fait accompli* look she had when presenting herself with that nose ring, aged fourteen. 'Sorry, Mum,' she adds, chewing her lip, just as she did then.

They roll up twenty minutes later and I watch, mouth gaping, eyes swivelling, as guitars, a whole drum kit, keyboard and amps the size of phone boxes are carried, sometimes by three people on shaky legs, into Dan's tiny home. Even Poppy manages to squeeze herself in.

After much banging and swearing and the occasional crash of a cymbal, they strike up with a 'ONE, TWO, THREE, FOUR!' I want to dive under our kitchen table but instead sit in an armchair and begin a slow countdown from one hundred, waiting for the first complaint. I'm at sixty-one when the doorbell rings. It's Veronica.

'Look, I'm *really* sorry,' I shout. 'I'll get them to–'

'I say, they're jolly good,' she yells back. I believe she's even jigging a little. 'May I come in?'

'Er, yes.'

She boogies down the hall and into the kitchen, and I can't decide whether to offer her a cup of tea or fetch her a soft drug from Troy Shed.

'Just what we need,' she says. 'Meg's arthritis is giving her gyp again, you see.'

I close the window in order to hear her better and, hopefully, get her drift. 'Just what you need for what?'

'*Robin Hood*, dear.'

I look at the clock – six thirty – and offer her a glass of wine.

'Oh, go on then. Mustn't get squiffy, though. Got Mrs Allsop's microwave cookery class tonight.'

She goes on to explain that Meg being in-disposed, the Upper Muckhill Players have been searching high and low for musical accompaniment.

'We thought of using a cassette player again,' she tells me, knocking back the wine in a couple of gulps. 'But the village has never quite recovered from the *Snow White* débâcle.'

I decide not to enquire, but refill her glass, wondering if After History – now treating us to a drum solo – would be altogether appropriate.

Poppy drifts in at this point. 'D'you mind?' she asks, rubbing her rummy. 'Baby doesn't like it. Going berserk, she is.'

'Or he.'

'Robina,' she whispers dreamily, staring at her lump as though it were transparent.

I click my fingers in front of her face. 'Earth calling Poppy.'

'Oh, right ... yeah. Or *he*.'

Veronica pats Poppy's arm. 'Don't worry, dear. All the best actresses stay in character.'

We talk about Veronica's proposal and I try to ascertain if any of the band can read music.

'I dunno. Not sure Phil can,' Poppy tells

us. 'He's got those, you know, coloured sticky labels on his keyboard, like I had when I was six. Middle C was red, I remember that.'

'All the better if they can play by ear,' Veronica chips in.

'Dan can't play a note till he's had two pints of lager.'

'Oh, I think we can run to that,' says Veronica, now looking anxiously at her watch. 'Duty calls.' She stands up with a trace of a sway. 'Fascinating subject, you know, microwave cookery.'

Poppy frowns. 'Don't you just like read the instructions on the back of the packet?'

'Ah, the young of today.' Veronica gives me a conspiratorial shake of the head, then turns to Poppy. 'You'd be amazed what you can do with brassicas in a microwave oven, dear. Why not come along to the class?'

Poppy shrugs. 'Yeah, alright.'

When things quieten later and Oliver has missed all the fun and dropped into bed, I pick up my journal.

Number of ideas for novel, I write. None. Wonder how others do it? 'Right, I'll have these huge plants called triffids...' Or, 'OK there's going to be this pig ... bit of a control freak.

Think I'll call him Napoleon.'

Just had quick look through the Liddleton Echo *for inspiration. Not much help, but 'Man rescues collie from blazing wine shop' got me wondering what the dog was doing in there in the first place. Looking for a cheeky Chablis to have with his Pal? Novel idea: new* Animal Farm, *set in an off-licence? Hm ... better go to bed.*

I decide the next day to check if Josh still has a pulse, his phone having been cut off weeks ago.

'Anyone home?' I call through the once-elegant Victorian letterbox. An aroma of dope and sweaty socks wafts towards me and soon a pair of droopy boxer shorts and a concave stomach make their way towards the door. I straighten up.

'Who is it?' comes an unfamiliar voice.

'Josh's mum,' I shout back.

'He's in the bath. Do you wanna come in and wait?'

'Yes, please.'

'OK.'

I wait for the door to open but instead, a few seconds later, a panel of the bay window beside me is thrust upwards and a drowsy young man with short but wild hair sticks his head out.

'Sorry about this,' he slurs. 'Only Josh locked up, then lost the last Chubb key. Did the same round the back too. Tosser.' He stands up and yawns, stretching his arms above his head, and for a moment I think his boxers might not stay up. 'It's best if you sort of dive in,' he then explains, holding the curtain to one side. 'You know, head first.'

I look down at my hips, then at the width of the window. 'Can I use that one?' I ask, pointing to the larger middle window.

'Nah. Fuckin stuck since we painted it.'

I have to make a decision here. If I squeeze in, which I might just do, I'd only need to put on a couple of ounces over the next half-hour and I'd be imprisoned in Josh's terraced house, for some time perhaps. I'd probably find myself spending hours mixing on his decks. I'd start growing illegal plants in the loft and penicillin on old dinner plates. I'd completely forget how one puts a toilet roll on its holder. I'd wear socks till I have to chisel them off, and my only adjective would be 'fuckin'. I don't suppose Oliver would consider taking me back.

'I'll just wait in the car.'

Ten minutes later Josh steps lithely through

the window, clean-shaven and amazingly smart, and bounces over. 'Alright?'

'Hello. Nice of you to dress up for me.'

'Got an interview.'

'Oh, right. What time?'

'Half-past.' He pulls his sleeve up and looks at a bare wrist where the last watch I bought him briefly lived. I've long since stopped giving Josh anything but food for birthdays and Christmas.

'It's OK, it's only ten to three,' I tell him.

'Yeah, right. Only the appointment was half-past two.'

'Oh Lord. Where have you got to go?'

'Dawson Street.'

'Jump in. I'll give you a lift.'

'Cheers.'

Five minutes later we pull up outside the shop whose name Josh has scribbled on a piece of paper. It used to be a butcher's, I remember, complete with dangling chunks of animal and a pungency that made you veer to the opposite pavement when passing. But now a deep blue façade bears the name 'Hammers', and instead of the blood-splattered, sausage-fingered former owner standing in the doorway puffing on a cigarette, there's Ali's lovely Hamish tapping a foot and looking irately up and down the street, his pale green shirt contrasting beautifully with the paintwork. I pull my coat collar up as far as it will go and slide towards the car floor.

'Good luck,' I whisper to Josh. 'I'll wait for you round the corner.' I give him a helpful nudge out the door and roar off in get-away driver fashion.

After cleverly reversing the Range Rover into a space made for a small Italian car, I scribble in my journal while I wait.

Current view, I write. *Two rows of Victorian houses at various stages of gentrification or disintegration. One hard-working owner with attractive emerald-green brickwork, white bay windows and a forest of ivy, is flanked by a front garden that grows supermarket trolleys and, on the other side, a sinister-looking house with what I'd imagine are permanent tablecloths at the windows. Beside me is a newly repointed home with small wellies on the doormat and a Playgroup Jumble Sale poster in the window. I bet that if I step inside I'll find once-glossed but now scuffed floorboards, a pine blanket box, the odd crumpled ethnic rug with a small plastic vehicle parked on it, magnetic letters on the fridge and a CD collection that includes a lot of African stuff, REM, Nigel Kennedy, all the David*

Grays and one Tracy Chapman. They probably take in foreign students from the better language schools as they think it's good for the children to engage with a variety of adults, and, besides, the money's bloody good if you give them dinner. They do, though, try to avoid French and Italian students, who they've found unable to adjust to Quorn in their three-week stays.

A young woman who looks in need of rehab, and quick, walks past and jolts me out of my reverie. I glance at the time and see forty minutes have passed, so jump from the Range Rover, check twice it's locked, then wander round to the shop. Through a gap in the window book display I see Josh in an apron hard at work with a cappuccino machine. Josh working! It's an odd but exhilarating sight.

'Absolutely not,' says Oliver, while I'm trying to direct his arms into a sheepskin coat one Saturday morning. 'There's bound to be a gaggle of eco-warriors with matted hair and Manchester accents. Some of us have a professional reputation to consider, you know.'

'Look, it's hardly going to make *Newsnight*. Come on.' I've conquered his left arm and got a tartan scarf halfway round his neck. 'Think of it as gentle persuasion rather than anarchic subversion. Poppy and Dan will be there.'

Damn, shouldn't have said that.

'Oh good. And their five dogs?' He laughs and I can see he's slowly coming round to the idea. 'This is ridiculous. I'm not even opposed to the bloody flying club.' He tugs gloves from his pocket. 'At the first sign of tear gas and people being dragged into armoured vehicles I'm leaving, OK?'

'I'm sure it'll be a very civil affair.' I look at my watch. 'We'd better go. The march leaves the green at eleven thirty.'

'You mean we're *walking?*' He looks truly horrified, as well someone who regularly drives to Ted's shop might.

'Oh, it's only a couple of miles. Just think of it as going to the car and back fifty times.'

'Veronica's idea,' says Jean Crowbar when we reach the green. She points us towards a Range Rover, attached to which is a large, rectangular cart on wheels. 'She thought, what with Meg's arthritis and Frank's pacemaker.'

The comfy front vehicle appears to be full, and people are beginning to clamber into the open trailer. Veronica swoops by. 'In you hop,' she says, patting Oliver's rear. 'Got your banners?'

I can't decide whether to laugh or cry. One glance at Oliver tells me which way he's going. Along with the rest of the chilly and bewildered protestors we lower ourselves gingerly on to the makeshift benches lining the cart, and by the time Poppy and Dan make a last-minute appearance there isn't a leg in the place not touching at least four others. The lengthy Dan sits opposite me, a large wriggling puppy on his lap and his knees close to my chin. Frank's soon pulling the Range Rover away in first gear and we begin rumbling and bumping along a road which has obviously been cobbled since I last used it. Oliver hasn't spoken for ten minutes but is nevertheless managing to let me know he'll be consulting a divorce lawyer on Monday. When, after a while, I sense him leaning over to whisper something in my ear, I brace myself.

'You don't suppose,' he says above the engine as we bounce up and down in perfect unison, 'that Saturday is Veronica's ethnic cleansing day?'

We disembark at the entrance to Potts Farm where we all, to a man, rub life back into our bottoms. I remember I'm supposed to be reporting on the event, so pull out my notebook and camera, and take a look around.

Mrs Allsop's already begun laying out a picnic of finger rolls. 'Egg and cress or potted crab,' she's telling interested parties. I see Dan's first in the queue. Veronica, heavily disguised in headscarf and dark glasses, is unfolding garden chairs for the hard of standing, while Frank, having wiped all the mud off his Range Rover, is now giving his wheel arches a bit of a buff.

'Ah yes,' sighs Oliver beside me, 'just like the old CND days.'

'STOP POTTS' seems to have been adopted as the campaign slogan. I decide to take a photo of a group already clustered together with placards and banners by the gate.

'Must have children in the shot,' Veronica cries out, then wheels a couple over. 'Now look very, very sad,' she tells them. 'Imagine your hamster's died, Hannah.' Hannah promptly bursts into tears. 'Perfect, dear.'

I notice a fellow failure from the panto auditions – grey ponytail, Yasser Arafat scarf. He's carrying a guitar and has settled himself on one of the trailer seats. Beside him a middle-aged woman in Doc Martens and a medley of primary colours lifts a megaphone to her face.

'WHAT DO WE WANT?' she asks us all.

'TO STOP POTTS,' shouts her friend.

'WHEN DO WE WANT IT?'

'NOW!'

We all soon get the hang of this and join in, but I can't help thinking it might be more effective if members of the heavily tipped-off press (real press) were here to record our fury. When the chanting eventually fizzles out, the guitar man breaks into 'We Shall Overcome'. We politely hear him out and give quiet applause at the end. With the exception, that is, of one person, who continues to whistle and clap loudly, long after we've stopped. The crowd turns, as one, to see Norman Potts propped on a shooting stick.

'Bloody good turn, eh?' he booms, and those in his vicinity begin inching away, as though a large, salivating bear had come to investigate the egg and cress rolls.

'Give us a bit of Jim Reeves, would you? The missus' favourite, he was.' (His first wife, presumably – Jessica, I'd imagine, being more of a Julio Iglesias woman.)

I decide to be brave and approach him.

'Ruby,' he greets me from several yards,

'how's our magazine coming along?' He stands up and offers me his shooting stick. It brings back memories of the time I tried to unicycle, and I decline.

'I was wondering if I might interview you some time, Norman. You know, get the other side of the story?'

'Certainly, my dear. Tell you what, come to supper with me and Trevor. Got plenty of beef in the deep freeze.'

I've heard Norman had to slaughter his entire herd, and images of blistered beasts float across my field of vision. 'That would be lovely.'

'And bring that husband of yours,' he adds with a nod towards the stooped and thoroughly miserable Oliver. 'Looks like he could do with a slap-up meal.'

'Mm.'

'Next Friday suit you? Seven o'clock?'

'Great.' I bid him farewell with a heavy heart. 'Ah,' I say as inspiration strikes. I turn back. 'I'm afraid we're both vegetarian.'

Norman shakes his head. 'Dear, dear. No wonder you're a mere slip of a thing.' He lifts an arm and bends it. 'You know,' he says, squeezing it hard with his other hand, 'you don't get muscles like these living on blinkin toffee.'

I think he means tofu.

'Afternoon, Jean,' he shouts as I walk away. 'How's your Lenny's waterworks now?'

'Oh, much better with the medication,' Jean tells us all.

'It's too much beer does it. Wouldn't catch me spending so much time in the pub with a charming wife like you at home.'

Jean giggles and Norman wanders over to Frank. Within minutes he's sorting out the wobbly roof rack Frank's been fussing over, receiving a hearty pat on the back for his trouble and a flasktop of refreshment from Veronica.

As Norman Potts does his rounds, people slowly fold up banners and garden chairs, and begin making for the trailer. The guitar gets slipped back into its cover and Mrs Allsop gives her tablecloth a good shaking.

'Whatever next?' I hear Norman saying to Poppy. 'You don't want that nipper arriving early, do you?' He's steering her away from the trailer by the elbow. 'Now just prop yourself on this handy seat and I'll fetch the Land Rover.'

After we've clambered into the cart, staying well away from Dan's knees, I get out my pad and chew on my pen while I try to think up copy. I thank Oliver for his suggestion of 'Potts crumbles in face of violent opposition' and arrive back at the village green with a blank page.

Sunday is big shop day. Oliver, Poppy, Dan and I all draw lots. Dan and I lose and set off together in the Range Rover; me with an array of debit and credit cards, and Dan with the ten-pound note Poppy fished out of her purse.

'We could like share a trolley?' suggests Dan when we arrive.

I guess he won't be buying much. 'OK.'

As I weave my way along aisles, chucking the usuals into the trolley, Dan shuffles behind, occasionally wandering off and coming back with a 'Cheap 'n' Cheerful' range item.

'Hey, forty p. for six instant soups,' he announces as another austerely packaged item goes in. 'Look, one ninety-nine for a zillion chicken pieces. Brilliant.' He plonks them on the pile.

'But, Dan, they've still got bits of feather stuck in them.'

'Yeah, well, at least you know it's not some soya rip-off. Well ... I don't think it is.' We both peer closely at the packet. 'Yeah,' whispers Dan. 'I reckon that's real blood, don't you?'

We're almost done. I'm perusing the Australian wines and Dan's picking up a six-pack, when someone says, in tones deep and lovely, 'Ruby?'

I turn round. 'Oh, Hamish. Hi.'

As automatically happens when one bumps into an acquaintance in the super-market, my eyes begin wandering over the goods in his trolley – fresh pasta, coriander in a pot, mangetout – while I ask him how he is; and his over mine – Hairy frozen chicken portions, 'Cheap 'n' Cheerful' fish paste, and instant mashed potato – as he tells me he's fine. I blush the colour of Dan's 'Cheap 'n' Cheerful' ketchup.

'Alright?'

'Oh, hello ... er...'

'Dan,' I remind Hamish, who met him briefly when visiting.

'That's right. How's ... er...'

'Pops? Yeah, she's alright. Rehearsing a lot, you know.'

'Rehearsing?'

'Maid Marion, right? In the village panto.'

Hamish turns to me. 'Isn't she...?' He forms a large arc in front of him with one hand.

'Long story.'

Dan places his lager in the trolley. 'Me and Phil's gonna be the orchestra.'

'Really?'

'I can get you discount on tickets, if you wanna come.'

Hamish hesitates only briefly. 'Love to.' He looks at his watch. 'Better dash, actually. We've started opening on Sunday afternoons.'

I want to ask how Josh is getting on but feel sure he only lasted an hour or so. Hamish reaches above me and a heady male perfume drifts my way.

'Got this fantastic new assistant,' he says, pulling one of the over-seven-pounds bottles I never even consider from the top shelf. 'Incredibly well read. Charms the pants off all the customers.'

Ah well, just as I thought.

Hamish turns his trolley a hundred and eighty degrees. 'Another relative of yours, I'm told.' He throws me that dazzling smile. 'Hard to believe you've got a son that age, Ruby. You were obviously a schoolgirl mum.'

'Yeah?' says Dan, looking startled.

I laugh off the compliment, but keep to myself that I was married and pregnant by twenty-one. Well, the other way round actually.

When we reach the checkout Dan ushers me through. 'Ladies first, right?' After filling five carrier bags my card gets swiped to the tune of just under sixty pounds. Dan fills four bags and is handed twenty-one pence change.

Oh crikey. Only two days to go and I still haven't told Oliver about dinner with Norman. I can't leave it any longer but decide to get him in a good mood first. As we sit sipping wine at the table, dinner over, I adopt a seductive pose, put my hand under the table and run it up his trouser leg. Oliver frowns and looks over at the calendar. 'Surely it's not that time of year again.'

'Have some more wine,' I say. I fill his glass with my spare hand, the other now negotiating a leather belt. Once I've successfully unbuckled and unbuttoned, I lift the tablecloth, toss my hair back wantonly and slowly lower myself to the floor.

'Um...' says Oliver quietly, 'as much as I love to live life on the edge, Roo,' he pushes his chair back, 'I think I might just lock the doors.'

With this he's up and carrying out a

thorough security patrol. I hear keys rattling, windows being slammed shut and curtains swishing across. I remain under the table for a while, but can't help feeling the moment's gone, so crawl out and join Oliver in the hall where he's securing the last of the front door bolts.

'Come on,' I say, and lead him upstairs.

I once read that the average time it takes a man to fall asleep after making love is eleven seconds. I glance at the numbers clicking away on the digital alarm clock and realise I must get in quick.

'We've been invited to Norman's for dinner.'

'Hm.' He's breathing slowly and heavily, arms wrapped around me. 'I know.'

'You know?'

'Saw it in your diary. Next to "Butter Oliver up".' More laboured breathing. 'Been looking forward to being butterrrr...'

Thought, I write while he snores endearingly beside me. *Perhaps I should encourage Oliver to diet, as am increasingly aware of his burgeoning spare tyre. Of course, one only has to think of the average Ricki Lake studio guest for Oliver to appear as slim as a shoelace, but I'm*

131

sure he'd be happier if he could see his feet with-
out having to breathe in and lean backwards.
Will make a point of discussing those late-night
Welsh rarebits he grown so fond of.

Oliver carries me from the car to Norman's front door – I, foolishly, having decided to wear heels and Norman, naturally, having a mulch of manure all the way to his house.

'Hello there,' says an early thirties and not-bad-looking man. Trevor, I presume. 'Come in.'

I point to the mud on my feet and ankles; the result of my jumping down from the Range Rover. 'I think I may need to…'

'Sorry about that. If you take your shoes off, I'll show you to Jessi– the dressing room upstairs.'

A flushed and jolly Norman appears in a plastic 'Aah, BISTO' apron and takes Oliver, also shoeless, into the living room, while I follow Trevor up a spotless wooden staircase, at the top of which he opens a door for me.

'Everything you need, I hope. If not, give a shout.'

'Thanks.' I close the door and set about removing tights and soaking them in an ornate, gold-tapped basin.

Jessica's room, eh? I take a good look

around. It's stylishly decorated and furnished – a bit DFS, with its vanity unit, ruched curtains and off-the-peg Monets – but nevertheless pleasant, and I find myself taking a little tour, inspecting ornaments and trying out a hand cream, then opening one of the fitted wardrobe doors. It gives a long, exaggerated squeak, like a *Goons Show* sound effect, and I'm hoping Trevor isn't on one knee with his ear at the keyhole. Inside the vast cupboard I see more clothes than I've owned in my entire life. More, perhaps, than Elton John has owned. Dresses, skirts, jackets – youngish, size twelvish. I shut the door quickly, wring my tights out, hang them over a radiator beside the basin and pad barefoot back down the stairs.

'Do you know,' I hear Oliver proclaim as I approach the living room, 'I can't remember the last time I ate meat.'

Trevor comes across as pretty educated and articulate and provides us with a persuasive argument for the flying club scheme; Norman just occasionally chipping in with, 'I told them there was nothin wrong with them cows', 'Bin in the family since eighteen twenty-three, this farm', and similar.

I can't help but be aware, as I sit and listen,

that Norman and Trevor tend to go in for high-volume conversation. I guess they're used to competing with farm machinery and light aircraft, but it does seem unnecessary in this small dining room, where the four of us are so close we could hold a séance. I notice Oliver's casually cupping one ear with a hand, and decide to do the same. It helps a bit.

'Anyway, the Civil Aviation Authority's still got to approve it,' Trevor tells us as Norman pours extremely meaty-looking gravy over my plate of vegetables. 'Checking the prevailing winds and so forth.'

While Trevor and Oliver move on to another topic I take in the contents of the orderly, polished room. No photographs of Jessica, I notice, but one of a lovely, grey-haired woman in a pale blue twinset.

'My Shirley,' Norman informs me. He picks up the framed picture and gives it a loving dust with his sleeve. 'Best woman ever walked the earth.'

'She looks nice.' I turn towards him. 'You married again, didn't you, Norman?'

Oops. The last time I induced the expression Norman now has on his face was when, two years ago, I told Oliver I might be pregnant.

'Are you all right?' I ask as he begins emitting an odd wheeze. 'Would you like some water, or something? Trevor ... your father's–'

Trevor leaps up, quickly pours a glass of water and holds it to his father's lips. 'WHERE ARE YOUR PILLS, DAD?'

Norman waves an arm towards the dresser.

'Did you mention Jessica?' whispers Trevor as he passes. I nod.

'Who?' asks Oliver.

'Tell you later.'

To allow Norman time to recover his dignity, I excuse myself and pop upstairs for my tights. As I reach for them I notice that the combination of heat and damp has caused the mirror above the wash basin to steam up, and that one or two letters are vaguely visible on the glass. I hurr on the mirror and the writing becomes clearer. 'Help,' it says.

I gulp audibly, give the mirror a wipe with a peach deep-pile towel and head downstairs, telling myself that Norman and Trevor have probably concocted one of those murder mystery parties for us, and that any moment now I'll hear a scream and a gunshot in a distant pantry.

'Nice bit of apple turnover?' Norman asks me when I've slipped back into my seat. His big shiny knife is poised over the steaming pudding, inches from my face.

'Mm, please.'

'So, who's this Jessica?' asks Oliver on the way home.

'Oh, Norman's second wife. She left him, apparently.'

There's no way I'd tell Oliver of my concern and subject myself to daily ridicule. Also, he tends to live by a noninterventionist code. 'What's it got to do with us if some guy knocked off his wife and scattered her dismembered bits around the county in black bin bags?' he'd say, almost convincing me. 'That's really their business, isn't it, Roo?'

It's Hallowe'en, and Oliver and I are preparing for Veronica's party. 'Prize for the best costume' the invitation says. From random enquiries around the village I gather that, in social acceptance terms, to arrive at this annual event in everyday clothes would be on a par with cutting your toenails in the Dog and Gun. Oliver's gone to all the trouble of buying a Margaret Thatcher mask.

'Scary, eh?' he says, holding it to his face. 'Thought I'd accessorise with these black jeans and polo neck.' He flings the said items on the bed.

I, on the other hand, am attaching a large, warty, rubber nose to my own, having already blacked out several teeth and painted moles on cheeks and chin. My bright green, frizzy wig is bringing on a headache and I'm wondering if I really want to top everything off with the two-foot pointy hat I spent the entire morning making. Oliver jumps out of his skin when I turn round and give him a gappy smile, so I guess I'm in the running for the prize.

'Welcome, welcome,' says Frank at the gate to their six-bedroomed residence. It's all heavy thatch and wonky leaded windows and I've coveted it since we moved here. 'Whoever you are,' he adds with a chortle. It strikes me that Frank has hardly entered into the spirit of things, dressed as he is in a checked zip-up jacket with furry collar, viscose trousers and what look like new white trainers – unless he's here as Starsky or Hutch, that is. 'You'll find punch over by

the pond and apple bobbing in the con-
servatory.'

The garden is adorned with lanterns,
throwing enough light on the gathering to
show us that almost everyone has come in
jeans and chunky sweaters. I'm relieved, but
only slightly, to see that a half-hearted effort
at a ghost – white sheet with eye holes – is
ladling liquid into a tableful of glasses.

As we approach the drinks, Oliver whips
his mask off and immediately blends in,
leaving me to receive unreserved praise for
my costume from every single person
present. I would smile as I thank them, but
first my tongue is frantically trying to rub
felt-tip off those three front teeth.

'Be a dear and fetch the camera, Frank,'
calls out the ghost. 'Must take a snap of
Ruby's sterling effort.'

Poppy and Dan amble through the gate just
as the unanimous decision has been taken
to proceed indoors, out of the now Arctic
evening. They're both wearing what they've
been in all day: the full, smocky, woollen
frock Poppy and I bought yesterday in
Evans, the outsize shop, and the dungarees
Dan does his carpentry in. They tell me Dan
got delayed at work, then apologise to

Veronica for being late.

'Oh, how absolutely super,' she says, standing back and looking them over. 'I can see you're a family that likes to dress up.' She turns to what's left of the crowd. 'Look everybody, Poppy and her young man have come as peasants.'

'Oh, go on,' Oliver's saying as he massages my temples at the dressing table. 'I've never done it with a green-haired woman.'

'But it's uncomfortable and it's given me a headache.'

'It'll only be for five minutes.'

'And what's in it for me?'

His hands head downwards. 'Anything you want.'

'Hm. Well, in that case...'

Oliver gives the wig a shake and places it for the time being on the bedside table, next to the framed pen-and-ink drawing of Upper Muckhill parish church, plus vicar, I've just won.

NOVEMBER

'Dumas?' I hear Josh say to a pretty girl with a hefty paperback in her hand. 'Great storyteller.' He hooks a book from a higher shelf and hands it to her. 'I'd recommend reading him in the original French, though.'

I try to recall if it was an E or an Ungraded Josh got for his French GCSE.

'Really?' she says, and looks up at him with a flirtatious tilt of the head. *'Ça perd quelque chose dans la traduction, peut-être?'*

Josh gives her a thoughtful nod and an enigmatic smile, then spots me and excuses himself. *'Mon mère,'* he explains.

'Ma, not *mon,'* I whisper when he comes over.

'Ah well.' He shrugs and runs fingers through his now vaguely styled hair. 'Good thing about working here is you get some fit women coming in. Coffee?'

'OK.'

In a far corner the fit Hamish catches my eye and waves. When he's finished with his customer he joins me on the stools at the counter and we chat about the shop, about Ali, Upper Muckhill. Josh hands me a veritable meal of a coffee.

'I hear you've embarked on a new career in journalism,' says Hamish. I think I detect mirth in his eyes.

'Well, I'm not quite in the corrupt dinner ladies league.'

'Ah, touché.'

'But I did a gripping review of the WI sugarcraft exhibition.'

'Really? It must be quite exhausting, the cut and thrust of country life.'

'Oh, one just gets used to the dramas.' I want to sip my coffee but rather than face Hamish with a frothy brown moustache, I drink from my spoon. 'You know,' I continue, 'only last week Mr Wilcox caused quite a furore by taking a pair of shears to Mr Turnbull's magnolia. Said it was obstructing the footpath, forcing him to stoop and put his back out again.'

Hamish grins and shakes his head. 'Just the kind of gritty stuff that never seems to come my way, unfortunately.'

'Actually...' I'm thinking of telling him about Jessica, but have a sudden vision of frogmen dragging the village pond, miles of that bright yellow ticker tape cordoning off fields, lines of policemen with sniffer dogs and Oliver having to undergo a DNA test.

'What?'

'Oh ... um...' My eyes flit around the shop while I attempt an instant decision. I suppose it would be nice to off-load this stuff on to an investigative journalist and concentrate on Brownie pack events. I open my bag and hand him the anonymous letter.

After reading it, he holds it up to the light, then sniffs it – now I'd never thought of doing that – narrows his eyes and strokes his perfect chin between thumb and forefinger. He calls Josh over. 'Pass me my magnifying glass and deerstalker,' I expect him to say, but he orders two more coffees (oh, no) and leads me towards a corner table.

My Hawkshead-clad brother is running a finger through an imaginary layer of dust on a kitchen shelf when Dan bounces in for Sunday lunch with an 'Alright?'

'This is my Uncle Tim,' says Poppy, who's creating cabbage and almonds à la Mrs Allsop in the microwave. 'This is Dan.'

'Pleased to meet you, Dan.' Tim goes over and holds out his hand.

Dan's a little nonplussed, but after wiping a palm on his trousers, manages an awkward shake and a 'Likewise.'

'So what do you do, Dan?' asks Tim.

'Carpenter, odd-jobbing.'

'Oh yes?'

'Doing up this record shop at the moment. You know, making racks for the vinyls and stuff.'

'Really?' Oliver and I say together. It's the first we've heard of it.

'Started yesterday. Cash in hand. Brilliant.'

Poppy pulls a face at Dan as she places her dish centre table. 'Uncle Tim works for the Inland Revenue.'

'The Exchequer, actually.'

'Hey, never met a real tax man before,' says Dan. He breaks into the Beatles' 'Taxman', accompanying himself with an air guitar, before the penny drops. We're all staring at him. 'Yeah, well, when I say cash in hand ... you know, that just means good money. It's all like above board.'

'Dan's also a musician,' I chip in. 'Done a couple of gigs now, haven't you?'

'Yeah. Yeah.' He sits at the table and nods nervously at Tim. 'Paid loads of tax on those.'

I ask Poppy to carve the joint – something Oliver normally does, but the rule-bound Tim, with his sailing in the Solent and chums in the House, always manages to bring out the rebel in me.

'Pass your plate, Uncle Tim,' she tells him, after hacking the meat into irregular chunks.

When he's given his cutlery a thorough going over with a napkin and cast an eye over his tilted plate, he asks Poppy for just a little and no fatty bits, thanks.

'So,' he says, turning to me, 'it looks as though Dad will be flying in for Christmas.'

Ah, now I get it. Tim's visits are rare, unable as he is to tolerate our casual relationship with Windolene and Hoover attachments.

'Yes, I got a letter too.'

Oliver and I have already decided we'd love to have Dad to stay for a couple of weeks. He'd be bored rigid at Tim's with nothing faulty to hammer, screw, glue or do a bit of soldering on.

'Better hide the secateurs, though,' Oliver said when I showed him the letter the other day. He took them out of a drawer and popped them on top of the tallest kitchen cupboard. 'Given two weeks and a free rein he could prune his way down to a Roman settlement, even in mid-winter.'

'So...' I say, nodding and smiling at Tim.

Tim nods and smiles back. 'So...'

'It's a shame we're so crowded here at Troy Cottage.'

'But didn't we–' begins Oliver until I thump his thigh.

'And you've got that attractive guest room, Tim. With the futon and everything.'

'Dad would hate sleeping on a futon.'

'No. I bet they're all the rage in southern Spain.'

'Claudia and I were actually hoping to get a spot of snorkelling in around then. Off the coast of–'

'Look,' says Poppy, banging down the carving knife. She's almost tearful. 'Grand-dad can have the puppy corner in Troy Shed. Can't he, Dan?'

'Yeah. They just like sleep with us anyway.'

'And we can put a curtain up so he can be private, right?'

I see this is getting out of hand and look to Oliver to untangle things.

'No, no,' he says. 'No need for that, Poppy.' He finishes building a hillock of roast potatoes on his plate and gives me a sly wink. 'You can take that rather nice Edwardian screen from the spare room.'

Tim raises his eyebrows. 'Spare room?'

'It's OK,' I say, more for Poppy's sake. 'We've already booked Dad in for full

English breakfasts. Polished up the tools.'

Tim leans back with relief writ large across his handsome, angular face – I've noticed him taking on a passing resemblance to Nigel Havers as he grows older – and slowly scans the room. 'Dad'll have something of a field day here, won't he?'

'Ha ha ha,' we all say.

I hear a protracted sigh and see Oliver casting a weary eye at the clock.

'I see the house next door's for sale,' says Tim when the rest of us are clearing up. He's rubbing at the window with a bit of damp kitchen roll to get a better look at it. The paper turns black, just as I feared. 'Rather fancy a weekend pad in the country.'

'It's sold!' cries Oliver, making us all jump.

'It's in quite a state,' I tell Tim. I'd have thought the semi-derelict place next door too much of a challenge for him, but I guess he'd pay for the best chaps to come in and squeeze every bit of character from it. The former resident was old Mrs Jarvis, kept alive to the age of ninety-four by the ladies of the village and a steady stream of hot Pyrex dishes. 'I said I've brought you a NICE BIT OF LIVER, Elsie,' I often heard when pottering in the vicinity of our two adolescent apple trees (or 'the orchard' as Oliver will insist on calling it). The cottage was on the market and ignored for months until a sudden boom brought us a constant background noise of shiny cars pulling up, walls being tapped and 'Oh look, Andy/Sarah/Tarquin, the original range/gaslamps/cesspit!'

'Sealed bids, Tim,' Oliver's saying sorrowfully. 'Too late to make an offer now. Shame.'

'I think it'd be rather good to have that young publisher woman move in,' says Oliver once everyone's gone and we're convalescing with large doses of wine. 'You know, the one I was chatting to last weekend?'

'At length, I recall.'

'Actually, she had some very interesting ideas on the post-postmodern novel.'

What he means is she had a very interesting skirt the length of a toothbrush and lips you could bounce on. When she was waiting for the estate agent to arrive, Oliver hacked at last year's brambles to make a path to the door for her, swinging our rusty old scythe like someone auditioning for *The Three Musketeers*. She thanked him gushingly and admiringly, not knowing,

150

of course, that I'd spend the next three days rubbing Deep Heat into his lower back.

Later, I recluse upstairs with my journal.

Siblings. Would there be fewer wars if everyone were an only child? Can't help thinking yes, as surely formative years spent fighting almost to the death over a spinning top, plus all the biting that involves, provides best training course for invading and pillaging in later life. Actually Tim and I never really fought, just seethed with mutual disapproval. Have always found him a priggish and anally tidy irritant, even as a child, when he regularly dusted his Roman soldier set and would only have one friend round at a time due to the limited seating in his bed-room. Being older by two years, I was supposed to set an example, but in fact Tim ended up in his early teens happily taking Mr Sheen into my room once a week for extra pocket money. Actually, since Mum died and Dad headed heartbroken for a new life abroad, Tim and I have grown closer, helped no doubt by the hundred-mile span between us.

Now, Oliver's an only child and I can't imagine him declaring war on a small Balkan state. Not unless he could do it without leaving home, anyway.

Ali phones one afternoon, requesting a 'chat'. 'We could go to that ghastly pub of yours,' she suggests.

She arrives around eight, and after we've half-heartedly invited Oliver along and feigned disappointment when he declines, we go and grab a table at the Dog and Gun.

'So how's it going with Hamish?' I ask. May as well get straight to the point of her visit.

Her face takes on a pained, man-trouble expression. 'I'm not sure I can handle it, Ruby.'

'Don't tell me, he takes off for weekends and doesn't invite you? Can't spend an entire night in your bed?'

'No, actually—'

'Alright?' calls out Dan from the bar.

'Oh, hi, Dan.'

'Here for the quiz?'

We look blankly at him and he points to a notice above us: 'Quiz Nite. Every Wednesday. Win a gallon of beer.'

I'm personally struggling with my half of lager, but it certainly appears a popular prize. The pub has filled to capacity since our arrival, and groups of four to six are forming around tables, hanging jackets on the backs of their chairs, rolling up sleeves and generally giving the impression that winning those eight pints means more than life itself. Dan carries an armful of drinks over to what I recognise as the rest of his band.

'Room for two little ones,' I hear Veronica trill behind us. Frank leaps up and moves chairs around to accommodate us.

'Oh, bloody hell,' whispers Ali. 'I'm crap at general knowledge.'

'Two pounds each, I'm afraid, ladies.' Veronica holds out a palm. 'But jolly good fun.'

We pay up while Frank dons his reading glasses and fills in the front page of an answer sheet. 'We call ourselves ACS,' he informs us. 'Always Come Second.'

Ali laughs. 'As the actress said to the—'

'Ali!'

Frank nods towards Dan. 'After History wins every week.'

'Really?' I look over at the quietly confident-looking group. Too late to change teams, I suppose.

Jean Crowbar joins us with her daughter, Gail, and while they go through the sleeve-rolling-up bit, I turn to Ali.

'So, what can't you handle?'

'Testing, testing,' booms a croaky Betty

over the microphone. 'One two, one two.'

'Hamish. He's just so ... so reliable and attentive. So, you know, nice. He even likes Beth. Planning a holiday for the three of us in the New Year.' She shakes her head over her drink. 'It's just too weird.'

'Hm, it is rather,' I say. 'Have you had it out with him? Said why can't he insult your neighbours and leave women's phone numbers lying around like a normal man?'

'So, what do you think, ladies?' Frank's asking us. 'James Dean or Marlon Brando?'

It seems the quiz has begun. Ali and I look at each other.

'James Dean,' we say together.

'Definitely,' adds Ali, and Veronica writes it down in a copperplate hand.

'What was the question?' I whisper.

'No idea.'

We come second – mostly due to Gail's remarkable grasp of current soap operas. While After History are collecting their beer tokens from Betty amid a ripple of un-enthusiastic applause from the other teams, the test of ACS heave on their coats.

'Same time next week then, Ruby?' asks Frank out of undeserved kindness.

Veronica's easing an Aran bobble hat over

her big hair. 'Why not bring that clever husband of yours along?'

'OK.' I try not to feel hurt.

Once they've gone, Ali and I resume our drinking. Being near to the door we're privy to snippets of conversation as people file out

'...me pigs to market in a coupla hours.'

'I told him, I said I worked like a Trojan for that harvest festival and what thanks...'

'...saw you gropin 'er in the bus shelter, ya dirty barrstard.'

Ali looks at me wide-eyed. 'How can you bear it here?'

What can I say? It would be like trying to explain the appeal of *Countdown* to an American game show fan with a beer in each hand and a wardrobe of vests. 'No, honestly, it's really good ... and you can win a teapot.'

Later. *Novel idea. Vicar bludgeoned to death with harvest festival marrow. Chief suspect, Hilary Watson – lifelong Trojan and flower lady.*

Ted and Hamish are unaware that I'm eavesdropping behind the rotating pantyhose stand. 'I'd just done the cash-and-carry run,' Ted's saying. 'So it must have been a Tuesday.'

'And how did she seem to you?'

'I tell you, that Jessica was a breath of fresh air to this village. Like nobody's been before nor since.' (Well, I do my best.) 'But that day she wasn't herself. Nor by a long chalk.'

'No?'

'Meg said to me, "That girl's been crying." I think the fair sex pick up on these things.' Ted clears his throat and lowers his volume. 'We're too busy mentally undressing them, aren't we? Eh?' I imagine a nudge and a wink taking place.

Hamish produces a laddish laugh. 'Can I give you my card? If you think of anything else that might help me track her down, just–'

'You're her cousin, you say?'

'That's right. But ... um ... keep this under your hat, will you, Ted? Don't really want Norman Potts having a seizure over it.'

'Mum's the word.' I picture him tapping the side of his nose.

Hamish leaves the shop without noticing me, and when he's gone and Ted's packing cigarettes tightly into the shelves behind the counter, I decide to have some fun and creep up with a pair of stockings in my hand.

'Hi,' I say.

Ted jumps before turning round to find

156

me holding the packet in front of him, the shapely thighs of the model inches from his startled face.

'Just these really sheer, black stockings, please, Ted.'

'Right you are.' He coughs and takes them from me, then fumbles around for the bar code.

'I don't suppose I could bring them back if they don't fit nicely?' I ask breathily, lifting my skirt a little and inspecting a leg. 'You just never know how they're going to look until you slip them on, do you?'

Ted gradually colours up and drops the stockings into a paper bag. 'So long as you've kept the receipt.'

On leaving the shop I curse myself for not buying what I'd set out for, but can hardly now go back in and present Ted with an arousing pack of butter.

'So do you think he mentally undresses, say, Veronica?' I ask Oliver later.

He has a long think about this, closes one eye and goes, 'Mm,' for a while. 'Well, I'm hardly *au fait* with Ted or any other male's sexual proclivities, but ... given a stab, I'd say no. I mean, there are all those cardies and scarves for a start. Then there'll be a petticoat or two and a cross-your-heart bra. A chap could exhaust himself thinking his way through all that.'

'So how about you?'

'What? No, no, I don't think Ted undresses me in his head.'

'Ha ha. I mean, do you...'

He becomes pensive again. 'You mean, apart from that rather delicious young weather girl who comes on after the local news on Tuesdays, Thursdays and every other Friday?'

I'm wishing I hadn't started this conversation. Oliver looks me up and down, then up again. 'Actually, I rather go the other way, you know, dress you all up a bit.' His features have taken on something of the Roger Moore and all of a sudden I feel the scratchiness of that gymslip.

I've squeezed my way into my so-called co-editor's house and he's apologising for his absenteeism. 'I've been awfully tied up with rehearsals.'

'How's it going?'

Toby clasps a handful of hair. 'One knows one's dealing with amateurs, of course, but all the same ... one absolutely despairs sometimes.' He manages to spot my discomfort. 'Poppy's superb, though.'

'You're not just saying that?'

'Gosh no. *Très* talented. Rather a shame she's got a bun in the oven.' He hands me several sheets of paper. 'Found the time to cobble this together, though.'

I look at the title – 'Rural Homophobia?' it says. 'By our Social Affairs Correspondent.' I flick through and discover to my horror that it's three and a half pages long – A4, single spacing. I'm more of a holiday-postcard-length journalist myself.

'Great,' I tell him. 'Thanks. Might have to do a wee bit of editing, though.'

'Well, if you must, swee– Ruby.' He takes it from me and turns to page two. 'But please, please, ensure this gets a mention. Here...'

I take a look. 'Gay antiques dealer, Tony Hardcastle (real name withheld), found himself the victim of discrimination when, after offering a local farmer a handsome sum for an early nineteenth-century port-manteau, discovered that the farmer had later sold the item to a heterosexual com-petitor at a lower price.'

'I take it this is you, Toby?'

'How very perspicacious of you. The farmer in question being the rustic Potts, of course.'

'Ah.'

'It was a trifle odd, actually.'

'Oh, yes?'

'Mm.' Toby stands up and paces the room – not an easy feat – arms folded across his chest. 'He was only selling the one item, despite that ramshackle place of his simply oozing with antique gems.'

I begin to wonder if we're talking about the same Farmer Potts. 'When was this?'

'Couple of years ago. I believe the place has undergone some refurbishment under the auspices of the delightful Trevor since then.'

'It's very comfortable now.'

'Oh, you've been?'

'Um, yes. To dinner.'

'Ha. How ridiculously courageous of you.' He sits at the table again and runs a finger up and down his largish nose. 'You know, one couldn't help thinking that portmanteau had an interesting history.'

'Oh?'

'I didn't inspect it too thoroughly. But even a cursory glance by a myopic numbskull couldn't miss that bloodstain.'

I try not to gasp. 'Who actually bought it then, Toby?'

He goes over to the old Welsh dresser

which spans the length of one wall, opens a drawer and flashes a card at me. I make a quick mental note of the address for Hamish, then bid Toby a hasty goodbye, before 23A Derwent Road, Liddleton seeps from my leaky, not-in-the-least-suited-to-pub-quizzes brain.

One Friday Josh arrives to chill in the country for the weekend. Late Saturday morning, with not enough sleep behind me, I look up 'chill' in Chambers. 'To cool: to preserve by cold,' it tells me. It doesn't say: 'To watch South Park videos until four a.m.: to cover all visible surfaces in bits of tobacco, grated cheese and lakes of Red Stripe: to swig directly from milk and other communal bottles then produce thunderous belch.'

'Come on, Josh,' I say after lunch, when I detect Oliver's jaw muscles repeatedly twitching. 'Let's go for a nice long walk. We can take the dogs.'

Dan, Ganja, plus the two boisterous male pups nobody would give homes to, join us, while Poppy has her obligatory nap, and we all set off together across the fields in faint drizzle, following the official footpath. Before long, due to Josh and Dan having

161

around twelve metres of leg between them and the energy that comes from sleeping till noon, Ganja and I find ourselves trailing way behind, breathless from taking twice as many steps as the others. They're soon out of sight, but I don't mind too much. As long as they're having a good time and Oliver's busy scouring the surfaces, I'm happy.

Ganja and I stop to take a little rest at the top of a hill but then spot the others in the distance, at the bottom of a grassy dip. They seem to be crouched and inspecting something, so we go and investigate.

'Magic mushrooms,' says Josh. He holds a scrawny little thing up for me to admire. 'Fuckin great, living in the country, if you ask me.'

I turn to Dan. 'Did you know about these?'

He gives me a cagey, 'Yeah.'

'You use a lot of mushrooms when you cook for us, don't you?'

'Yeah, I do. But not these.' He pops another one in the bag he's obviously brought along especially. 'Apart from–'

'What?'

'Well. You know when we had that dead brilliant game of Trivial Pursuit?'

'Ye-ess.'

'I reckon I got a few mushrooms muddled that evening.'

'Was that when Oliver never stopped going on about how beautifully vibrant the colours on the board were?'

'Right, yeah. And you put your hand on my leg and said you really loved me, right?'

So I did. 'Might be a good idea to take mushrooms off the menu, Dan. You know, what with Poppy's condition.'

'Spect you're right. We don't wanna give birth to a space cadet, do we?'

'Quite,' I say, and find myself quietly considering Dan's genes for the first time and hoping Poppy's might be dominant.

'Where are the dogs?' asks Josh. He stands up and turns full circle. 'Dogs!' he calls out.

Dan joins in. 'Dogs!'

They're nowhere in sight and I have a fleeting déjà vu sensation. 'Let's check those woods,' I suggest. 'I think Ganja went that way.'

'I dunno,' says Josh, shoving his hands in his trouser pockets and hunching his shoulders. 'I've read that farmers fuckin shoot you if you don't stick to the footpaths.'

'Oh, nonsense. Anyway they don't shoot at people they've had to dinner. Come on.'

We discover the three of them scurrying around in a large clearing, sniffing at the ground and occasionally stopping to scratch at the soil.

'Hey, what you doing, guys?' asks Dan.

'Perhaps they're looking for doggy magic mushrooms,' says Josh.

Dan nods with a serious expression. 'Hey, maybe there's like a body under there?'

I laugh loudly and for far too long at his suggestion, then go and grab one of the dogs by its collar. The ground, I notice, is relatively soft beneath my walking boots, despite being strewn with the debris of several seasons.

'Look what Ganja's found,' calls out Dan, and an icy tingle creeps up my spine. It's a Julio Iglesias CD, I know it is. I turn to see him trying to pull a floppy dead rabbit from the dog's jaws.

'Come on, girl. Give it to me. Rabbit stew for supper if you let go.'

'Wow,' I hear Josh say quietly behind me. 'This is so fuckin rural, man.'

Early Sunday evening, I'm showing Josh the articles I've either written or accumulated for the first month's magazine.

'Great, yeah. But you don't wanna get

ripped off by fuckin typesetters and all that. Just e-mail it through to me at the shop and I'll desktop publish it for you. For a small fee. A mate of mine'll print a few samples for you. He owes me one.'

'You can do that stuff?'

'Yeah. They encourage you to take all these courses when you're unemployed. You know, improve your CV-writing skills, introduction to boiler maintenance, that kind of bollocks. Anyway DTP was good. Had this safe teacher, said I had a flair for it.'

Oliver's outside revving up the engine, and has been for a good five minutes, so I thrust a few sheets of paper at Josh and tell him to show me a sample of his work, before ushering him out and kissing him goodbye. We pick up his two bin bags of clean laundry and chuck them on to the back seat.

'Couldn't just stop at the supermarket, could we?' he asks a fuming Oliver. 'Only it was my turn to shop last week and they'll fuckin kill me if I don't do it today.'

Oliver now manages a smile. 'But it's too late, Josh. They close at four on Sundays. What bad luck.'

Oliver says he'd rather have a daily chest

wax for the rest of his life than suffer the humiliation of losing to Dan's quiz team.

'I take it that's a no, then?'

'Absolutely.'

Poor Oliver. I may have been lumbered with lousy spatial ability, but he's had to endure the handicap of a male ego for forty-five years.

I trot over to Troy Shed. 'Fancy trying your hand at the pub quiz?' I ask Poppy. She's lying on the sofa reading, using her tummy as a bookrest, a half-eaten box of Milk Tray beside her.

'Yeah, alright.'

It takes her an age to get up, kiss the animals goodbye and lock up, and by the time we reach the Dog and Gun, Betty's already repeating the first question.

'Where in the body would you find the greatest concentration of synovial fluid?'

'That's easy,' says Poppy as we take our seats. 'It's the knee, right?'

'Sshhh,' hiss Always Come Second, fingers at our lips. We look around to see if anyone heard her.

'Oh right, sorry.'

I go and get us a couple of soft drinks and return when Poppy's saying, 'Peru,' in a quiet but authoritative way.

'Sure?'

She nods and we all listen to the next question. 'Ernest Hemingway,' she tells us immediately.

'I was actually going to say that,' says a slightly piqued Veronica. 'Or that other chap, you know, Gatsby.' I watch her misspell both Ernest and Hemingway, and hope it won't lose us points.

At the end of the first round of ten questions we exchange answer sheets with the nearest team, and as Betty painstakingly gives the correct answers the mood of ACS builds to what is probably an all-time high.

When asked for our score, Frank calls out a resounding, 'TEN!' for Betty to note.

She looks to the far corner. 'After History?'

One of them mumbles something.

'Sorry, dear?'

'Nine!'

Everyone looks our way and a murmur works its way around the pub before Betty hoists herself back on her stool – grunting into the mike as she does so – and launches into round two.

During the half-time break, when we're so pleased with ourselves we can barely sit still and it's drinks on Frank, and Veronica's doing her relaxation breathing, Oliver rolls up – 'Just as an observer, you understand' – and takes a detached position at the bar. However, by the time we're receiving a standing ovation from the other teams (bar one) and collecting our beer tokens, he's managed to sidle over to our table and even gives a nod and a small wave to the applauding throng.

'Who's going to drink all this beer then?' I ask the team.

'None for me and babe,' says Poppy.

'G and T man myself,' Frank tells us.

'I'm friggin starvin,' says Gail.

I go to the bar, and as After History are skulking past, jackets zipped up to noses, hands deep in pockets, I talk Betty into exchanging our beer tokens for six packets of crisps. The boys stop in their tracks and stare in disbelief, as though I'd just set fire to a couple of World Cup Final tickets. I give them a smug smile and my condolences, then go back and dish out the crisps, giving Poppy my packet too for being so clever.

'Same time next week then, team,' commands Veronica.

We all nod, including Oliver. He rubs his hands together. 'We'll show them again, eh?'

Sudden recollection of Poppy first week at school when she fell deeply in love with her reception class teacher, Miss Blacksmith: an energetic woman in thick tights who'd obviously missed her calling as university lecturer.

'What did you do today?' I asked Poppy on day three or four. 'I writed a book,' she told me and got it out of her bag. She was soon to be five, so I wasn't expecting Middlemarch, *but was amazed at the quality of her ten pages on the Castles of Britain. On page one was Warwick. 'Crenellations,' she'd written with an arrow to the top of the wall. The dictionary told me they were notches in a parapet. After looking up 'parapet' I felt ready to move on to page two.*

Next week it was, 'Miss Blacksmiff teached us about ammonites.'

'Oh yes?' said Jeremy and I, pulling faces at each other and shrugging. 'Tell us all about them then, Poppy.'

Just when we thought our daughter might be ready for Oxbridge by the age of six, Miss Blacksmith gave a term's notice and was sadly replaced by the newly qualified Mr Collins, who wrote on her first report that Poppy needed to be more 'carefull' with her spelling.

In a teashop in Liddleton with doilies and

dainty white toast racks and the aroma of Welsh rarebit, Hamish and I are getting our heads together. I can't say it's unpleasant. We're both wearing raincoats with the collars turned up, adding an extra frisson to our furtive meeting.

'So, what have we got?' asks Hamish. He's pulled a reporter's pad from an inside pocket and is flicking pages over. 'Seemed upset. Popular, but didn't say goodbye to anyone. Cry for help on mirror. Left her clothes behind.'

I'm sitting side on to Hamish, staring at a cute lock of dark hair behind his left ear. 'Norman panics when she's mentioned,' I say when he turns to me, then go on to tell him about how Norman flew from the auditions just when the song was contemplating murder.

He looks at me askance. 'You mean you actually *sang* "Ruby Don't Take Your Love to Town"?'

I nod. 'Mm.'

'In front of people?'

Don't blush. I clear my throat and continue, 'Bloodstain on the portmanteau.'

'Checked that out. No longer in the country, apparently. Let's see, what else is there? Oh yes, possible shallow grave on

Potts' land.'

'One tea,' says a portly blonde waitress suddenly beside us in neat black and white uniform. 'And a filter coffee for you, sir.'

I'm convinced she overheard us as her eyes are now darting between Hamish and me in the manner of someone who's about to slip out the back to a telephone and whisper things to the local constabulary.

'Thanks,' I say sweetly.

'Her maiden name was McKenzie,' continues an unaware Hamish. 'Married twice.'

Our waitress is pretending to clear the next table, while I grimace at Hamish and gesture towards her.

'What? Oh.'

'So it's a good film then, is it? *Shallow Grave?*' I've completely lost him but continue anyway. 'Have you seen that new one with, oh, whatsisname, in it?' My mind scratches around for the title of a recent film, but so cut off have I been from the world it can't come up with one. These days I feel I've had a cultural experience if I peruse Ted's postcard selection.

The waitress glides away to a newly arrived party of four, shaking their umbrellas and looking around for a table.

'Anyway,' says Hamish, 'did an Internet

search. It just came up with Jessie Mc-Kenzie's Health Club in Inverness.'

'Oh?'

'Turned out to be a man.'

'Ah.'

Before we leave I place a five-pound note on the table, under the condiments.

Hamish blinks at it. 'You don't tip that well in my place.'

'Hush money,' I whisper.

'Could just draw attention to us.'

'Good thinking.' I pick up the note and put a one-pound coin in its place, then turn to see our waitress staring at me, arms folded over her plentiful bosom, face creased into a perplexed expression.

'Bye. Thanks,' I call out to her when we reach the door.

Once outside we open our umbrellas and agree to keep each other informed of developments.

'If it's Jessica Potts you're after,' a voice suddenly hisses from the rear – I turn to see our waitress leaning through the open door – 'you want to have a word with that hairdresser of hers.'

'Tina?'

'That's the one.' She gives a firm nod and

bobs back into the café.

'How extraordinary,' whispers Hamish.

During the six-mile drive home, I ponder on our strange new lead. Perhaps Tina was a close confidante of Jessica's, as many a hairdresser is of many a client, and knows more than she let on. Or maybe Jessica topped herself after a particularly hideous perm. What's more likely, I decide, as I swing the Range Rover into the drive, is that young Maximilian is behind the whole thing.

I've noticed in recent years that Bonfire Night has extended itself into a whole season, beginning the minute Hallowe'en's over and petering our with a few leftover bangers in mid-November. Upper Muckhill, it seems, has signed up to this trend, and Oliver and I are about to attend our fifth fireworks party – this time a Parish Council-organised affair, which means I should really write a line or two about it.

'I do believe,' Oliver's saying, 'that we're born with so many "Ooos" and so many "Aaahs".' He's knocking back a second gin and tonic. 'And that I have used all mine up in the past few weeks.' He slops a little more gin in his glass. 'So, if you hear someone admiring the fireworks with an "Eeee" tonight, I'm not just being perverse, you understand.'

'OK.' I'm only half listening, searching as I am for the list of questions I've prepared for Tina. Having got them, I return to the kitchen to find Oliver refilling his glass and immediately adopt nagging-wife stance. 'Look. If you're going to get drunk you can't come.'

'Promise?'

I go alone and mingle with familiar faces, my eyes constantly sweeping the crowd for Tina's. Once the display starts, I sit on a rusty old chair by the cricket pavilion, savouring a polystyrene cup of Mrs Allsop's season's vegetables soup and listening to the crowd's somewhat predictable noises. Before long I hear a definite 'Psst,' behind me. I turn to see what I think is Hamish. It's his coat, but it doesn't seem to be his hair.

'Psst,' he says again.

'Hamish?'

'Yes. Come here.'

I join him in the dark, but it's not so dark that I can't see he's been totally shorn. I'm unable to stifle a gasp. 'What happened?'

'Paid Tina a visit. Thought I'd get a trim

while I was there.'

'But she did mine really nicely. You should get your money back.'

'I did. Turns out she's never really got the hang of men. Can only do a number one.'

He looks just like Maximilian. 'So, did you find out anything?'

'Um, only that she thinks they're probably going to her mum for Christmas.'

'Right ... but that's if her dad's had his operation, isn't it? Otherwise they'll be–'

'Having her brother and his family over?'

'That's it.'

We both stand nodding. 'Nothing new, then?' I say.

'Uh-uh. I was only in there three or four minutes. Maybe you could go and have a shampoo and set. Might take an hour or so. Have a natter while you're under the dryer.'

Hamish has obviously never been under one. This all seems somewhere beyond the call of duty but I find myself agreeing to do it. He fishes in his pocket and hands me a twenty-pound note.

'Here you are. It's on me.'

Twenty pounds, eh? Could probably have it done twice for that. 'Thanks. But if I end up looking like Shirley Temple I'll be suing, OK?'

'I've called it *Menstrual Cycle*,' Ali's telling Poppy and me. We take three steps back, the better to grasp the concept of her new piece. Before us an old pushbike leans slightly to one side on its little stand, on top of a white board with a large, blood-red splodge painted in the middle.

'Cool,' says Poppy. 'And what's this one?'

'Oh, that's a protest about battery farming.'

They go over to something constructed out of cardboard egg trays and barbed wire, while I'm left wondering if it's me, or what.

'It's entitled *It's No Yoke*.'

'Brilliant.'

Ali's daughter, Beth – ceiling height and willowy, long, baby-white, blonde hair – wafts in and announces that there's a pot of ginseng tea on the go.

'Oh my God! Poppy!' she cries, and flies across the room with arms open.

'Hi, Beth.'

They embrace as best they can, what with Poppy now being as wide as Beth is tall.

'Wow,' Beth says over and over. She's got her hands on Poppy's bump. 'That must feel *so weird*. It's just like amazing that someone my age is going to have a baby. Hey, Mum,

176

can I get pregnant too?'

'Only when I sell some of my work, love.'

'Huh,' snorts Beth. She hooks her arm through Poppy's and leads her into the kitchen. 'In that case I'm gonna die childless.'

Poppy throws me a distressed look over her shoulder. I don't think she wants the ginseng tea either.

'No, thanks,' says Poppy when Beth offers her a top-up. She's got that bilious expression I've seen so often recently. 'So anyway,' she tells Ali, 'we're just using this old *Babes in the Wood* set, right? Which is like peeling paint and sellotaped together.'

'Would you like some more, Ruby?'

The pot is heading towards me so I quickly slap one hand over my cup. 'Uh-uh. Got to drive, ha ha.'

'So, yeah,' continues Poppy. 'It would be really good if you could sort of make us a decent set.'

'No money in it, I suppose?' asks Ali.

'Don't think so. Veronica sent me to beg a carton of milk off Ted the other day.'

'It'll be crap if *she* does it,' chips in the angelic-looking Beth. She curls a lip at her mother then gets up and goes over to the

Sanyo where she carefully chooses some music-to-irritate and puts it on at full volume.

Ali has to raise her voice. 'Could form part of my portfolio, I suppose.'

Poppy frowns. 'Won't that be a bit heavy?'

'Photos,' she shouts.

'Oh right. Shall I put in a word then?'

'Sure.'

So, that's Poppy, Dan and possibly Ali involved in the panto. All we need now is for Oliver to redesign the village hall and Josh to do interval espressos. During a lull in the music I ask Beth what she's doing these days. She switches off the stereo and rejoins us.

'Art A level. Evening class.'

'Oh right. Are you enjoying it?'

She curls that lip again. 'Got a complete wanker teaching us but it's something to do for a year.' She briefly inspects the ends of her hair then flicks them back. 'God, this place is *sooo* boring. I can't wait to get away.'

I'm about to forage for my cheque book to help her on her way when Ali leans over and strokes her daughter's face with the back of a finger. 'I'll be heartbroken when she goes.'

Beth rolls her eyes. 'Wanna go upstairs?' she asks Poppy.

It's odd to be in Ali's company and not be listening to tales of emotional abuse. After the girls disappear we sink into capacious armchairs and find ourselves discussing a TV documentary we both watched, then the new city traffic scheme. It's so odd, in fact, that after some time I'm compelled to ask how Hamish is.

'Great. Well, I think he is. He's a bit busy at the moment.'

'Oh yes?'

'Sniffing out some story. Says it's hush-hush.'

'How exciting.'

Ali's lovingly stroking the two sleek cats on her lap. 'You and Oliver should come over for dinner soon.'

'That'd be nice,' I say, studiously ignoring the chubby and odorous one that's staring me in the face while it pummels my chest and dribbles.

'Then I'd get to see Hamish,' she adds. Why is she staring at me through narrowed eyes, I wonder. 'Think he's got a bit of a soft spot for you.'

'Oh rubbish, he barely knows me.' Quick, change the subject. 'So what's on at the, um, cinema at the moment? Maybe we could go

and see something together? You know how
Oliver hates to drag himself beyond the
cottage walls.'

I heat Poppy's heavy footsteps on the
stairs and make a show of glancing at my
watch. 'Perhaps we should be off before
rush hour.'

'But it's Saturday.'

'Of course.'

Beth glides gracefully into the room. 'No
he doesn't. He looks like a dickhead.
Literally, yeah?'

'Well, I think he looks a lot better,' says
Poppy.

'Who are you talking about?' asks Ali.

Beth sneers. 'Hamish and his stupid haircut.'

'It's very nice.' Ali tells them. 'So when did
you see him, Poppy?'

Poppy eases herself into a comfy armchair
and while she has a little think my old cat
flops himself on to the floor, pads across the
room and takes up residence on her tummy.

'Oh yeah, I know,' she says. 'When he was
talking to Mum behind the cricket pavilion
the other night. It was a bit dark there but I
thought he looked really good.'

We leave an hour later after I've taken Ali
into a quiet room, calmed her down, told

her the story and sworn her to secrecy. 'Otherwise it might get out of hand. You know – *News of the World* reporters crawling over the village, parading as thatchers while their tool bags are secretly filming.'

We're five minutes from Ali's, inching through the city at ten miles an hour, when Poppy announces that she desperately needs the loo again. She wriggles in the passenger seat while I turn down a side street.

'Here we are. We're quite near Josh's. I'll take you there.' I'm simultaneously praying that someone's in, and shuddering at the thought of what awaits her in Josh's bathroom. Not an attraction the National Trust has been clamouring for, I'd imagine, although possibly a Site of Special Scientific Interest.

It turns out Josh has moved, but a young man sporting blue lips and a hooded coat tells us it's cool for Poppy to use the toilet, only there's no light because the electric's been cut off. Probably for the best, I decide, as I accompany her into the icy darkness. Before we leave I ask where Josh has gone.

'Not sure. But I think he's living over that place he works in.'

'Oh right, thanks.'

The boy shivers, pulls his hood over his brow and throws himself into a lengthy sniff. It's all I can do not to bundle him into the Range Rover and take him home for hot broth. 'If you see Josh,' he says as he exhales, 'tell him Saddam and his posse's after him for that money, yeah? He'll know what it's about.'

I stare stupidly for a while, wondering if I've been jerked into a parallel universe. 'Saddam,' I repeat with a couple of nods. 'Right.'

I close the day with my journal, neglected of late owing to channelling my energy into interviewing a visiting vicar, knocking Frank's article on Upper Muckhill's rodent life into shape, and worse.

Winter days in a village, I scribble, *seem to come to an end just when you're stretching and yawning and thinking of what you have to do today. Mums hurry their children home from school before darkness descends and, from the end of October, Ted closes his shop at four thirty. Fires are lit, a bit of telly is watched and then – unless it's pub quiz night – somewhere between nine and ten, fires are doused and the cat's shown the door. This I discovered when deliver-*

ing Frank's rewritten piece in the dead of Upper Muckhill night – eight forty-five. Around thirty chains and bolts and locks were undone before Veronica creaked her old oak door open a foot or so to reveal a brushed nylon nightie and a fringe wrapped round a curler. Was mildly repri-manded for having given them a nasty fright as one only expects bad news at this late hour. Walking back past unlit houses, I found it hard to get my head around the fact people in the city were just setting off for the cinema, so on arriv-ing home, picked up the car keys and asked Oliver what we needed from the 24-hour supermarket. He stopped dousing the fire, lifted the sleeve of his towelling robe to see the time, suggested I have my hormone balance checked, and said, 'Actually, we are running pretty low on Horlicks.'

'Just off for a lap dancing session with Jean Crowbar,' says Oliver one chilly, late Nov-ember morning. 'Better make sure I've got everything. Dirty mac, five-pound note to tuck in her stocking.'

He means laptop. 'Why exactly are you doing this, Oliver?' It's hardly in character for him to be helping out a fellow human being for no personal gain.

'Well ... Jean told me that her Gail's screwing her married and corrupt boss at the computer shop and can therefore get hold of knocked-off laptops and sell them to any villager with a spare fifty quid. Not in those precise words, you understand.'

'Ah.' That explains why half the village is on-line.

'Anyway. I'll just give Jean a quick lesson in Windows, then slip in my order. Back in half an hour.'

After he's gone I take a last look in the mirror at my hairstyle – the one I've had since the age of five, basically – then drag myself out of the house and head for Tina's place. I'm reluctant to do this, to say the least, and wonder en route whether I'll have to switch to smart M&S outfits to match my new hairstyle, as they do in those women's mags where sexy, casually dressed, young-looking women with nice natural hair are made over into the kind of secretary you wouldn't mind your husband having.

'Shall I put a few layers in?' Tina asks. 'Give it a bit of body?'

'Um.'

'Make it easier to put the rollers in too.'

'Well...'

184

She's already lifting a portion of my hair between two fingers and running the scissors along. 'You could do with a softer look with your features.'

I wonder what she means but daren't enquire. 'So, got your Christmas organised?' I ask instead.

'Thought I had till bloody Darren started up.'

'Darren?'

'Me ex. Maximilian's dad.'

'Right.'

Tina shakes her anxious-looking head. 'Says he wants his son for Christmas,' she tells me with a weighty sigh. I'm finding it hard to see why she's looking so distressed; surely that would be her best present ever? I see a lock of hair the size of a small mouse plummet to the floor and feel my stomach tighten.

'So when did you split up?'

Tina goes quiet for a while and I wonder if I shouldn't have asked. 'Ages ago now,' she says. 'When I found out about him and...'

'Hm?'

She points at the photograph of Jessica Potts.

'No!' I stare at her in the mirror, jaw in lap.

Tina nods. 'It done my head in, I tell ya.'

'I'm not surprised. But you and Jessica seem to have stayed friends.'

'Weren't for a while. But then I met my Pauly and realised she done me a gynormous favour.'

She pulls strands of hair together under my chin to check one side isn't shorter than the other, forcing me to pause for a while before asking, 'Did Norman find out?'

'Oh yeah, I'll say. Went ballistic, he did.' She wheels a small trolley containing assorted foam curlers towards me and I realise I'll soon be incommunicado under the big pink dryer next to the ironing board. Just as it's getting interesting.

'Er, I was wondering about highlights, Tina. What do you think?'

'It depends really,' she says, holding up a length of hair and inspecting it. ''Sup to you. I mean if you're happy with hair the colour of ... of...'

'Day-old dishwater?'

It takes Tina a good few minutes to recover from my wry wit, and when she goes off to turn the Chris de Burgh tape over and mix up the peroxide solution with a plastic spoon, it dawns on me I might be able to eke this out till Maximilian needs to be fetched from school.

Oliver walks through the front door just as I'm coming out of my office-in-the-wall. He stops in his tracks, reverses out, looks up at the front of the house and comes back in.

'Just checking I've got Troy Cottage,' he says, 'not Dolly Parton's place.'

'Very funny.'

He takes his coat off and follows me into the kitchen where he slowly circles me, then stands with his hands on his hips. 'I have to say you're looking pretty hot, Roo.'

'Am I really?' This is due in part to the little red number, stockings and high heels I felt a compulsion to pop into the moment I got home. It's funny how a small hairdo can make you want to dress like a Las Vegas hooker. I go over to the mirror by the back door. God, I look weird.

'Blimey,' Tina said just before releasing me from her chair. 'Know who you're the spitting of now?'

I looked at the full, fluffy, highlighted mass surrounding my face and shrugged.

'Her.' She pointed to Jessica's photograph.

'Well, hardly!' I protested.

'Dead ringer.'

I wished she hadn't used that word.

When I wake the next morning, after a night with the suddenly insatiable Oliver, and stumble into the bathroom, I can see why Jessica went to Tina twice a week. I'm definitely more Dolly the Sheep than Dolly Parton today. I go downstairs and potter in the kitchen, jumping every time I see my reflection, then try to rouse Oliver with a strong coffee. He's due at Jean Crowbar's for her second day of training.

'I believe they call it computer dyslexia,' he tells me through a yawn. 'Happens to women of a certain age after years of following complex knitting patterns.' He peers at me through one sleepy eye. 'Mm, you look different.' He takes a sip of coffee. 'What was that programme that used to be on, about women in a prisoner-of-war camp? You know, where they looked bedraggled and ravaged all the time?'

'Excuse me?'

'It's very appealing, actually. Come here.'

'What about Jean's cutting and pasting?' I take his coffee off him and put it out of harm's way.

'Given the choice between a quickie with the young Dolly Parton and a smart new laptop com–' his eyes wander over to the alarm clock, then begin darting from side to side, '–puter.'

I get up and pass back the coffee. 'Croissant?'

'Please.'

I'm about to interview a clairvoyant for the magazine. She's called Miss T. Ree and has recently set up a consultancy in Little Crompton.

'You'd think she'd come up with a better name than that,' said Oliver before I left this afternoon. 'You know, I.C. Danger, or something.' He then spent half an hour or so ranting about the gullibility and utter patheticness of people who rely on astrology and tarot and all that tosh to prop up their insecure and meaningless little lives.

'Oh, I don't know,' I managed to say, eventually. 'It's no different from believing in a God you've never met. And I don't hear you calling the vicar and his flower ladies deluded cretins.'

That shut him up. But only temporarily. 'No, no,' he continued. 'Religion's different. I mean, my parents went to church and you could hardly call them flaky.'

While I was reversing out of the drive he came running over. 'You wouldn't just mention those funny twinges I've been getting in my, you know, nether region?' He held on to the open window while he recovered his breath. 'If it's curtains I'd rather you kept it from me, though.'

Miss T. Ree is around sixty, but with her maroon velvet catsuit and bandanna-wrapped jet-black hair could at some distance pass for a groovy young thing from the Kings Road, circa 1967. She greets me at the door of her bungalow, where a note on the step says, 'No milk after Friday, thanks.' She's obviously foreseen some fatal personal incident, I decide, and try to crack a joke to that effect.

'Got a Psychic Fair in Cleethorpes this weekend,' she informs me.

'That's nice. And are you going to get lots of clients and enjoy good weather?' I really must stop this.

'Most probably. We're always successful in Cleethorpes, for some reason. I think they're going through a bit of a repression up there.'

'Do you mean rece–'

'This way, dear.'

She takes me into the living room, where I immediately sink four inches into the carpet. Miss Ree goes on to weave us through a leatherette three-piece suite, past an ornate gold-edged hostess trolley, two Degas prints and a collection of glass animals on a gratuitous shelf in the hall – until we come to a sun, moon and stars motif curtain across a doorway. All of a sudden I smell joss sticks and hear the strains of a slightly crackly version of 'Aquarius.'

'Just take a seat,' she says, holding the curtain to one side and revealing a small room bathed in ultrared light. 'I'll just go and turn the heating up.'

'But I'm really only here to—'

'Choose the colour of bean bag you feel most drawn to.'

'Right.'

I step inside, the curtain falls back into place behind me, and I spend several moments trying to work out what she means. There are five bean bags and they all look a sickly red in this light. I choose the middle one of a row of three, set up my cassette recorder and wonder how on earth I'm going to read the questions on my pad. I'm squinting at them when she returns.

'Ah, you chose the yellow, I see. A wee bit low in spirits, are we?'

I've heard about this. Tricking punters

into leaking little clues. 'I don't know if you remember me saying I wanted to interview you for our magazine?'

'Yes, dear.' She sits opposite me, picks up a pack of tarot cards which she holds to her chest, and appears to go into a trance.

'I'm not actually here for a consul–'

Her eyes spring open and she stares above me at the wall behind. 'I see an elderly man.' I turn around to see if I can see him too. 'He will be journeying towards you soon.'

'Oh, that'll be my fa–' Damn.

'Aaahh... and also a, now what is it... a girl or a boy. A boy, I believe.'

'Oh, really? Is it going to be a boy?'

The corner of her mouth twitches. 'And another boy ... no ... a young man. Smartly dressed, affluent, successful in his career.' She lowers her head and looks penetratingly into my eyes. 'A relative, perhaps?'

'My son?' I say, laughing and slapping a thigh.

She casts a glance at my left hand. 'Your husband will continue to provide love and companionship for ... oh dear ... well, for a while, anyway.'

I catch my breath and point to my groin. 'Is it?'

She nods.

'And so,' she says a few minutes later, laying the unused cards down and smiling appreciatively at me, 'I see you continuing to develop your creative and communicative skills in the written form. You will enjoy a warm family Christmas with your father – and ... do I see a new member of the family arriving in the near future?'

I nod.

'Do you perhaps have difficulty relating to a child's lifestyle? Your son?'

I nod again.

'I have a feeling your husband is experiencing one or two little health worries?'

I raise my eyebrows.

'An early check-up is always a good idea.'

I nod.

'That's the end of our session, dear,' she says.

What? People pay twenty-five pounds for that? Even I'm feeling a bit cheated as I bend down to switch off the cassette that's been secretly recording at my feet, heave myself out of the bean bag and follow her into the glare of a hundred-watt bulb. She says, 'I think that should be efficient for an article, don't you, dear?'

'Do you mean suff–'

'After all, with my name I shouldn't be giving too much away about myself. Were you wanting a photograph?'

'Please.

I get her to pose languidly against the celestial curtain, then gather up my belongings before being led to the front door, where Miss T. Ree's hand all of a sudden falls on my shoulder. Her eyes turn saucer-like and adopt a faraway look. 'You have a tall plant with long, sharp, pointed leaves in the alcove of your lounge, don't you?'

'Ye-es.'

'Just behind your favourite armchair?'

'But how do you—'

'Knives in your back, dear. Bad feng shui.'

'Really?'

'Bury it in the garden.'

'OK.'

'And another thing.'

'What?' I ask nervously.

She rubs her left temple in a circular fashion with the tips of three fingers, as though trying to tune in better. 'The number twenty-three will open doors,' she tells me dreamily, before rather abruptly closing her own.

'But we paid a bloody fortune for that

plant,' Oliver's saying, hands rigidly at his waist. He's refusing to help me dig a hole in the semi-frozen soil in the dark. 'Just because some fraudster happened to inadvertently hit on a recognisable fact.'

'OK, listen,' I tell him when I've given up and we go back into the house. I surreptitiously find the spot on the cassette where Miss Ree is on a roll. '... family Christmas with your father,' she's saying. I see Oliver's ears prick up and he listens through to the end, when the colour, I notice, begins fading from his sceptical features.

'Did you tell her about my...?'

'No.' (Not exactly.)

'What does she mean, an early check-up is always a good idea? As opposed to a far-too-late-one, I suppose. Where's the phone book?'

'Two double one, four five nine. Doctor Spencer.'

'Right.' He jots it down. 'It's a woman, isn't it?'

'Yep. She's rather gorgeous actually. Looks about eighteen.'

'Really?' He picks up the phone and taps in the number, glancing down at his groin, then into the mirror with a grin and a twitch of the eyebrows.

Poppy saunters into the kitchen one Saturday morning carrying the communal mobile phone. 'Josh just rang,' she tells us. 'He's invited us all to dinner tonight.'

Oliver turns to me wide-eyed and steadies himself with a hand on the worktop.

'Oh come on,' I say, blocking from my mind the time I visited Josh and saw maggots in a saucepan on the draining board. 'It won't be that bad.'

Poppy agrees with me. 'And he's really good at Thai curries.'

Oliver's hand flies to his stomach.

'Perhaps we can take a packed meal along for you.'

He looks relieved. 'And my own cutlery?'

There are two doors: one to the shop and the other a buzzer-operated affair.

'Hello?' comes Josh's tinny voice through the intercom.

Dan bends down and shouts, 'Easy, Josh.'

'Jesus. Just deafen me, won't you?'

The buzzer buzzes and we all troop in, Oliver at the rear with his Tupperware boxes. At the top of a flight of dark green carpeted stairs an open door leads us towards a table laid for around ten.

'Wow, brilliant sofa,' says Poppy, pointing to the far end of the room. She kicks off her shoes and pads over satin finish floorboards and lowers herself slowly, hand in the small of her back. In front of her is a matt black coffee table on which sit one book and two remote controls, side by side and perfectly parallel. She adjusts the cushion behind her: one of four, all plumped and perched at the same angle. To her left, off-white linen curtains hang from a wooden pole and at her feet lies a spotless rug in assorted primary colours. Beside the sofa, fresh tiger lilies spring from a frosted-glass vase and are effectively illuminated by the small white lamp I've had my eye on in Habitat for some time.

Josh comes out of the kitchen in a pinny and says, 'Hey, you alright, Mum?'

'Mm.'

Oliver breathes in the aroma of tomatoes, garlic and basil. 'Something smells good. Treating us to Italian, eh, Josh?' He slips his packed dinner out on to the landing.

'Yeah, my speciality.'

I hand him our bottle of wine. 'Nice place,' I say hoarsely.

'Thanks.' He reads the label, says, 'Not bad,' and places it at the back of a collection of others on a pale grey unit that runs almost the length of one wall.

Dan's already sitting at the table and ripping open a bread roll.

'Hey,' says Josh, snatching it from his hand and placing it on a pristine white side plate. 'Gotta wait for the boss to arrive.'

'Oh right, sorry. Only Pops wouldn't let me have any dinner before we came out.'

'Is Hamish coming then?' I ask.

'Yeah. And Ali and Beth.' Blimey. 'Need a hand?'

'Nah. It's all sorted.'

'Your hair's looking very nice,' Hamish whispers in a corner towards ten o'clock, after we've gorged ourselves on Josh's delicious and beautifully presented pasta dish, fresh fruit salad and posh ice cream, and are about to begin a game of charades. 'Does that mean you've seen Tina?'

'Yes.' I take a folded envelope out of my pocket. 'Here you are.'

'Oh, thanks.' He runs a hand through his own, now slightly spiky, hair. 'What do you think?' he asks. 'Shall I keep it like this?'

I take a step back and assess. He looks adorable. 'Yep. Definitely.'

He glides towards me and bows his head.

'Why did you tell Ali about Jessica?'

'She thought you and I were having an illicit affair.'

'Ha!' he says, moving almost indiscernibly closer.

'Ridiculous, eh?' I get a whiff of Calvin Klein's Eternity for Men and a small flutter in the pit of my stomach.

'Fatal Attraction!' calls out Ali.

'Yeah, that's right,' says Poppy. She bows to her audience and takes her seat again.

Hamish and I look at each other, leap apart, and go and join our respective teams.

When the game's over Josh brings out the whisky. 'Single malt, of course. I think you'll find it pleasing. Hamish?'

'Yes, please.'

Josh pours some into an appropriate glass. My, how well-equipped this place is. All Hamish's doing, apparently.

'Mum? Oh no, you loathe it.'

'And I'm driving.'

'Poppy, I don't suppose...'

She shakes her sleepy head.

'Beth?'

Beth sticks her fingers down her throat.

'Oliver?'

'Don't mind if I do, Josh.'

Dan holds out his beer glass for filling, but Josh tuts, calls him a philistine and exchanges it for a smaller one.

'A toast, I think,' says Hamish. He stands and holds up his glass. 'To the new flat.'

'New flat, new flat, flat,' say we, those with glasses lifting them towards Josh then taking a genteel sip.

Josh meanwhile hoists the whisky bottle to his pursed lips, takes several glugs, swallows audibly, grimaces, blinks away the tears, says, 'Aaahh,' and releases a loud burp then a smaller one. He wipes his nose with a sleeve and looks up to find he has an audience.

'Oh fuck,' he says. 'I mean…'

We all quickly find something to talk about. 'Well, he almost pulled it off,' I hear Oliver say to himself.

Journal – *Am intrigued by Miss T Ree's number twenty-three business and, as a consequence, have found myself behaving in a worrying fashion: changing my lucky number, for a start; changing my cashcard pin number, credit card pin number, Callminder pin number, and so on. Buying twenty-three National Lottery tickets, all with the number twenty-three on them. I berated myself for days after that.*

'STOP POTTS! Campaign. Join us for a day of Non-Violent Direct Action,' says the poster in Ted's window. 'Bring a tree.' Three of us are standing there wondering if it's a spelling mistake. I decide to go home and phone Veronica for clarification.

'The committee thought we might sway Norman Potts if we, I mean they, I mean, you – have to disassociate myself, you understand – plant young trees on Trevor's airstrip.'

'Won't that be trespass?' I ask. 'Not to say vandalism?'

'Well, it's hardly vandalism. After all, we'd, I mean you'd, be creating a dear little spinney.'

'Right.' In solid mid-winter soil? She's obviously lost all sense of the feasible.

After putting down the phone, I go over to Troy Shed and ask if I can borrow a dog.

'Yeah, have three,' says Poppy. 'They keep jumping all over me when I'm practising my birth scene.'

I'm not sure if she means the real one or what, but decide to take the two boys off her (and the exhausted-looking Ganja's) hands, and soon find myself being yanked towards the large flat area that will one day be abuzz with light aircraft and people who spend their other days working in Swaps and Derivatives. When we eventually get there I let the dogs off their leads and they immediately bound towards the makeshift hangar which houses Trevor's little plane. I pray he's not in there, but of course he is, a tool in one hand and a pained expression on his oil-smeared face.

'God, these dogs!' I pant. 'I'm so sorry.'

'Don't worry. I just wish they could help me fix this dodgy injector.'

I go over to the front of the plane where Trevor has one arm buried in its innards.

'Watch the propeller,' he warns me. 'It could take your arm off, you know.'

I have a sudden image of Jessica's coiffed head flying through the air. 'Right, thanks,' I say, staring inside the machine at the actual nuts and bolts that he obviously relies on to keep him airborne. Talk about brave. 'Gosh,' I say helpfully.

'She's a lovely old thing,' grunts Trevor. 'But been coughing a lot lately.' He pulls his arm out and wipes his hand on an oily cloth. 'Want to have a sit inside?'

I eye him suspiciously. This wouldn't be a trick, would it? Switch on the ignition, spin the propeller round and push her off into oblivion. That'll teach her not to go snooping around.

'Can I?'

'What do you mean, you want to go up for a flight with Trevor?' asks Oliver later. 'Are you mad, woman? But more importantly, where do you keep your life policy?'

'Oh you know, in the thingy.'

'We'll go to Spain or somewhere if you want to fly.'

'But it was just so ... oh, I don't know ... sort of small and scary, I suppose. Just sitting in there was exciting.'

'Are you saying you don't have enough excitement in your life? Didn't you help judge the WI cake contest last week?'

'Yes, but we all knew Mrs Allsop would win.'

'I can see that would take some of the fun out of it.'

'Anyway, he said he would take me up if I wanted. When the something or other's mended.'

Oliver potters about for a while shuffling papers around, flicking through circulars, crumpling old envelopes, whistling a bit. 'He's quite nice-looking, wouldn't you say?'

'Who?'

'In a kind of agrarian way.'

'Oh, for crying out loud, Oliver. Not everything's about sex, you know.'

'Ha! What could be more sexual than a penis-shaped object erecting itself into the air?'

I can see what he means. 'Well, there's no need to lose sleep,' I tell him. 'I could never go for a man who tucks his jumper into his trousers.'

Frank and I stagger into Ted's shop under armsful of the first issue of *Grapevine*, Veronica's name for the magazine. Oliver suggested the *Village Organ*, but then decided he held that title himself.

'Think you can shift this lot, Ted?' puffs Frank. I'm slightly worried about his pacemaker and quickly offer to fetch the rest. I return to see Ted flicking through *Grapevine*'s eight pages.

'Where's my advertisement, then?' he asks.

Frank perches himself on a stack of empty milk crates and recovers his breath. 'On the back with the others.'

'Right you are.'

I pick up a copy and turn it over. Although

I know every word of the magazine, I haven't yet checked out Frank's ads.

'Shop on the Green,' I see. 'Open six days a week. Gourmet items from around the globe.' That's the bananas and Danish bacon, I suppose. 'Off-licence.' Short and to the point. Least said the better. 'Wide range of videos for rental.' I think they missed out the words 'Bruce' and 'Willis'.

'Dan's Your Man,' catches my eye in a bottom corner. 'Carpentry and General Repairs.' It's followed by our mobile number.

'They look great,' I tell Frank while I read on. 'Country Loving. Upper Muckhill and District's new Introduction Agency. Total Discretion. Free hairdo when you join. Call Tina on...' Not that discreet. Surely all male members will be walking round with number one haircuts.

'Had a little help from your son,' says Frank.

I see Ted turn to the letters page. Letters which go something like: 'May I say how pleased I am that the folk of Upper Muckhill will be given a voice...' or, 'I'm researching the history of the supposedly haunted vicarage, and would be interested to hear any stories...' All made up by me, of course, and signed 'W. F.' or 'Name and address withheld'.

'Seventy pence a piece, you say?' Ted turns to the front cover and fans us with his eyebrows. 'Bit steep.'

'Tell people that some of the money will go to a worthy cause.' Me, that is.

Jean Crowbar comes in. 'Oo, I say, it's a bit pricey, isn't it?' She fiddles in her big, clip-top purse for ages, muttering, 'My Gail can get me six reams of office paper for that.'

'Thanks,' I say. Our first sale!

While I'm creating a hey-come-and-buy-us display by the newspapers, Frank takes Jean into a corner with a sweep of an arm. 'About this office paper, Jean...'

What I'd do, I write later, *if Ted took a long sabbatical and asked me to hold the fort. Get rid of: 1) curled and yellowing Players No. 6 advertisement sprawled across window; 2) all tinned pears, starting with the rusty ones; 3) pile of 1961 knitting patterns displaying young men in primary-coloured cardigans and scooter helmets (might be worth a bit); and 4) everything else. Replace with, 1) Thai restaurant.*

DECEMBER

'Hi, it's Hamish,' he says over the phone.

'Hello, Ali.'

'What? Oh, I get it.'

Oliver's in the far corner of the room laughing uproariously at the turgid journal in his hand while pretending not to be watching The Simpsons.

'News from the front.'

'What's that then?'

'Well, apparently Jessica was so badly injured from a supposed fall off her horse two days after Norman found out about her affair with Tina's bloke, that she had to go to hospital.'

'Oh, this and that,' I say. 'We got the first issue of the magazine out this week. Mm. Yeah, yeah. How's Beth?'

'Had to have stitches.'

'Well, I expect it's just a phase.'

'You are listening, aren't you?'

'Of course I am.'

'And what's more, she was seeing some-one else within a month.'

'Blimey. No wonder Norman–'

'Aah ha haa,' roars Oliver.

'Careful,' says Hamish. 'All this came from their ex-charlady.'

'You and Hamish must come over for dinner soon,' I say loudly. 'How about Saturday?'

'Do you mean that?'

'No, not really.'

'Speak to you later.'

'Look forward to it. Bye. Yeah. Bye, Ali.'

'Beginning to wonder about you,' says a frowning, stroking-his-chin Oliver when we're trying to decide what to have for dinner.

"What?'

'You know, you were being almost flirtatious with Ali on the phone earlier. Giggling, preening your hair, sucking suggestively on the end of a forefinger.'

'Don't be ridiculous.'

He pops a cork from a bottle and pours two large glasses. 'Nothing to be ashamed of, Roo. I'm not averse to a bit of girl-on-girl myself.'

I pull a face and mull over this perversion while I sip my wine, wondering why it doesn't quite work for women. I mean, as far as I recall I've not once fantasised about say, Pierce Brosnan and Jeremy Paxman, tumbling naked together and going 'Oh, yes' a lot on black satin sheets or a forest floor. But I'm thinking maybe I should give it a go, so I conjure them up and concentrate for a while. No, nothing stirs. Of course, for a closer comparison with Oliver's fantasies, it would be Pierce and Jeremy's seventeen-year-old sons frolicking together.

Later. *Novel idea. Lesbian, country-based detectives... Fosdyke and Butcher? Keen horsewomen. Get Oliver to write sex scenes.*

Ali turns up the next evening with Beth in tow. 'We've just come to do some work on the panto set. Want to watch?'

'OK.' I grab three of Oliver's jumpers, guessing there'll be a subzero wind-chill factor in the village hall. I'm right. As soon as we arrive I hand them out.

'Can I have that thick one?' says a shivering Beth. 'I'm not as fat as you two.'

Veronica shows us what Ali has to work with, which is basically sad-looking, cut-out trees, seven or eight feet high, an appalling backdrop of woods and distant hills, and props the church playgroup obviously made. When Ali's stopped laughing she rolls up Oliver's sleeves and levers lids off the tins of Dulux she brought with her.

'Let's get cracking' she says to Beth, handing her a paintbrush. 'Everything lime green, OK?'

Oh dear, not sure I can watch. I wander off and find Poppy having a costume fitting backstage – i.e. the village hall kitchenette. She's in a long cherry-red velvet affair and felt shoes, and her hair's been plaited and interwoven with little rosebuds.

'Like it?' she asks.

'You look fantastic,' I tell her, which she does. Although I can't help thinking she might clash with the new set. But then, what won't? Jean Crowbar's kneeling at Poppy's hem with a mouthful of pins. So much work, I think. And all for something that's bound to be met with widescale derision.

'Need a hand?' I ask, praying she doesn't. I try not to go anywhere near needle and thread since spending an entire domestic science lesson inadvertently stitching my armhole facing to my Peter Pan collar and becoming the object of great hilarity when Miss Tilsley pinned it to the cork board as 'a lesson to you all'.

'Pshwshwsh,' says Jean.

'Oh, OK. I'll go and help the others then.'

She was probably asking if I could just slip-stitch the zip into place along the selvedges, taking care to match the notches. I hurry away before I see any bias binding.

'This is just the first stage, of course,' Ali's telling us an hour and a half later.

Veronica takes sunglasses from her handbag and slips them on. 'Ah, that's better.'

'The fresh, bright green symbolising spring and–' she gestures to Poppy's tummy – 'new life.'

'Oh, I say, how clever.'

Ali unrolls a poster of Bill Gates, leaps on stage and Blu-Tacks it high on the backdrop. 'Very, very rich person.'

'Ye-ess,' we all say, elbow in one hand, chin in the other.

She moves to front stage and swishes back the curtain to reveal an image of a starving African child. 'Very, very poor person.' It goes a bit quiet while she waits for a reaction.

'Oh, right, I geddit,' says Poppy. 'Robbing the rich to feed the poor, yeah?'

'Ah, splendid,' chirrups Veronica. 'Just the ticket. Adds a little depth to Toby's frightful script.' She peeks over her shoulder. 'I didn't say that, of course.'

We all quietly cough. 'Um...' continues Veronica, 'it is safe, isn't it, dear? The scenery?'

'I think so,' Ali tells her with a shrug.

'Only one can never quite forget 1998 and *Snow White*.'

Several people dip their heads as if in prayer and murmur, 'No.'

Back at home, I'm trying to shove two paint-splattered jumpers into the washing machine before Oliver spots them, but unfortunately get caught in the act. He tugs at them and holds them up for inspection.

'Christallbloodymighty, Roo.'

'Oh, all in a good cause,' I say cheerily, in the hope that he might realise he's being churlish and mean-spirited. No such luck. He stomps to the door, saying he'll just have to wear that nice maroon jumper Paula made him, won't he, then?

'But you promised. And these don't look too bad.'

He turns and scowls. 'If I wanted to wear lime green sweaters I'd go to ... to ... the Wednesday market.'

'But you do.'

'Well ... Mothercare then!'

He's stopped growling by the time Ali and Beth pop in to say goodbye and, 'Thanks for the jumpers, Oliver. Sorry about the paint.'

'Bah. Just a couple of old things,' he says, and on seeing Beth goes into something of a Leslie Phillips routine. 'Well, he*llo*. How about a drink? I've got a rather nice Chilean Cabernet.'

Ali starts heading for their car. 'Better not. Things to do.'

'See you Saturday then?' he calls out from the back door.

'What?'

Damn. I hurry them along down the path. 'You're coming to dinner,' I hiss. 'I mean would you like to come to dinner, Saturday?'

'You too, I hope, Beth,' yells Oliver.

'You're behaving oddly, Roo,' says Ali. 'It's got something to do with that missing woman, hasn't it?'

'Sort of.'

'Yeah, I heard something about her tonight.'

'Oh?'

She stops by the car and fumbles for keys in a pocket. 'Did I give them to you, Beth?'

'Durr, like I can drive? Jesus, hurry up. It's freezing.'

I produce my brightest smile and say, 'It is a bit nippy, isn't it?' then turn to Ali. 'What did you hear?'

'Um, now what was it? Um... Oh bugger, it's gone. Like the keys, ha ha. Ah, here they are.' She walks round the car and unlocks Beth's door first. 'No, just can't remember.'

'Give me a ring if it comes back, will you?'

'Sure.'

'Bye, Beth,' I call out after her door has been firmly slammed. May an army of vipers visit you in the night. 'Bye. Nice to see you both.'

I wake sharply from a strange dream in which Miss T. Ree is dancing with snakes. 'Of course!' I say, sitting bolt upright and causing the duvet to fall away from Oliver and wake him too.

'What the–'

'Miss T. Ree,' I whisper.

He heaves the duvet back his way. 'Chrissake.'

The clock tells me it's three fifty-one. Hell, I'll never sleep now. I slip out of bed, pull on a thick towelling robe and tiptoe to the living room where I jot down a few notes before finding myself being shaken by the shoulder and waking to bright winter sunshine.

'Tea up,' says Oliver. He puts a mug on the floor beside the sofa. 'What was all that about in the night? Having out-of-control light aircraft dreams, were we?' He goes off chuckling to himself.

I pay an early call on Tina, who's getting Maximilian ready for school. He's been sitting at our feet in the hall while we chatted, putting his shoes on.

'Look, I know it's an odd request,' I say with a kind of pleading expression, 'but I'd be really grateful.'

'I said *your* shoelaces, Maximilian.' She turns to me. 'Sorry about that, but he's a right little prankster these days. Aren't you, Maxi? Now undo the lady's laces.'

I look down to see my boots tied together. 'What a scamp you are,' I say, bravely patting his shaved head and forcing a smile. Tina pads off to the salon in her moccasins while I sort my feet out, then returns with the photo.

'Here you are,' she says, tentatively handing it to me. 'You will take care of it, won't you? Only I come second in that contest. Best day of my life.'

'Of course. Thanks.' I slip it inside the envelope I brought along especially. 'See you later.'

'Yeah, ta-da. Now see our guest to the gate, Ma–'

'No, no. No need.'

I'm relieved to see a note saying, 'One pint of semi-skimmed and half a doz. eggs, please' on Miss Ree's doorstep. She's not in Cleethorpes, Scunthorpe or Mablethorpe then. I ring the bell and after some time a woman with short blonde hair, enormous tortoiseshell glasses, cream belted cardigan and shiny, pretend-denim jeans opens the frosted glass door.

'Um. Is Miss–'

'Oh, hello, dear. Do come in, that's a nasty old wind out there. Is it about the magazine again?'

The voice is the same, but that's all. 'Miss T. Ree?'

'Valerie, actually, when I'm off duty.'

'I was rather hoping you'd be on duty.'

'Well, I could go and change.'

'Is it necessary?'

'All the same to me, dear. Only the clients tend to like all the mystical stuff. They're a bit septic otherwise.'

'Do you mean scepti–'

'Come along. We'll sit in the lounge.' She

goes through and plumps up a shiny cushion, waves an arm for me to seat myself, then takes the other chair. 'Now what can I do you for?'

Oh dear, it doesn't feel right. I want velvet and patchouli, not cold leatherette and lavender furniture polish and someone saying 'do you for'. I hold out the photograph of Jessica. 'I was wondering if you could help me find this woman? I'll pay you for your time, of course.'

After taking it from me she changes her glasses for an identical pair pulled from a cardigan pocket. 'Ah yes. I've done this sort of thing for the police a few times.'

'Really?' I don't want to ask if she was successful, she might think I'm being septic.

Valerie gazes at the picture and wriggles around in her noisy armchair while she concentrates. This goes on for some time so I sink back and watch her tropical fish swimming past a deep-sea diver and in and out of a shipwreck. It's quite mesmerising actually with its repetitive blub, blub, blubbing of bubbles. But then all of a sudden the photograph is being thrust back at me.

'You'll find her very close to home,' Valerie tells me matter-of-factly. '*Very* close.' She stands up, turns and prods her cushion and announces that there'll be no charge. Something tells me our session's over.

'How's the article about me coming along?' she adds.

Oh God, I long ago scrapped that idea. 'Fine, fine. Should be in the next issue.'

'You binned it, didn't you, dear?'

'Yes.'

It's Saturday night. I've had far too much to drink and am telling our guests, with some embellishment, about the time the cat gave birth in Josh's bed while he was having one of those marathon lie-ins nobody over eighteen can manage. Said he kept feeling this sort of wriggling by his tummy and wondered what it was. He was about thirteen and it was the first time I heard him swear. 'Fuck,' he kept saying all the way down the stairs in his underpants.

'Hasn't stopped since,' adds Oliver.

'Really?' says Hamish. 'I haven't noticed.'

'I suppose he's hardly likely to tell customers something's a fucking good read.'

I wouldn't be so sure. When I offer to make coffee, Hamish asks if I need a hand. I tell him I think I can manage that little task but he offers again with something of an insistent gaze.

'OK.'

We take it in turns to lift cups from their hooks and place them on their saucers. 'You're right,' I tell him. 'I couldn't have done this without you.'

'Can we meet up in the week?' he asks quietly. 'Have another review, knock a few ideas around.'

The alcohol has loosened my tongue enough for me to tell Hamish about my visit to Miss Ree, but I'm not so drunk that I don't expect him to guffaw and say, 'A clairvoyant? God, you women.'

But, 'What a brilliantly inspired piece of detective work,' he whispers instead, lifting his hand and pulling back a wisp of hair that's floated its way towards my nose. 'You're a little jewel, Ruby.'

Not very original, but lovely coming from Hamish.

He thinks I'm going to look into those conker-coloured eyes and respond with a flirtatious chuckle. Which actually I'm about to do, but Oliver yells why don't we have some of those choc mint crispy things with our coffee and I say OK and Ali calls out just a black decaff for her please and I say OK and lovely Hamish in his green cord shirt with a touch of dark chest hair showing takes the tray of cups through.

'Bye, Ali,' I say. Peck on one cheek, peck on the other. 'Thanks for coming.'

Hamish looms before me. 'Bye, Hamish.' Kiss on one cheek, protracted kiss on the other. 'Thanks for coming.'

'Thursday, two o'clock, back room of the Queen's Head, Wilkstone,' he whispers.

'OK.' I seem to be running my hand over his hip.

'Better go and write it down, Ruby. You might be a bit drunk.'

Journal entry, found the next morning and immediately slashed through with large black marker pen.

Queen's Back Room 12 oclock?? Wiltshire thursday. Hamihs darling take me to a vacant guest room and Well, never mind.

December can be such a trying time. In Ted's shop I stop in my tracks when I hear Mrs. Allsop announce that she wrapped all her presents last night.

'Done everything now except the mince pies,' she adds with an irritating little sniff.

I look at my watch, which tells me, just as

I thought, that it's only the seventh of December. After momentary panic, I decide she's probably also signed Mr Allsop's Valentine card and got a cupboard full of Easter eggs, and should perhaps be pitied. I relax again – a whole two and a half weeks to go.

'Ken Pritchard's had to stop taking turkey orders, I hear,' says Ted. 'Sold the lot. Beautiful birds they are.'

Mm, well there's always Tesco.

'Not like that supermarket rubbish.'

Veronica flies in. 'Ah, Ruby,' she says. 'Here you are. Save me delivering it.' She hands me an invitation to 'Christmas Drinks with Veronica and Frank'.

'We can look forward to receiving one from you and Oliver, I take it?' She's sort of smiling and half-winking but it feels like an order.

I pay for my items with a heavy heart, desperate to be out of here before someone rushes in and announces that Christmas Day will be on the eighth of December this year. There's only one thing for it, I think on leaving the shop, and I head for the mobile library van. Nothing like a good book to take your mind off things you should be doing. And, of course, there's nothing like a good book in the mobile library. I wander around picking things off shelves and sighing heavily, when the librarian – I always think of her as a Geraldine – says, 'You might like this one,' in a very loud whisper. 'It was in the bestsellers.'

'Oh really?' My heart does a little skip for joy, but it turns out to be one of the tidal wave of 'I'm thirty and I'm still single and what's more my tits are sagging' novels that women who are thirty, single and sagging can't get enough of.

'Thanks,' I say quietly, giving it back. 'But I've already read it.' Not true.

'It's good, isn't it?' whispers the thirty-something Geraldine. She flicks through its pages. 'What did you think of that Martin?'

'Martin? Oh God, complete rat.' I shake my head in dismay. 'He treated her *so* badly.'

Geraldine nods and pushes her glasses up her nose. 'He promised her so much.'

'Then suddenly turned cold and with-drew.'

She looks distressed, puts the book down, and begins wringing her fingers. Better cheer her up. 'But it was good that she ended up falling in love with the guy who was her platonic best friend through all the bad times and had always secretly adored her.'

'That was rather a nice twist, wasn't it?' sighs Geraldine.

I see the library van driver – fortyish, Fair Isle tank top his mum might have knitted – who's obviously heard us in this silent little room, look up from his newspaper and stare in a lovelorn manner at Geraldine.

'I'll just take this one,' I say, handing her *Original Christmas Decorations in an Hour*, half hoping they just mean a quick trip to Habitat.

I get home to a phone message from Dad. 'Just to let you know I'll be arriving on the seventeenth. No need to send the limo, I'll make my own way to Mucklestone.'

'Mucklestone?' I say to Oliver.

He thinks he's seen it. 'Shropshire maybe, or Staffordshire. Wherever it is, I'm sure it's a very nice place to spend Christmas.'

'The seventeenth? Oh God, so much to do.'

'Such as?'

'Oh, you know ... buying all the bloody presents, making the pudding, creating cute little handmade Christmas cards and an impressive table decoration with holly and silver spray, stuffing the turkey I haven't ordered yet...'

'A touch out of character, *n'est ce pas?*'

'I know, but what if Veronica or someone calls in? They're hardly going to say, "Oh, how delightful!" to that balding, two-foot silver tinsel tree we always drag out.'

'I think it went to Oxfam, actually.'

'See.'

'See what?'

He potters around in the kitchen for a while, while I stay in my grrr-I-hate-Christmas pose at the table.

'Look, I'm not too busy at the moment,' he says. 'Why don't we go to M&S tomorrow? Do a one-stop shop? Eh?'

Thursday. Two o'clock. Back room of the Queen Head. Wilkstone. 'Er. I've actually said I'll um interview someone tomorrow.'

'Oh, yes? Who?'

Think, think. 'A taxidermist.'

Oliver wanders over to the wine rack. 'Well, that's one of your problems solved then,' he says with a grin. 'You can get him to stuff a turkey for us.'

Hamish and I are eking out our two halves of Guinness and I'm trying hard to ignore the unexpected army of butterflies in my tummy.

'Hm...'

'So...'

'Not that much progress really.'

'Seems not.'

My eyes drift around the uninspiring and completely empty little room we've found ourselves in: brown patterned wallpaper, wonky pictures of old mills, plastic flowers on the windowsills. The drabness of the surroundings only serves to make Hamish appear more godlike, so I avoid looking at him. 'Game of darts?' I venture.

'Why not? First one to get a bull's-eye has a wish granted. Right?'

'Are you any good?'

'Hopeless.'

'OK then.'

His third throw is a bull's-eye. 'Well, that's quick progress,' I protest while he takes the darts from the board, then comes and hands them to me. I sense he's grinning.

'What's your wish then?' I add, staring nonchalantly at a nearby toby jug.

'Oh...' he says, one of his hands moving towards my face, then changing its mind. 'It'll keep.'

The surprise element of country pubs, I write on my return. *One never knows when approaching an ancient, stone, mullion-windowed hostelry –*

one that Charles I maybe bedded down in on occasion – whether one will be greeted with crackling log fire, sturdy old tables with pews and the aroma of roasting game, or (as invariably happens) pool table, split red plastic benches, a group of surly youngsters in the corner and a faint whiff of the urinals. Oliver and I have visited quite a few now, but because they're all so similarly and delightfully attractive on the outside, can never quite remember which pubs have an enticing wall-sized menu, and which, at a push, will serve you a dripping sandwich on a cracked plate. When we go out now, Oliver jots down details in a small book. For Christmas might get him a waterproof plastic pocket with 'Pub Notebook' on it to hang around his neck.

On Saturday, Poppy, Dan and I are shivering and stamping our feet in the long queue outside the village hall. It's two minutes to eleven, a dusting of snow is settling on the ground, and in front of us Jean Crowbar is sharpening her elbows ready for Upper Muckhill's Christmas Bazaar and Rummage Sale. She takes out three empty carrier bags, flicks them open and hooks them on to her left arm.

'Got to get in quick if you're going to snap up the bargains,' she informs us, taking the ten pence entrance fee from her big purse. 'Gail's on the ladies' clothes stall. Says there's some lovely bits and pieces.'

'Really?' I can imagine. Matted little jumpers you feel you have to buy when you see they're from Next, jeans with threadbare crotches and almost white knees. Things with shoulder pads. I'm only here for a Christmas pudding I can pass off as my own.

People keep looking at their watches and there's more and more of a buzz as the seconds tick their way towards eleven. When we reach four minutes past, however, the buzz has turned into a communal grumble and one or two small children are beginning to grizzle. Jean says she hopes they're not having a crisis in there and I wonder what that could possibly be. Mrs Allsop's cranberry jelly hasn't quite set, perhaps. We do eventually start making our way, first slowly, then with increasing speed towards the tiny table just inside the door where Frank sits with his cash tin and doesn't blink when I hand him a five-pound note for the three of us but takes an age to count out four pounds seventy in tens and twenties.

I make a beeline for the cake stall, but can't help noticing people are crowded six deep over in the far corner. It occurs to me that Gail might be flogging computers at giveaway prices, so I decide to investigate. It takes the strength and ruthlessness of a full back to get to the front, but I manage it and discover a mountain range of nearly new clothes tumbling around in the mêlée. Women are constantly jostling for a better position, butting neighbours out of the way, then leaning territorially over the stall with elbows held high. Items are being snatched from others' hands then flung over a shoulder or tucked under an arm. All this takes place in near silence, which is the strange thing. Two teenage girls with gritted teeth are having a tug of war over some flimsy little item, but not uttering a word. I watch in disbelief for a while, gradually discarding my long-held belief that women would do a better job of running the world. We'd just have lots of very quiet wars, I expect. I push up my coat sleeves. May as well join in.

Before long a rather nice little black dress catches my eye and my hand reaches it a nanosecond before someone else's. It's soft and expensive-looking, with an unusual thin red piping. I don't recognise the label, so it must be good. I wave it at Veronica and ask how much and she tells me she thinks a pound would be reasonable.

'OK, I'll take it.'

'We've got some super things this year,' she tells me. 'Mostly Norman Potts' kind donation.'

I instantly drop the dress and look around me in disgust at all the hands scrambling for Jessica's clothes – 'Wrong size,' I say – then push my way out to where it's far easier to breathe, and have a lengthy shudder while wiping both hands on my coat. I suppose a lot of stuff at jumble sales comes from dead people, but all the same...

I leave half an hour later with two puddings and an iced-and-decorated-with-Nativity-scene cake. Plus an unsolicited kiss from a Santa with eyebrows not unlike Ted's.

Back at home Poppy and Dan are full of their bargains, tipping bags on to the kitchen table.

'Dan bought these wicked boots. Look.'

'Great.'

'And I got these sleepsuits and an activity centre for babe. It just needs a bit of a Jif.'

'Mm.' It certainly does.

'And this sexy nightie for when I like get

my figure back.'

Dan's face lights up.

'Oh yeah,' says Poppy. 'And this for you, Mum. Thought it looked like you.' She hands me the little black dress I threw back. 'It was only twenty p.'

'Oh, right. Thanks.' Twenty pence!

I stand up and hold it against me. It's very soft Jersey – low neckline, three-quarter-length sleeves – and looks as though it might hang beautifully. Oh, what the hell, it could have come from anyone.

How relieved I am to have home-made puddings and cake under my belt. Not cheating, just being practical and avoiding hours of tedious recipe following. Have long believed that the world is divided into two types of people – those who use recipes and those who don't. Well, three types, if you count the ones who never cook. Folk who refer to a cookbook for anything from scrambled egg upwards, would also, I'd imagine, tend to have nicely written diary entries for the next eight weeks: Tea with Miriam – Return library books – Picket Chinese Embassy – Bikini line wax (remember ibuprofen) – My birthday! – and so on. They'd know exactly where in the house they can lay their hands on a paperclip, and probably stick to

one or two tried-and-tested formats in bed. I,
needless to say, fall into the second category. I
couldn't tell you where the car keys are right
now, nor what I'm doing this evening, let alone
three weeks Sunday. A recipe-user getting
together with a non-recipe person may well be a
recipe (ha ha) for boudoir disaster. 'Take off my
belt and do what with it, Deirdre? Mm, let me
just see if that's in the manual.' I may be wrong,
of course.

The headmistress of the village school has
asked me to write a glowing review of their
carol service and nativity play. Living as
they are under permanent threat of closure,
owing to there being as many teachers as
there are pupils, any media support is
extremely welcome, she says.

I arrive with my reporter's notebook just
before two, and savour the smell of disin-
fectant and plimsolls, as mums, babies,
grannies, a few dads and I enter the old
Victorian building and pass down a short
corridor to the hall. I see tiny coats with
gloves dangling on elastic, gym bags and
assorted packed lunch boxes, and I'm
momentarily thrown back to the time I
forgot to hard-boil Poppy's egg and got her
into her first and only bit of trouble at

school when she cracked it all over Dominic's Wagon Wheel.

We file into the hall where the lucky early-bird parents have grabbed the seats made for adult bottoms, leaving a couple of rows of doll's-house chairs at the front for the rest of us. I lower myself with as much dignity as I can scrape up to a position six inches from the floor. It's what to do with one's legs, really.

'Oh, wotcha,' says Tina, plonking herself beside me and going unselfconsciously into a half-lotus position. She messes about in a canvas bag for a while and pulls out a camera. 'Now where's my Maxi?'

He's not hard to spot, despite the costume, what with his tongue protruding in our direction. She gives him a little wave and a good luck thumbs-up.

Before I know it we're all standing and singing 'Away in a Manger' and I've got a big lump in my throat. It gets bigger when all the sweet little tots in their shepherd and wise men outfits, with wide-open mouths and chins held high, sing, 'The CAttle are GLOWing...' at the beginning of verse two. It's an effort not to weep copiously, just as it's always been at these events. Poppy's acting debut was as Mary in the infants' school. She didn't have any lines but held the doll beautifully. I sobbed out loud at one point.

While the vicar comes on and tells us that Christmas isn't just about getting the latest trendy toy, you know, Tina whispers to me, 'If you're thinking of having your hair done for Christmas, better tell me. Filling up fast.'

'Oh, OK.'

'Got spaces on Sat'dee. Two o'clock alright?'

'Um. Yes. Thanks.'

Oh good, that should perk up my sex life again, I'm thinking, just as the vicar's telling me life isn't only about doing things we enjoy. 'Think of all the boys and girls in the world who don't have anything to play with,' he says, hands forming a cradle on his stomach. 'Can you imagine what that's like?'

'NO,' they chorus for a full seven seconds.

'No? Well, I'll tell you what you could do. You could try giving up the thing you enjoy most for a while and see how it feels to go without.'

'Not friggin likely,' says Tina.

After a 'Silent Night' where we all sing at a different pace, the Nativity play gets under way and small voices are projected at a volume they'd be sent to their rooms for at home. When Maximilian appears and booms to Joseph and Mary that there's no room at the inn then waves them away with a snarl and a clenched fist, Tina takes a snap.

'Brilliant casting' I write on my pad.

'My source tells me Jessica might have had a bit of a thing with Trevor too,' whispers Hamish when I've actually only rung the shop to talk to Josh.

'Really?' Nothing surprises me now, but, my God, the energy of the woman.

'Want to check it out?'

'OK.' How the hell do I do that?

'Thanks. What would I do without you, Ruby?'

I wish he wouldn't say my name that way. It's most unsettling. 'Bye,' I say back, and try to recall why I'm calling Josh.

I find Trevor in his ramshackle hangar, more or less in the position I left him in a month ago. 'Anyone home?' I say with a pretend knock where the door should be. The dogs charge in.

'Ah, hello.' He pulls an arm out of the

machine and wipes his hand. 'Not come to ask for a flight, have you?'

'No, no.' Just to ask if you screwed Jessica.

He brushes items off a small bench running along one wall. 'Have a seat.'

'Thanks.'

After settling myself down on the narrow plank of wood I wonder what we can talk about. 'I suppose I should warn you the protesters are planning to plant trees on your runway.'

'Guessed as much from the posters. Bloody barmy idea.' He picks up a tin kettle covered in black grease and takes it over to where a bottle of water, assorted chipped and grimy mugs and a Primus stove sit on the floor. 'Just let them try, that's what I say. Cup of coffee?'

Only if you hold me down and peg my nose. 'No, thanks, Trevor.'

'Hey, dogs!' I say when they almost trip him up. I'd call them by their names, but 'Hendrix' and 'Cobain' refuse to trip easily off my tongue.

Trevor laughs and gives them both a playful ruffle. 'You're no trouble, are you?' One of them flings himself with some force at Trevor's chest.

'Sit!' I shout, and remarkably they do. For

a matter of seconds. Then they're off again sniffing and rummaging.

'Should be getting a CAA decision soon,' says Trevor. He puts a match to the little stove. 'Better do before our investor changes his mind.'

'Investor?'

'Well, me and Dad could hardly start a flying club ourselves. All our foot-and-mouth compensation went on clearing debts. If we had a penny between us, I'd get someone in to fix this damned plane.'

And buy some new mugs maybe.

I'm trying to work out a way of casually weaving Jessica into the conversation, when Cobain trots over with what looks like an expensive pink and purple silk scarf in his mouth, plonks himself at my feet and, between paws and teeth, begins to rip the thing to shreds.

'No!' I tell him. 'Bad dog. Give it to me. Drop! Bad dog. Drop!' He eventually gets the message and I pick up the tattered item and give it a shake. 'Not yours I take it, Trevor?'

'Jessica's,' he says with a dismissive shrug.

I stand up and take it over to him. 'She might want it one day.'

'No she won't.' He seems pretty certain

238

and a small shiver tickles the back of my neck.

'So ... did you and Jessica ever...?'

'What?' His eyes flash sharply at mine and his face slowly turns crimson.

I stretch out my hand and tap the fuselage. 'You know, go up together. In this.'

He turns away to hide his blush. 'No, no. Terrified of flying, she was.'

I note his use of the past tense and give him a big smile. 'Better get these two out of your hair.' I clap my hands and head for the door shouting, 'Come on, Goldie, come on, Blackie,' at which they come bounding over as if they'd never known any other names.

Half a dozen privileged people have been invited to watch a dress rehearsal of *Robin, Queen of Sherwood*.

'Queen?' says Ali, while flicking through the programme. 'Well, Robin must swing both ways if he's managed to get Maid Marion pregnant.'

'Actually I think there may be a dispute over paternity. But I'd hate to give the story away, even if I knew it.' Or cared.

'Alright?' calls out Dan from the orchestra pit, a small roped-off area by the door to the toilets. He and Phil are looking very presentable in Lincoln-green outfits and I try to remember if I've ever seen Dan in anything but washed-out white (grey) or faded black (grey). Must buy him something colourful for Christmas. They spend some time tuning the guitar and warming up the keyboard before Veronica bursts through the curtains and announces that the final dress rehearsal for the Upper Muckhill Players' eleventh – yes eleventh – annual Christmas production will begin.

A slightly lacklustre 'Robin Hood, Robin Hood, riding through the glen...' hails from the orchestra pit and the curtains jerk themselves open to reveal Bill Gates surveying a lime-green Sherwood Forest. Young Julian then runs on stage in a felt and feather hat and a rather too short tunic, and raps one or two lines about that no-good gangster, the Sheriff of Nottingham. I look over to where Toby sits, chewing on a thumb and shaking his head, and feel enormous pity for him.

The star of the show is, thank God, Poppy, who delivers her appalling lines with aplomb and even manages to look slim again after little Robina makes an appearance. Toby applauds every time she leaves the stage.

'So,' says Ali at the end, when the six of us

have clapped as much as six people can. 'I'm not sure I get it. Was Friar Tuck, careful how you say that, the father or what?'

Why's she asking me? I switched off after thirty seconds and made Christmas present lists on my knee in the dark. 'I suppose he just wanted to Triar Fuck.'

'Oh, I see. Broken celibacy vows, universal corruption...'

I look at her and sigh. Sometimes I think everyone in the whole world, apart from myself and Trevor McDonald, is slightly unsound of mind.

Christmas shopping turns out to be twice as bad as I feared. The streets are carpeted with people as equally fraught as I, but, to make matters worse, chronic indecision sets in the moment I join a queue to pay for what, just two minutes before, seemed the perfect gift. This results in me eventually putting back the hooded Lincoln-green top for Dan, *Create Your Own Wild Garden* for Dad, and other ill-chosen items. I leave the city some three hours later with yet another watch for Josh and – inexplicably – a rather pricey lipstick for myself. I never wear lipstick.

'Oh yes,' says Oliver when I try it out in

the living-room mirror, run my tongue over the unfamiliar taste, squeeze lips together, then frown at the blood-red result. 'Very girl-next-door meets dominatrix.' He's stopped sawing the top off the Trafalgar Square-size Christmas tree he brought home for our squat living room and is watching me with some interest.

'Actually, I was hoping it would look Christmassy.'

'Yeah, yeah, it does.'

'Oh good.' I smile at my festive image and decide I'll wear it to Veronica and Frank's drinks next week.

Oliver cocks his head. 'Christmas in Soho maybe.'

It's strange, I write upstairs, *while Oliver covers the living room in pine needles, how things take on either greater or lesser significance in the country. When young Jonathan West returned from six months in India last week, we were all invited to the village hall to watch the video he made and eat samosas. All arranged by Mr and Mrs West to honour their son's terrific achievement. In the city, if you come across a nineteen-year-old you haven't seen around for a while you say, 'India or Thailand?' They'll tell you which and sum it up in one word —*

'Amazing' – *before you move on. If on the other hand, the entire Cabinet should one day be slain by a crazed gunman, the main topic of conversation in Ted's shop would no doubt be Mrs Faulkner's nasty tumble on the ice yesterday.*

The aroma wafting my way from Tina's cooker tells me it's Brussels sprouts season.

'Shall I use the big rollers again? Like what we done last time?'

'I think I'd just like a trim, actually, Tina.'

'Oh, go on. Glam yourself up a bit. Christmas, innit?'

'Umm...' I'm not sure I want to go home looking sexy and chic, turning Oliver all predatory and salivating again. Not with my father arriving later today, and some time near midnight no doubt suggesting a nice game of whist before we all turn in.

'I could touch up your highlights while we're at it?'

'Oh, go on, then.'

'I managed to get an extra ticket for Granddad,' Poppy's telling us later.

'He could have had mine,' mumbles Oliver.

The Upper Muckhill Players are subjecting themselves to public ridicule this evening in the first of their five-night run.

'So, that's one for you, Mum.'

'Thanks.'

'One for you, Oliver.'

Silence.

'Thanks,' I say.

'And one for Granddad if he gets here on time.'

'Should do.'

'Wangled the front row for you all.'

'You shouldn't have,' we both say.

While Oliver's hitting the bottle around five p.m., I phone Veronica and ask if I might possibly be allowed to go on stage and ask this evening's audience to contribute their amusing Christmas stories to *Grapevine*.

'I don't see why not, dear. After the show, rather than before, I'd say. Wouldn't you?'

'OK.'

Jolly good. That'll save me having to write a January issue. I put the phone down and turn around to see Oliver topping up a G and T.

'Oliver!'

'Look, if I've got to endure this bloody thing tonight...'

'It's good. You'll enjoy it.'

'Changed your tune a bit, haven't you?'

'Well, you know. In retrospect one sees the underlying messages, clever use of irony...'

'Clever use of my best sweaters, more like.'

I'm upstairs slipping into my dry-cleaned jumble sale dress – better look smart if I'm stepping on stage – when the phone rings.

'What the hell are you doing *there?*' I hear Oliver shout. He usually goes up a couple of decibels with alcohol. 'Well, don't move, Ken. I'll come and pick you up.'

Ah, it's Dad. I clip-clop down the stairs on my heels, admiring the way my just-above-the-knee dress ripples as I move, and say, 'No way are you driving, Oliver.' I grab the Range Rover keys from their hook before he can. 'Where is he?'

'Worcester railway station.'

'What! Why?'

'Don't ask me.'

I click out to the hall and, as I try to decide on a coat, a hand which definitely isn't mine slithers up my satin-finish tights.

'You look fantastic,' breathes a ginny voice.

Actually, I feel quite good; so does that hand. I reach back and stroke Oliver's head. 'Do you think we've got time?'

'Don't see why not. Last opportunity to let

our hair down for a while.' When he stayed with us shortly after Oliver and I got together, Dad offered over breakfast one morning to give that blinkin' noisy bed of ours a bit of a looking at.

'Yes, well,' I say, second thoughts beginning to creep in, 'I can't let my hair down too much. Just paid twelve pounds for this, you know.'

Oliver says he'll be gentle with it.

For most of the journey I have the accelerator slammed to the floor in a guilty, record-breaking sprint to Worcester, but on arrival – knuckles still pretty white – Dad's nowhere in sight. Not, that is, until I spot the small figure in a familiar tweed jacket bent under a propped-up bonnet. I park haphazardly and illegally, and rush over to him.

'Hello, love,' he says, giving me a kiss and a bear hug. 'How's my little girl then? Looking a picture, I see.'

'Country living,' I explain. 'How are you?'

'Never been better. This is Patricia, by the way. Having a spot of trouble with her plugs and points. Should have it sorted out in a tick.'

'Hi.'

I look at the time and tap my foot. Seven fifty. The panto's probably under way. Oliver will be resolutely refusing to 'Oh, yes he is,' along with the others and Poppy will be wondering why she can't see me in the audience.

It takes around five minutes for Patricia's car to spring to life, and for Dad to drop the bonnet with a satisfied clonk, shake Patricia's grateful hand, pick up his two suitcases and heave himself up into the Range Rover.

Back in our drive again after what feels like an eternity, I switch off the engine and give him a gentle shake. 'We're here, Dad. Wake up.'

He's one of those truly blessed people who are as bright as a button and able to hold an intelligent conversation the moment their eyes pop open. 'Hey, nice place,' he says without so much as a yawn or a scratch of the armpit. 'Got it damp-proofed, have you?'

We take his things into the house. Dad has a quick instant coffee while tapping the odd wall or pipe, and I knock back a large glass and a half of Shiraz, before we hurry down to the village hall where we encounter a just-about-to-close door.

'Come in,' whispers Frank. 'Second half's just starting.' He twiddles with a dimmer switch and the lighting slowly, if not totally smoothly, recedes. Dad and I stand for a while adjusting to the darkness while the curtains jerk hurriedly open and a loud communal gasp fills the hall. There on stage, in full Maid Marion costume and an appalling waist-length wig, is Jean Crowbar. She's cradling a Tiny Tears doll and reading a script at arm's length, glasses perched on the end of her nose.

'And I'm going to call her Robina,' she shouts.

'What's going on?' I ask Frank, who just shrugs.

I ease the creaky door open again and rush round on wobbly high heels, Dad in tow, to the back entrance where I find Poppy sitting on the step, shivering, arms folded across her stomach.

'Hey, Granddad.'

He bends and gives her an awkward hug. 'You all right, love?'

'What is it?' I ask.

'Just a bit of tummy ache. Something I ate, I reckon.'

I get her to describe the pains and Dad

and I give each other an uh-oh look. 'OK, don't move,' I tell her. 'I'll go and get Dan.'

It takes Frank a while to get to the orchestra pit, what with all the coats, bags and assorted small children cluttering the aisle, but eventually he taps Dan's shoulder and whispers in his ear. Meanwhile, I stand on tiptoe at the back of the hall and watch Oliver flinging his head back with laughter, then shouting at the Sheriff of Nottingham, hands cupped around his mouth.

'Oh, cool, cool. Like this is it. OK, just chill, Pops. It's gonna be alright, yeah? Deep breaths,' rambles Dan as we help Poppy get to the road where Dad – 'Give us the keys to that monstrosity of yours, Ruby. You've been drinking' – is going to pick them up and wind his way along fifteen miles of unfamiliar little roads in the dark. Dan says he'd drive only he wants to be in the back in case someone has to do an emergency delivery.

It really doesn't bear thinking about.

'Do you want me to come?' I ask Poppy.

'No. 'Salright. They wouldn't let you like be there anyway.'

'Ring us, won't you, Dan?'

'Yeah, yeah.'

'Got the mobile?'

'Yeah, yeah.'

Dad draws up and we hoist Poppy with her cherry-red velvet dress and tousled, rosebud-adorned hair into the back, while Dan stands patting his pockets.

Ah, got it,' he says, pulling out a penknife and holding it up to me. 'Just in case I've got to cut the rope, yeah?'

'Cord, Dan.'

'Right.'

I bid them goodbye and good luck, and they pull away in an over-revved first gear, leaving me hoping they're not on their way to Preston or King's Lynn.

I wander round to the back of the hall, coat wrapped tight against the cold, thinking about grandmotherhood and feeling a bit bad for not having knitted half a dozen cream-coloured matinée coats with ribbons woven through, like any decent granny-to-be. It's obviously going to take me a while to get into this role, but no doubt I'll soon be boring everyone rigid with photographs and telling Poppy she shouldn't sleep the baby on its back. Once inside and hunting around for Poppy's things, Veronica suddenly appears and bears down on me.

'Ah, there you are, Ruby. Ready to go on soon?'

'What?'

'Your announcement?'

Oh crikey. 'Yes, of course.'

I spend some time freshening up my makeup (a bit of lipstick, why not?) and checking my tights for ladders, then once the cast has finished all its curtain calls and the applause and whistling has begun to wane, I step on to the back of the stage and walk over to the closed curtains. Ah, my big moment at last. I pull them apart a little and step through into a very shaky spotlight.

'Hello, ladies and gentlemen,' I project (quite well I think) and they all quieten down. 'I'd just like a word before you all leave.'

'Oh, God bless the Lord!' cries a voice near the back.

I look up to see something of a commotion and a person scrambling over chairs and people.

'Jessica!'

It's Norman. What's he doing?

'My lovely, lovely Jessica,' he booms, now stumbling over the children who didn't move quickly enough. 'You've come back!'

I look down at my dress and run fingers through my hair. *You'll find her close to home. Very close.* Shit. Now what do I do? Poor

Norman's going to have a heart attack and die and the first night of *Robin, Queen of Sherwood* will go down in the annals as *the* one to have been at.

I close my eyes and wait for Norman, now clambering up on to the stage, to realise it's just boring old me in all this, when Hamish – where did he come from? – manages to catch up with him, take him to one side and have a quiet word. Veronica swishes through the curtains with a fold-up chair – she must always carry a supply – and I try to compose myself and continue with my announcement over the hubbub.

'Anyway.' I clear my throat and a hush descends again. 'I just wanted to say that if any of you would like to send me your amusing or unusual Christmas stories, they'd be most welcome.'

A wave of titters follows and a hundred and twenty heads turn to Norman. Well, that's one for a start, we're all thinking.

'I remembered what it was I heard about Jessica,' Ali tells us over our sparkling wine and vol-au-vents at the first-night party.

'What?'

'Someone said they saw her serving behind a Clinique counter in Salisbury.'

I nod for a while, sigh, raise my eyebrows at an embarrassed Hamish and go off to phone the hospital.

FEBRUARY

We should be knee-deep in snow but in fact spring is making a premature appearance, throwing both man and nature into confusion. Jean Crowbar's brought her A-line sundresses out of winter storage and daffodils are peeking tentatively above ground by our front door. 'Not yet, you silly billies,' I keep telling them. 'It's just Jack Frost playing nasty tricks.'

I've begun talking like this since little Grace appeared on the scene in the middle of December. 'Who's a boo-full li'll baby then? Yee-eess,' and similar keep issuing from my mouth and causing Oliver to leave the *Observer* open on the Soulmates page with the odd woman's ad circled.

At present I'm sitting at my desk in Troy Shed with the two words 'Chapter' and 'One' and a bleeping cursor before me, as I have been every day for a fortnight. Sometimes I make 'Chapter One' bigger and bolder, or try it in a different font, before finally shutting down the computer, sauntering back to Troy Cottage and telling Oliver it's going really well.

When in need of a distraction I write something short and snappy for *Grapevine*. 'One village resident, who wishes to remain anonymous, claims to have sighted a UFO hovering above the church spire on the night of the fifth. "It was quite big and had these really bright searchlights zooming all over Upper Muckhill," she told our Science Correspondent. Perhaps some of you spotted it too? Or maybe you've had an abduction experience? Call, fax or e-mail.'

Actually we've had one or two real events, but I'm reluctant to report them for fear I might find myself tied to a stake with kindling at my feet – Veronica being detained overnight at Liddleton police station for trespass and criminal damage, for example. All to no purpose it turns out, the Civil Aviation Authority having finally refused Norman permission for his flying school. He promptly found himself a buyer for the farm and rumours flew round that a country club was at the design stage. Then the unmortgageable house next door to us displayed a SOLD sign, and within a fortnight Norman and Trevor rolled up in a cattle truck and began unloading their possessions: items of reproduction furniture, surround-sound TV, brand-new cooker I'd kill for, and not one chest freezer, but three. 'UP YOUR END, TREVOR,' we and the whole village heard. 'DON'T WANT ALL THAT BEEF TUMBLING OUT.' Oliver and I spent the rest of that day investigating double glazing.

Next came huge sheets of corrugated iron and then a horsebox; all parked by our shared fence and blocking light from the kitchen. On day three, when we watched Norman lead two goats and a Rotovator up the garden path, Oliver got on to a lawyer to find out if our property was now officially 'blighted'.

As for Veronica, well, she's got a lot of time on her hands now she's resigned her council seat, and is throwing herself into a new venture – the Upper Muckhill Players' Summer Production. It was going to be *Abigail's Party*, last I heard, Toby having been given an enforced sabbatical. Jean's up for the title role.

I drum my fingers on the desk then get up and go over to the book shelves where, for want of anything better to do, I pick up the letter I received in the New Year from Jessica McKenzie. 'Dear Mrs Grant, I believe you and your friend have been making enquiries about my whereabouts,' it begins. Turns out she's living in Wiltshire with an animal feed salesman with whom she had a 'heart-wrenching affair' during her otherwise happy marriage. 'I was ever so fond of Norman, but I just couldn't get along with all that beef and Jim Reeves. Please tell him I'm well and that he's free to give all my things to charity. Apart from that little black and red dress. He'll know the one.' (He does now.)

I glance at the time. Oh good, only twenty minutes to go. I promised I'd look after Grace for an hour while Poppy helps out in the shop. Shortly after Christmas, I talked Ted into letting his empty upstairs flat to Poppy and Dan. It was the horror on the health visitor's face the first time she came to check up on the baby that did it. As she drove away with the mobile at her head I thought I lip-read the words 'high priority' and 'care order'. Oliver, inevitably, found it hard to hide his glee over Poppy and Dan's move, cracking open the best wine – 'Been saving this for a special occasion' – and dashing off to the supermarket for no other reason than to gather cardboard boxes for them.

Dum-de-dum. I rummage at the back of my desk drawer and pull out the card from

Hamish, in which he apologises for the wild-goose chase, hopes we'll keep in touch and signs off with 'Much love'. Actually he phones once or twice a week, but I still like looking at the card. There's a kind of abstract bird on the front which could be a goose, I suppose.

Wild Goose, I find myself doodling in strange curly letters. *Wildgoose*. I need a heroine. *Letitia Wildgoose ... Lily Wildgoose...*?

Ten minutes to go. Big sigh. I type up a couple of items sent in for our 'Handy Tips' column. 'Don't throw away those giant-size soap powder containers, as with just one or two snips they make excellent box files.'

This one was addressed to 'Ruby Grunt', so solving one little mystery: 'A good squirt of washing-up liquid in your children's bathwater will guarantee a clean and shiny bath afterwards – and no scum ring!' Just itchy children. That came from Norman's ex-cleaner.

Several people sent in 'Don't waste money on fake tan creams. For that sun-kissed look simply rub legs with a wet teabag.' Might try that one. Presumably you can go for different shades.

Helen, how come your legs are so much browner than mine?

Darjeeling.

Ah.

OK, back to the novel. I spend some time converting 'Chapter' and 'One' into Brush Script. It's a bit ostentatious, but it makes a change.

My eyes have been lingering on Jessica's letter for a while, when, in something of a surprise move, my fingers lower themselves on to the keys and begin to type, 'When destitute beef farmer Nigel Potter first set eyes on Jemima McIntosh, all thoughts of foot-and-mouth disease rushed from his head, like barley from a split sack.'

Hey, not bad.

PART TWO

JUNE

Dad's in the garden with the long-handled shears, making the edge of the lawn so defined you feel you'd gash yourself if you touched it. He's in his old army shorts, a pair of sandals and nothing else, looking deceptively frail and vulnerable. Oliver's sweating buckets up in the boxroom, drawing plans for what I believe to be Veronica and Frank's completely unnecessary extension. ('Not at all,' said Oliver over breakfast this morning, the mega-K fee dancing in his eyes. 'I think everyone should have a function room.') The dogs are panting in the coolest spots in the house and garden, tongues lolling, and I'm in Troy Shed trying to write up an interview with local celeb, Brenda Wagstaff – metallic blonde, shortish and a valued customer at Evans, I'd imagine – who recently and somewhat miraculously won *Stars In Their Eyes* as Kate Bush. It's very hot.

'So what was it like when you went back to work at the fruit-packing factory, Brenda?'

Aaargh, it's no good. Must have liquid.

'Tea's the best thing for cooling you

down,' puffs Dad when I pass him and offer iced juice. 'Put an extra sugar in, there's a good girl. Shall we have it under the new pergola?'

I call to Oliver, but there's no answer, so tiptoe up the stairs to find him sprawled naked on our bed, eyes closed and a copy of Dostoevsky's *The Idiot* spread-eagled on his thigh.

'We're having tea in the garden,' I whisper.

'It just isn't natural, Roo,' he mumbles.

'Well, you can have something cold if you prefer.'

'This sodding weather.' He rolls his head towards me, picks up *The Idiot* and limply fans himself. 'I mean, how's a person supposed to design a function room when his ruler's melting?'

I hand Oliver his shorts and tell him I'll fill the paddling pool for him. 'You're an angel,' he rasps, and attempts a smile. I stroke his red cheek and cock my head consolingly. What bad luck to be fair-haired, pale-skinned and so utterly pathetic in this glorious heatwave.

I find Dad and Dan squeezed into the shade of the only thing Dad hasn't pruned to a stub, our lovely – 'Don't you dare, Dad!' –

lilac bush. They've filled the paddling pool for Grace, who looks just as the Buddha might have done had he gone in for Mothercare sunhats and a permanent dribble. She gets all excited when she sees me coming – how nice that somebody does – bashing rhythmically at the water with chubby little hands and twisting to left and right like an enthusiastic aerobics teacher.

'Here comes Granny with the tea,' says Dad.

I automatically look back over my shoulder to see who's following, but, of course, he's referring to me. Must have a word with him about that. Oliver and I thought we'd rather like to be called Mops and Pops, or Ruby and Ollie, or... well... *anything* but Granny and Granddad – particularly as Oliver isn't remotely blood related (one hopes).

Here he is now. He lumbers across the garden and dives into the remaining bit of shade. Dad tut-tuts and shakes his head. 'You should have been in Egypt in 'fifty-six. I tell you, it was so bloomin' hot–'

'We know!' cry Oliver and I.

'Yeah well, I don't,' says Dan. 'What was it like then, Mr ... er...'

'Just call me Ken.'

Dan's eyes dart from side to side while he thinks about this. Or perhaps he's just trying to place Egypt. 'A mate of mine went on holiday there too. Saw the whatsits ... pyramids.'

'Holiday! I'm talking Suez, son. I tell you, that bloomin tinpot Nasser–'

'More tea, Dad?' I interject swiftly. 'Digestive?' Not Suez, please.

'Lawn's looking good, Ken,' says Oliver, to help me out. 'You'll have to give us a few tips.'

Dad says, 'Secret tool,' and winks, then pulls out his Swiss army knife and rubs the dry mud off between thumb and forefinger. 'Best little edger there is.'

'Sue is what?' asks Dan.

We all turn to him. He's looking at Dad.

'You said, Sue is...'

'Ah.' Dad rests a grandfatherly arm on Dan's bony, vested shoulder. 'Well, you see, son, it all started in nineteen fifty-six... Well no, as a matter of fact it began in nineteen forty-eight, when...'

'Shall we?' I ask Oliver, nodding towards the pergola.

'Only if you give me a piggyback.'

When we reach the canopy of frighten-ingly expensive climbers Dad's woven through his fretwork, Oliver stretches, exhales, falls helplessly into a padded chair and pats my hand gratefully. 'Wasn't too heavy, was I?'

'Not at all.'

I take my zippy new car (how nice not to be driving a tank) to the teashop in Liddleton, where Hamish hands me back my computer disk. There's an odd twinkly thing going on with his eyes.

'She's ... er...' – he clears his throat, 'quite a woman.

'Mm?'

'Your heroine.'

I finish a mouthful of Danish pastry. 'You think so?'

'Mm. I, er ... particularly liked that scene in the barn where she sits on the chief suspect's face while she's giving him–'

'Yes, all right, Hamish!' I look around and behind me. 'There are pensioners present, you know.'

He leans across the table and whispers, 'Talk about a promiscuous, unfaithful little trollop.'

Oh dear, not quite what I'd intended to create. Independent and resourceful was how I saw her. 'She loves her boyfriend very

much,' I insist quietly. 'It's just that sometimes, you know, in the line of duty, she has
to ... um...'

'Screw herself senseless?'

'Well yes.' I lean back in my chair,
deflated. 'I'll obviously have to rewrite the
damn thing.'

'*No!*' says Hamish, snatching the disk
from me. 'Leave her alone. She's terrific.'
He slips my entire novel into his shirt
pocket. 'I mean, even I'd be driven to a
heinous crime if I thought Lydia Wildgoose
might turn up in camiknickers to screw
information out of me.'

'Hamish!' cries a hoarse and jolly voice
from the distance. 'Thought it was you!'

One by one chairs are scraped closer to
tables to let a man the size of a helicopter
make his way towards us. He arrives
breathless and perspiring. 'How the devil
are you?'

Hamish stands and a very male, hand-
shaking, arm-clasping greeting takes place.
'Victor. Good to see you!' Something in
Hamish's face tells me it's not that good.
'Do join us. This is Ruby,' he says, gesturing
my way. 'A friend.'

Victor's huge hand looms towards me and
I brace myself for a spell in a plaster cast.

(Limp and clammy, it turns out.) A third chair is produced and I'm given a potted history of their friendship, beginning with their being at school together. 'Surely not!' I stop myself blurting out. Where Victor could be anywhere between fifty and sixty, Hamish will look just past adolescence for the rest of his life.

'Victor's in estate agency and property management,' Hamish tells me, and with that Victor's off – last year's boom, this year's mini slump, tales of wayward tenants, how much you can ask for a house in Cheltenham during the races and, oh, so much more.

After twenty minutes, just when I'm beginning to forget what my voice sounds like and whether Hamish can say anything but 'You don't say?', Victor heaves himself up and ambles to the gents.

'Sorry about this,' says Hamish.

'You'd think his tongue would get repetitive strain injury.'

'If you want to slip away...'

'OK.' I point to his chest. 'May I?'

'What? Oh right.' He hands over the disk and winks. 'Got a copy anyway.'

'What I *really* wanted was your opinion on the investigative stuff I mean, did it seem

273

authentic, feasible? Did the clues all tie in?'

He looks vacantly at me for a while. 'Yes. Excellent.'

'You skipped those bits, didn't you?'

'Ah, there you are, Victor. Another coffee?'

'CALLING ALL WOMEN,' says Veronica's notice in Ted's window. 'Important and terribly exciting meeting for the Ladies (only!) of the Village. 7.30 pm, Friday 9th, in Veronica Weatherall's sitting room (temporary function room).'

I consider giving it a miss. She probably wants sandwich-makers for the Upper Muckhill cricket team. And besides, would I call myself a lady? I read it again. 'Terribly exciting'....? Can't be sandwiches, then – unless they're ciabatta filled with smoked salmon, cream cheese and a smattering of dill. '7.30 Friday, V's,' I scribble on my cheque book.

'Maybe it's one of them knicker parties,' says Tina over my shoulder. 'You know, where you get all carried away and end up paying a soddin fortune for a bit of string with lace sewn on.'

No, I don't know, actually. But I guess they're similar to Tupperware parties where you decide the future would be unendurable without that lettuce shaker.

'Veronica?' I ask Tina with a quizzical look.

'Yeah, well, she's a bit of a dark horse, if you ask me. Ere, Maximilian. Git ere!' I turn to see her son slipping matches into his pocket and blowing frantically at smoke wafting from the Upper Muckhill litter bin. She goes over and tugs at his T-shirt. 'What have I told you about that?'

Inside the shop, I ask Poppy what she's reading. She lifts her book from beneath the counter and continues to chew on an ice-lolly stick. 'Hobbes,' she says, flashing the cover at me. *Leviathan.*

'Any good?'

'Brilliant. It's about obeying the law, yeah? Hobbes says like if you don't you'll just get fucked over, so you may as well.'

'Really?' Pretty obvious, I'd say. Perhaps I'm wasting my time on my two local rags and (apparently soft porn) novel, and should try my hand at a political theory treatise. 'Is this preparatory reading?'

'Yeah, political thought. It's wicked. Did you want those teabags?'

'Please.'

I watch her scan them, Hobbes in one

hand and a contented Grace asleep beside her, and am full of wonder. I remember new motherhood as a fraught and frantic time when my brains drained away with my breast milk. Poppy, on the other hand, has signed up for a Politics and Economics degree. 'What kind of jobs would that lead to?' I asked her when she first told me. 'Maybe Chancellor of the Exchequer?' she said, deadly serious. I laughed, but who knows? She's never yet given me the wrong change in the shop.

'Mornin, my dears,' hails Norman, making all four of Grace's limbs jump in the air. She gives a little grizzle and goes back to sleep. Oliver and I are never going to get used to our neighbours' volume, and neither perhaps will the rest of the village. Felicity Cousins, three lanes away, said she once heard Norman asking Trevor to pass the mustard.

'Thought you might like to sell this lot,' Norman's now saying to Poppy. He plonks a boxful of small round pats of cheese onto the counter.

'I dunno,' says Poppy, peering in and sniffing. 'A lot of people think goat's cheese tastes like old socks.'

'Yes, well, it's a bit of an acquired taste, I'll

give you that.'

I'm biting my tongue. Those two goats don't know how close they've come to a Range Rover ride to a distant county – Oliver at the wheel sporting a Jack Nicholson expression.

'Here you are, Ruby,' says Norman, delving into the box, then handing me three packs. 'Let's call it compensation for them trousers young Gertie took a liking to.'

A pile of goat's cheese for Oliver's new chinos, ripped to the point of comic on the rotary washing line? It's hard to look grateful, but I give him a lame 'Thanks' and excuse myself. 'Got to see a dog about a man.'

Four eyebrows are raised at me.

'Barking Mad? You know? The ventriloquist's doll, or dog rather?'

No, they don't know.

'Well, he's, I mean *it's*, got this campaign going to bring ventriloquists back onto our television screens.'

'I wonder what happened to Orville?' says Poppy, who was keen on things lurid and fluffy for most of her childhood. 'Probably really old now,' she adds mournfully. Norman rubs his chin and frowns. 'Older than Emu, you reckon?'

I leave them discussing what live longer, ducks or emus, and put it down to the heat.

It's Friday and it's hot. 'Ladies, ladies,' shouts Veronica, with a couple of deafening claps. 'Come along now, I'm sure there's floor space for everyone.'

I've only been here ten minutes and already my left buttock's lost all feeling. I switch to the right and curse Veronica, who could easily have used the village hall.

She's clapping again. 'Frank and I were hoping to have our function room up and running soon, but I'm afraid we're suffering something of a delay at the design stage.'

Thirty people look my way.

'However, you've all found a space, I see. No, no, I wouldn't rely on that occasional table, Sandra. Not with your water retention, dear.'

A florid Sandra heaves herself up, and joins another large lady leaning against a wall.

Veronica then stares us all into silence, one by one, as teachers are taught to do, and a hush descends.

'Good evening, ladies,' she enunciates.

I'm tempted to start a chorus of, 'Goood-eeev-ning-miiss-izzz-Weeaa-ther-aall', but we all just nod and smile at the woman towering above us and shift our bottoms on her parquet flooring.

'Thank you so much for coming. I'll get straight to the point, shall I? As we're all sweltering in this rather small room. Of course, once we've got our function room...' She pauses to let everyone dart their eyes at me again and mumble, then presses on. 'As you may know, I've worked tirelessly for the past year for the charity Mobiles for the Elderly.'

We all nod.

She tilts her head and treats us to a sincere Thatcherite smile. 'Your support and contributions so far have been most appreciated. But you know, it's *terribly* hard to think of new fund-raising ideas all the time.'

Now we all nod with a sympathetic expression, hurriedly thinking up reasons why we can't shake a tin outside Sainsbury's for two hours a month.

'However, Frank and I have come up with a super idea. Fun, zany...'

She's going to produce giant mobile phone costumes, I know it.

'...and a jolly good little earner to boot.' She slowly scans the room to prolong our suspense. 'In the light of the success of the recent spate of WI and other ... um ... what shall we call them, Frank?'

We swivel our heads to the only male in the room. Frank clears his throat and stands upright. 'Glamour calendars, dear?'

At this there's a communal squeal, followed by a cacophony of giggles and chatter. Veronica claps three times and we settle down as best we can until Tracy Ledger calls out, 'If you thinks oi'm posin' in nothin' but a coupla Brillo pads, you're mistook.'

And then of course we're off again.

Veronica cups hands around her mouth. 'Frank, Frank! Do come and help me out.'

Frank weaves his way over to the inglenook and manages to command our attention. 'No need to panic, ladies,' he tells us calmly. 'What Veronica and I had in mind–' he throws her a deferential glance – 'was that we'd get the Upper Muckhill *chaps* to do it. The posing, that is.'

It's a good five minutes before he can carry on, after six people have offered to be the photographer, and Jean Crowbar has volunteered her services in the wardrobe department and we've all wiped away the tears.

'I'm sure all your husbands, boyfriends,

sons and so on have got a trade or profession or even a hobby that might provide appropriate props.'

Oliver's melting ruler comes to mind.

'My boyfriend keeps sheep,' we hear. 'Would that do?'

Frank blushes and Veronica takes the helm again. 'Cricket, allotments, DIY. If your hubby's a carpenter, for example, he could pose behind his Black and Decker workmate.'

'Or his power drill?' suggests Tina, to general hilarity.

'I reckon a two-inch nail'd do for my Pete,' comes a voice from the back, and everyone turns to stare at the unfortunate woman.

Of course, we're all wondering if Frank's going to pose, but none of us likes to ask. Until Tina does, that is.

'Unfortunately, our GP's advised against it,' Veronica tells us, and Frank shrugs and throws his hands up in the air, as if to say, 'What's a chap with a pacemaker to do?'

'Now then, ladies,' eventually concludes our leader, pulling herself to full height and pointing her chin at the ceiling.

I sense a rallying cry coming on.

'Go back to your homes and *persuade!*'

Later, I'm secretly observing Oliver in his armchair, flicking through the channels with a cheese sandwich balanced on both knees. Profession – architect. Possible props – drawing board (too big) –twelve-inch ruler (too long) – pencil (too narrow) – five pencils (maybe). I move on to his hobbies and hit a brick wall.

'Oliver?'

'Mm?'

'Do you realise you don't have any hobbies?'

His eyes remain on the TV. 'Children, scout leaders and the institutionalised have hobbies.'

'Interests then.'

'Yes, I do. I'm interested in ... well, my work.'

I shake my head. 'Uh uh.'

'Nature?'

'Watching wildlife programmes doesn't count.'

He chews on his sandwich for a while. 'And I read.'

So he does! I leave my chair quietly, slip from the room, creep upstairs and rummage in Oliver's bedside cabinet until I find *The Idiot*. I close my eyes and recapture the image. No, can't use that. I rummage some more. No ... no ... no. *Remembrance of Things Past?*... Better not. I come across *Just How Big?* (small subtitle *Was the Big Bang?*) Perfect. It's a City Library book, I see. And overdue. 'Better hide it then,' I say out loud, and shove it in my tampons drawer.

I'm in Troy Shed writing up an interview: 'Ventriloquist's dummy Barking Mad (known to those who've met him as Garking Gad) is determined to bring this "popular and much-missed form of entertainment" away from the end of the pier and back on to our TV screens' – when the mobile rings.

'Hi, it's me,' says Hamish.

'Hi, how are you?'

'Not too good, actually. I've just heard that Victor's dead.'

'Victor?'

'You met him in the teashop.'

'Victor! You're kidding!'

'Yes, I often joke about friends and acquaintances dying.'

'What happened?'

'Electrocuted himself in the bath, apparently. Could have been suicide, but–'

'Suicide? But he was so jolly. I'm sorry, Hamish. Was he a close friend?'

'Not really. Just a Winchester chum. We

met there when we were seven.'

'Were you boarders?'

'Fraid so.'

Poor little chaps. I wonder why someone doesn't found a public school that takes children the moment their umbilical cords are cut. They'd surely have a waiting list as long as Surrey. 'That must have been fun?' I venture.

'Fun? It was hell.'

'Oh. Well … poor old Victor. Quite a nice man really.'

'Yes.'

'Do you think he just couldn't live with all the hatred and derision? You know, being an estate agent.'

'Possibly. But … well, I'm not sure it was suicide. Or even an accident.'

'Oh, Hamish. For God's sake don't go all PI over this. Remember how much time and energy we wasted over Jessica Potts.'

He laughs. 'Now, that was fun.'

'Ha!'

'Just answer me this, Ruby.'

'Mm?'

'Who in their right mind would have an electric fire perched on the edge of their bath in this weather? Not somebody with Victor's body fat, that's for sure.'

I could suddenly feel that clammy hand-shake. 'Perhaps he had flu or something.'

'Perhaps.'

'Or maybe he did top himself.'

'Maybe. But who'd choose to do it that way?'

I shudder at the thought of all that pain, when ten paracetamol would do the trick.

It's hard to get back to Barking Mad, now that Victor and his girth frying in the bath has lodged itself in my mind, but I do some-how manage it.

'"I'm right behind Barking in his cam-paign," said owner, manager and straight man, Danny Dee, discreetly slipping an arm inside the doll and bringing it to life. "You get he is!" Barking then told me, with a creepy roll of the eyes. 'Better take out 'creepy' and put mischievous'. Victor! So completely alive just the other day, and now ... 'I was then treated to a rendering of "How Gluch is that Gloggy in the Glin-dow?" whilst Danny knocked back a pint of water. It was around this point I lost the will to live.' I'm deleting most of that when Oliver thumps just once on my door and barges in, all-over furious and not trying to hide it.

'I've just had a call from Veronica.'

'Oh?'

'Saying she'd like to see me naked behind a small-scale model of their function room.'

'Ah.'

'You might have bloody told me about this calendar plot, Roo.'

'Sorry.'

'It all got very embarrassing, I can tell you.'

'Oh dear. What did you say?'

'I thought she'd hit the gin and was having a bit of flirty fun. You know how she can be sometimes.'

'Not really.'

'You just go along with it. So I said, "Ha ha," and how I'd often pictured her mud wrestling in only those gumboots of hers.'

'We'll have to move house.'

'No, no. It all got straightened out, and she filled me in on this ridiculous calendar idea. Anyway, Roo, if you think I'm–'

'Look, if they can do it in Ambridge–'

'Huh! And have you ever *seen The Archers*' calendar?'

'Well ... no.'

'Quite.'

'Oh, go on. Think of all those old people without mobile phones.'

'And what's supposed to be in it for me?'

I fish out the leaflet Veronica handed us all as we filed out of her stifling room. 'Free advertising of your business, for a start.'

'Oh, big deal.'

'And personal guidance on how to show off your best attributes from last year's Glamour Model of the Year, Melanie Parsons.'

His eyes do a little jig and he takes the leaflet. 'Not Melanie "Just call me Melons" Parsons?'

How does he know these things?

He flops himself down on the sofa bed and reads the leaflet. I see he's now torn.

'Anyone making a brew?' calls Dad, his head poking through a Troy Shed window. I shoot Oliver a look, and he shoves the leaflet under one leg. Dad's motto being 'Count me in', he's bound to be first in the naked men queue, holding a polyanthus at just the right height.

I give up on ventriloquism and we all traipse over to the kitchen where Dad tells us over tea that 'Young Jean' has just told him about this calendar project, and seeing as how his extended holiday has made him an honorary resident, she thinks he might well stand a chance of getting into it.

'What do you mean, "stand a chance"?' asks Oliver with a snort. 'We're hardly going to be fighting duels at dawn to be Mr April.'

'Got a list of eighteen wannabes already, I heard.'

'And only twelve places?'

'Obviously,' I chip in.

'Reckon I'm going to sign up,' says Dad, heaping more sugar into his tea. 'The way I see it is, if you're not actually *in* the calendar, folk will think you just weren't attractive enough to get chosen. They won't know you didn't volunteer in the first place.'

'Good point,' says Oliver, taking out the leaflet with its terrible sketch of voluptuous Melanie Parsons, done by Frank or someone, and rubbing his chin.

While he's thinking, my eyes idly scan the kitchen bookshelf for prop contenders. *Ready in Five Minutes, How to Defrost Safely, Cook It on a Griddle* – I can see we're going to be spoiled for choice.

Reflections, I scrawl illegibly. (How hard it is to use a pen these days.) *If rural life is supposed to be slow and leisurely, how come it appears at the same time to fly by like the wind? Over a year in Upper Muckhill and still people are asking how we're settling in to Bert's place.*

If, in the minds of the villagers, Oliver and I moved in only yesterday, then it must seem to them that England won the World Cup last month and young Princess Elizabeth came to the throne just before Christmas. Would try to get Oliver's head round this conundrum but he's presently on the Internet ordering a weights machine.

I wander down the road one afternoon and knock tentatively on the door of Bankside Cottage.

'Anyone in?' I call out. 'Josh?'

It's two fifteen.

'Josh?' I try again, and it suddenly occurs to me it might be his signing day. But a toilet flushes, feet thump down wooden stairs and the door opens. He stares vacantly for a while, so I help him out. 'It's Mum.'

He takes my arm and looks at my watch. 'Christ, is that the time?'

I'm invited in and I follow him down the hall, studiously avoiding the four carrier bags of empty beer cans. Ah, not quite empty it appears as my sandal enters a warm, frothy puddle and half slips away beneath me. 'Oops, ha ha,' I say. It's like going round the Fun House at the fair. But free!

'Coffee?' asks Josh.

I take in the carpet of crusty, unwashed crockery in the living room. Cups crammed with cigarette butts, a chicken carcass in the fireplace. 'Uh-uh. Just a flying visit.'

Josh picks up a Coke can, shakes it and takes a swig. We go through the kitchen, where I try not to breathe in, and into the garden where, beneath the canopy of intertwined elder trees, he stamps down an area of waist-high grass for us to sit on, then offers me the Coke can.

'No, thanks.' I lower myself gingerly, trying not to have a claustrophobia attack. 'We've got a scythe if you want to borrow it.'

'Yeah, you said.' He yawns again and rubs both eyes with his knuckles. 'I was up all night working.'

'Oh, I'm sorry.'

'Nah, it's alright. Loads to do. This bloke wants us to find him an original pair of bonce bouncers, circa 1981, preferably hearts and in pristine condition. They're all fuckin nutters these people, I tell you.'

'Mm.' They must be if they're dishing out their credit cards numbers to www.no-sweat!.com, which is basically Josh and part-time Luke – twice a guest of Her Majesty's Prisons.

'Anyway ... the reason I'm here is that I was wondering if you'd make us a website.'

'What, you and Oliver?'

'No, no, Upper Muckhill.'

'Oh, right.' He runs his tongue along his cigarette paper. 'Yeah, for a price. Fuckin dangerous things, though, you know, village websites. Especially ones you can post messages on.'

'But that would be the whole point of it. It would give me material for *Grapevine*, and when absolutely everyone's on-line, maybe replace it.'

Josh nods, drags on the cigarette and says, 'You know ... what this village could do with is a cybercafé,' as he exhales.

I laugh dismissively, but then think, *Hey!* Jean Crowbar's daughter could get us some cheap computers... Josh could make ridiculous coffees ... all those sullen boys who more or less live under the bus shelter would have somewhere to go and overthrow military dictatorships. If I mention an Internet café to Veronica, we'd be sure to have one up and running in weeks. Although at the moment she *is* pretty busy knocking *Abigail's Party* into shape, organising naked men, pestering Oliver about her extension every ten minutes and generally running the world. But all the same...

'Mum? ... Mum?'

'Mm?'

'I said, Benny reckons we should make a pond. Over there by the shed. What do you think?'

'Benny?' I ask.

'Oh, right, yeah. My new housemate since yesterday. Well, actually, his dad owns this place.'

'Uh-huh.'

'Hey!' Josh shouts at the house. 'Benny! Get up, you lazy git. Come and meet my mum.'

I hear a long groan and a few banging noises, the toilet flushing again, then the kitchen tap running a long time, before Benny – six foot four, as dark as Bournville chocolate, and crowned by long, beaded dreadlocks – appears semi-naked at the door. 'Good morning,' he says with a broad white-toothed smile.

Josh introduces us. 'This is my mum. This is Benny.'

'Hi,' I say with a nod.

Benny pads over the flattened grass on his bare brown feet and holds out a hand. 'How do you do?' he says plummily, giving me a no-nonsense shake.

'How do you do?' I reply regally, going along with the joke.

'Benny was at Eton,' explains Josh.

'Oh, I see.'

'Anyone for char?' Benny asks, sashaying back to the house in his twelve-inch towel.

'Love one,' I say, suddenly thirsty.

I hurry home to my journal.

So pleased Josh has got a nice new friend and is no longer involved with people he owes money to who have posses. Have to own up to having mixed feelings when he first told me over the phone that his mate's dad had a place dirt cheap to let in Upper Muckhill.

'Fuckin amazing coincidence, man.'

'Yes,' I replied in strangled voice.

'Good thing about running a successful, Internet-based business,' he went on, 'is that you can do it anywhere. Fuckin bed, even.'

'Business?'

'Oh, yeah. Left the bookshop,' he said. My heart plummeted. 'Why, Josh?'

'Well...' he said, drawing on whatever he was smoking. 'You could say I felt the need to develop my entrepreneurial skills.'

'Really?' I said.

'Or you could say I pissed Hamish off so many times by being late that he said he'd sack

me if I wasn't your son and it all got too fuckin tense.'

'Right.'

Think Benny – First Class Honours in Art History, very tidy bedroom, I noticed on way to loo – will be a good influence on Josh. Says he's hoping to do a D.Phil at Oxford, but will spend a year working and saving money first. When I left he was making his way round the living room with a bin bag, singing a Bob Marley song in a voice he must never let Veronica hear. Super, Benjamin! Now tell me, have you ever done any Gilbert and Sullivan?'

JULY

Jean Crowbar's blocking the aisle in Ted's shop. I look over her shoulder at the *Cosmo*, or whatever it is she's reading, and see '50 Tricks for Outstanding Orgasms'.

Fifty? I can think of one, and 'outstanding' might be pushing it. 'After you with that, Jean,' I whisper, making her jerk and slap the magazine shut. She hands it to me with a rut and says, 'Load of old codswallop.'

'Thanks.'

I'm on number eight, which involves contortions I'd have to pay Oliver for, when a voice over *my* shoulder says, 'Doing a bit of research, are we?'

I jerk and slap the magazine shut. 'Hamish! What are you doing here?'

'Ahh, nothing would keep me from the Upper Muckhill summer fête. The carnival's just making its way up the street, you know. Aren't you going to join the cheering throng?'

'I should really. My father's supposed to be in it.' I go over to the till. 'Just this magazine, please, Ted.'

'Right you are, Ruby,' he says, but then

decides to inspect the lingerie ad on the back and read the entire front cover, while I casually drum fingers on the counter. I expect Ted's one of these people who open a letter only after they've tried to work out whose handwriting it is, squinted at where and what time it was posted, felt for interesting contents and propped it against their egg cup for half an hour. 'Three pounds seventy, if you please,' he eventually says as the scanner beeps.

'What!' I grab the magazine, check the price and tell Ted to forget it. Who needs outstanding anyway?

Seven infants in big heads are pretending to be dwarfs, and Leanne Perring – fifteen, and, according to the graffiti, a bit of a pushover – is Snow White. A tinny version of 'Hi ho, hi ho...' is belting out of speakers. As usual with these events, I'm both amazed and appalled. All those hours doing things with crepe paper, all that stapling and setting up the sound system, and getting the kids to act like Sleepy or Grumpy...

'Do you remember,' I hear a nearby woman shout to her friend, 'when the Upper Muckhill Players did *Snow White*?'

The friend nods and grins and they both

start whooping with laughter, hugging their stomachs, gasping for breath and eventually mopping away tears on their sleeves.

'What hap–' I begin to ask them, but Hamish cries, 'Look, Ruby, this one's terrific,' as *Star Wars* passes by on a float with a hole in its exhaust. 'Wish I'd brought my camera.'

I frown at him and wonder if it's just me. However, after we've waved and cheered and whistled at Dad parading as Alan Titchmarsh – thick black wig, spade in hand, buxom young woman holding hose – I sense Hamish's interest waning and watch a nervous foot tapping. 'Look, can we go somewhere and talk?' he eventually asks.

'OK.'

I lead us by a back route to Troy Cottage where I call up to Oliver that Hamish is here. 'He's come for the fête.'

'Down in a minute. Bloody sweltering up here.'

I pour us some juice, which we take out into the garden, where Hamish says, 'Hey, nice ... um...'

'Pergola.'

'That's it.'

When we've settled ourselves on the padded seats he gets straight to the point.

'I've been making some enquiries about Victor.'

Uh-oh.

'It's all *very* mysterious.' He turns to me and makes serious eye contact. 'I was wondering if you and I could maybe–'

'No.'

'Why not? We make a great investigative team.'

'Oh, rubbish.'

'OK, we were a bit off the track with Jessica Potts.'

'Shh,' I say, pointing to where Norman and Trevor are noisily cobbling together something on the other side of our new leylandii hedge.

'OVER TO THE LEFT, TREV.'

'RIGHT YOU ARE.'

Bang, bang, bang, bang.

'I RECKON WE'LL BE ABLE TO GET A NICE BARBECUE GOING BY DINNER TIME.'

Barbecued goat, hopefully.

Hamish rests his chin on his fingers and stares at me. 'I just don't believe Victor's was accidental death, or suicide.'

'Mm? Look, I'm sorry, Hamish, I've got far more productive things to do.' I lean back in my chair and stretch out my bare legs. 'There's sunbathing, for a start.'

He goes quiet for a while, sips at his drink and looks so deliciously forlorn in his lovely pinkish-brown shirt that I'm wrestling with a change of heart. 'Poor old Victor,' he whispers.

'Mm. Horrible way to go.'

He throws me a hopeful look.

'But an *accident*, Hamish.'

He sighs heavily and we both watch Oliver make his way towards us in a floppy sunhat. He tumbles into a chair and fans himself with the bottom of his T-shirt. He says, 'Didn't have you down as a guess-the-weight-of-Mrs-Allsop's-fruit-cake man, Hamish.'

'Sorry?'

Oliver rubs his hands together and bobs his eyebrows up and down. 'Thought I might try and catch those majorettes later, though.'

Hamish shakes off thoughts of Victor. 'Ah, the fête. Well, they can give you a feel for a place, these events. You know, before you buy somewhere.'

My jaw drops. 'A *house?*'

His eyes are resolutely refusing to meet mine, I notice. 'Mm. I'm tired of the city. And, now that Ali and I are no longer... It's a nice village.'

'Great idea!' says Oliver, pouring himself some orange juice. 'Only make it soon, then you'll qualify for entry into the calendar.'

I give an involuntary yelp at the very idea, while Oliver explains. I hear Melanie Parsons mentioned four times. 'Anyway, there are so many applicants now, it's been decided that the women of the village are going to vote for the best twelve.'

While I'm visualising Hamish with a kind of Philip Marlowe look – off-the-shoulder and off-everything-else raincoat, smouldering cigarette – he wriggles himself upright, clears his throat and crosses his legs tightly. Hope I wasn't staring.

'Actually, I was also considering Little Crompton,' he tells us.

Oliver shakes his head. 'Uh-uh. Caravan site and no pub.'

'Old Buckton?'

'Next to the railway line.'

'Oh.'

The sound of distant drumming reaches us and I see Oliver's ears rise half an inch. He hurriedly downs the rest of his drink and stands up. 'Suppose I'd better enter into the spirit of things,' he says resignedly, before crossing the garden in something of a controlled sprint.

'So ... how's the shop?' I ask Hamish, before he gets back to Victor.

'Fine, fine. We're missing Josh, though. I guess he'll never really be a nine-to-five man.'

'Not unless you mean nine p.m. to five a.m..' I tell him about the daily schedule at Bankside Cottage, or Sleepy Hollow, as Oliver calls it.

Hamish goes quiet for a while, then says, 'And how's Ali?'

I groan. 'Constantly phoning and complaining about Bloody Greg.'

'In her element, then?' He chuckles to himself and runs a finger around the rim of his glass. 'I did *try* to be what she wanted, you know. Once, I didn't phone her for a whole day.'

'You bastard!'

We laugh and fall silent again. 'Oh, *go* on, Ruby.'

'*No.*'

Seven p.m., sitting alone in nice, cool (owing to three-foot-thick walls and mini orchard by window) living room with journal.

Ali, I ask myself where is she coming from? Met Bloody Greg when I called in the other day.

He tallish, fair-haired, quite nice-looking, but what you might call guarded. He runs his own graphic design business from home which he told me is in the country but wouldn't be specific when I asked where. Apparently Ali doesn't know either. Throughout our impromptu supper he didn't stop jangling his car keys in an OK-I'm-here-but-I'm-off-any-minute manner. When he excused himself for the loo, we heard him making a mobile call. After he eventually shot out the door with no kiss and an 'I'll call you', Ali took a pin and fair-haired boy rag doll from a cupboard and gave Greg a blinding headache.

'I may be a bit dense,' I said, 'but I can't understand why you dumped wonderful Hamish for that uptight control freak.'

'Oh, it's easy,' she said, jabbing the pin in once more, just to be sure. 'My therapist says I can only get turned on by men who are like my mother.'

I frowned and willed her to stop as I was developing a bit of a headache. 'But Greg isn't small, dark and cuddly and a Friend of Kettle-wick Library.'

'You know what I mean,' she said, suddenly coming over all dreamy and lovingly stroking the doll's lower half in a rather shocking way. 'Have I told you the sex is fanTAstic?'

'Many times,' I said, but now I'd met him

304

found it hard to see Greg as a thoughtful lover,
what with those keys constantly jangling by
your ear or digging in your back. But, what do
I know, maybe they add an exciting dimension.
Could suggest it to Oliver when his heat-induced
libido problem gets sorted out.

I'm in Ted's shop, or Poppy's shop, as we
now like to think of it – Ted being almost
permanently 'Off to the cash-and-carry'
with a golf bag slung over one shoulder –
when Benny walks in, all dreads and beads,
tie-dyed vest and glossy black flesh.

'Ah, hello again,' he cries, and comes over
and kisses both my cheeks from his great
height. He surveys the handful of customers
who seem to have frozen mid-action.

'Gosh, what a delightful little shop,' he
proclaims, and I wonder if he's looking at
the one I'm looking at.

The only person moving is Poppy, who
seems a little flustered; pulling a strap back
on to her shoulder, rearranging her hair
with one hand, straightening her back, then
breaking into a sweet smile. 'Hi, Benny,' she
says huskily.

'Hello, Poppy. How are you?'

The door ding-a-lings as a new customer
enters and suddenly everyone is galvanised

back into action, placing that tin of custard in the basket, finishing the sentence they'd been halfway through.

I hear Poppy telling Benny about our family lunch this Sunday. 'Why don't you like come? That'd be alright, wouldn't it, Mum?' she says without taking her eyes off him.

'Sure.'

Benny frowns and shakes his head. 'Ah, but a family lunch? I'm not sure.'

'I think you'd fit in really nicely,' insists Poppy. Her eyes drop to his shorts and she colours up. 'I mean...'

'In that case, I'd love to,' Benny tells her.

'Just come when you feel like it.' This time she grimaces. 'I mean...'

Oh dear, poor Poppy. Usually so composed. Better step in. 'Any time after twelve, Benny.'

'Terrific. I'll look forward to it. Shall I bring anything?'

'Just Josh, if you can manage it.'

'Right you are.' He asks Poppy for green Rizlas, which has young Janine Granger tittering for some reason, and takes his leave with a 'Cheerio.'

What a poppet.

Back home, I ring my brother. 'Hi, Tim.'

'Hi there. How are things?'

'Fine, fine. And you?'

'Fine.'

'We were just wondering...' *Don't bring Claudia... Don't bring Claudia...* 'if you'd be able to come to lunch this Sunday?' *Please, please, don't bring Claudia.*

'Mmm, I'd love to. Can I bring Claudia?'

'Of course.'

'One-ish?'

'Yep. Perfect. See you then.'

'Bye.'

'Bye.'

Bugger.

Have recently struck up a friendship with Barbara who has three grown-up children, but who says, given her life again, wouldn't on the whole bother. We've taken to walking our dogs together, partly to prevent 'Wife goes missing while walking dog' headlines, but also for the company. The English countryside is all very nice, but let's face it, after you've sighed contentedly at one or two vistas, there isn't a lot more to do for the next hour and a half, apart from put one foot in front of the other.

'It's when they say they'd really like a

greenhouse you know you're on that down-
ward spiral,' Barbara's now telling me. I
think she's talking about husbands. 'Before
long you're driving to the coast to look at
the sea from the car. A flask of tea in your
hand and a tartan blanket on your knees
because you've opened the window an inch.'

'Mm.'

'Conversation gets to consist of, "I got us
a nice bit of haddock for our tea," and "That
William G. Stewart never gets any older,
does he?"'

'Uh-huh.'

'After about twenty years of this, he'll pop
off with a bad heart, or something, and
when you're packing up his sports jackets
for Help the Aged, you'll ponder wistfully
on how you'd really wanted to go and do
VSO when the children left home.'

'Right,' I squeeze in. A conversation with
Barbara tends to be a monologue.

'Anyway, I asked if they had it in a size
sixteen, and this girl looked at me like I
ought to be culled or something.'

'Sorry?'

'You know, that dress for Gordon's office
do.'

'Ah yes.'

It's quite hard work, but, as I said, preferable to sudden death.

'How's your son's business doing?' she asks.

'Oh, very well. He and his partner have just g–'

'I told Peter last week – Peter's the middle one – that if he doesn't get off his butt soon and get qualified, he'll end up like his Uncle Alan.'

'Uncle Alan?' I ask obligingly. That should keep her going for twenty minutes.

We eventually round the last corner and Troy Cottage looms into sight. When we reach my back gate, Barbara lowers her voice and nods in Dad's direction. 'Now if I thought Gordon was going to be like your father, Ruby – you know, active, fit, interesting – I wouldn't be considering leaving him at all.'

'You're thinking of *leaving* him?'

'Hello, Ken,' she calls out with a Mexican wave of four fingers. Then in a whisper to me, 'I'd love a cuppa.'

'Um, yeah, OK.'

While I'm brewing up and watering the dogs, Barbara disappears to the bathroom, re-emerging some five minutes later in Burnt Orange lipstick with part of her dyed brown hair back-combed into a small hillock. I suddenly have a vision of her as a tarty sixth-former, circa 1960.

'I'll take your father's out to him, shall I?' she asks, whipping two mugs from the worktop.

'Thanks.'

Some time later, I look through the window to see how Dad's coping with her, but, in fact, see *him* talking nineteen to the dozen and Barbara listening intently and regularly flinging her rigid hair back with laughter. This is most unfair. By now Oliver has crept up behind me and we both take in the little scene in the garden.

'I'm not sure I want Barbara as my step-mother,' I say.

'Her husband probably wouldn't be too keen either. What's his name? Donald?'

'Gordon.'

'Nice chap.'

'Yeah?'

'Mm. Got this terrific greenhouse he was showing me round the other day. You know I wouldn't mind–'

'No no *no*. Absolutely not. We haven't got room.'

'Steady on now, Roo.'

Just when you think it couldn't get any

hotter, the sun manages to notch up another degree or two. Even in Scotland, apparently, people are abandoning their cardigans. Oliver's permanently tetchy, snapping at clients on the phone and leaving the house only to take a spin in the air-conditioned Range Rover. A more or less useless fan whirrs away on my desk, redistributing the piping hot air, while I'm trying to write an article for an autumn supplement to the *Liddleton Echo* entitled 'Ten Musts for Home Insulation'. Now let me see, number three, number three. Ah yes. 'Lagging the tank. Any good DIY store will...' Oh, sod this. I get Lydia Wildgoose – the sequel – up on screen. *Lydia Rides Again*, Hamish calls it. When I left it yesterday (page four) somebody was knocking on Lydia's office door. She had no idea who, and neither did I. But this morning, upon waking to brilliant sunshine, and suddenly inspired by Barking Mad, I decided it was going to be a Lord Charles-type ventriloquist's doll, monocle and all. But – and this bit I loved – no ventriloquist! Over breakfast, I shared the idea with Oliver, who said, 'Ah yes, very Kafkaesque,' and went back to his newspaper.

'Come in,' called Lydia.

On receiving no response, she stood up, eased her short, navy skirt down over her firm thighs, and stepped purposefully on three-inch heels across the buffed oak floor of her office. She swung the door towards her. 'Hello, can I–' Her eyes slowly fell to the strange little man, no higher than her silk-stockinged knees. 'Uuhh!' she cried.

After bowing from the waist at her, the little man's eyes then made a noisy clonk as he raised his gaze. 'Giss Gildgoose?'

Maybe not. Delete, delete, delete. 'Miss Wildgoo–' The mobile rings. 'Hi, it's me,' says Hamish.

'Hi.'

'Want to come and see a cottage with me? Dewdrop Lane. This afternoon.'

'I don't know. I'm quite busy.'

'I'd appreciate your advice. I know nothing about these dilapidated old properties.'

'Whereas I'm living in one, you mean?'

He politely ignores me. 'It's number four. I'm meeting the estate agent there.'

'Number four. Oh, I know, Marjorie Bradshaw's place. She died. It's been on the market for ages.'

'Meet you there at one thirty?'

'Oh, OK.'

The shiny red Peugeot crunches to a halt at our feet in the gravelly lane. 'Sorry I'm late,' says the tall, slim, possibly bleached-blond, late-twenties man. He pulls a suit jacket from its hanger behind the passenger seat, slips his arms in and holds out a hand. 'Miles Fletcher-Maycock.' We shake and introduce ourselves as speedily as possible, desperate to get out of the sun. Miles pats his pockets for the keys, then clicks up the path on his noisy shoes.

'Have many people seen it?' asks Hamish.

'No, no. Just come on the market.' Miles then spends some time wiggling the key in the old lock. 'It's always a bit tricky, this one.'

Hamish and I exchange a knowing look.

'So Mrs Bradshaw's daughter tells me,' he adds quickly. He chews on his bottom lip whilst fiddling, and after giving the door a hefty whack with his shoulder, tumbles into the hallway with a 'Eureka'.

Hamish and I wander round silently for five minutes or so. Somebody's been in and emptied the place, but a few touching remnants of the widowed Marjorie Bradshaw's life have been missed: a bottle of brown sauce on a kitchen shelf, a tube of

Steradent and a hairnet in the bathroom. It makes me hope my children will be thorough when emptying their inherited house and not leave *Living with Flatulence* on display.

I pass Hamish and notice he's carrying around the same fixed expression of horror as I am. It seems the Bradshaws had cared nor a jot about maintaining the character and dignity of a three-hundred-year-old cottage, deciding rather that what couldn't be clad in mock pine must be daubed with the spikiest Artex known to man.

'Needs a bit of work,' Miles Fletcher-Maycock helpfully points out. 'But you've got your basics. Wiring's good. Central heating.' He indicates the boiler that someone has criminally installed in a corner of the living room, just above the wall-length Cotswold stone fireplace. 'That's why it's such a good price.'

'A quarter of a million is a good price?' asks Hamish, his eyes fixed on a particularly garish chandelier.

'Well, just under. Two thirty.'

'Can we see the garden?' I ask.

'Ye-ep.' A narrow passage leads us to the back door, which Miles opens, with a pained expression, on to a huge expanse of dazzling concrete. The only thing the Bradshaws had thought to plant in their garden was a rotary washing line. Hamish sighs. 'It doesn't get any better, does it?'

Miles fiddles with the ring on his little finger and in a low voice says, 'Tell the truth, they're getting desperate. You'd probably get it for under two hundred. But...' he looks over both shoulders, 'I haven't said that.' A loud ding-dong from the front door makes us start. 'Ah, that'll be the next viewing. Excuse me.'

Hamish and I stand cross-armed for a while, discussing possible uses for the garden – netball court, car park – then make our way back through the house, where we find a young couple bouncing around the living room, obviously enraptured. 'Oh *look*, Adam,' cries the young woman, 'a sixties partition.'

'Hey,' says her partner. He goes over and strokes the plywood. 'I've only seen these in photographs.'

'And to think, some people rip that kind of stuff out,' exclaims Miles, who seems to have cheered up considerably.

Adam shakes his head. 'Criminal. Have you had any offers?'

'Quite a few, actually,' Miles tells them,

after a sheepish glance in our direction. 'All around the asking price.'

'Better get in quick then,' says the woman, all starry-eyed as she wanders off to the kitchen. 'Ohmygod!' she cries when she gets there, just as I almost did. 'Polystyrene ceiling tiles!'

Adam catches his breath and hurries in with a 'No!'

Hamish stands stroking his chin, his eyes scanning the room. 'Actually, it's not *that* bad.' He calls Miles over. 'OK,' he says in hushed tones, 'one ninety.'

Miles shoves his hands in his trouser pockets and gives Hamish a withering look. 'Sensible offers only, I think.'

The hottest Saturday since records began and Veronica decides to hold a barn dance this evening in aid of Mobiles for the Elderly. 'Poor old Mr Longbottom was trapped under his lawnmower for hours last week,' she's telling a shopful of people. We're all here to enjoy Ted's all-year-round January temperatures, not even pretending to shop. 'Now if he'd had a nifty little phone tucked in his cardigan pocket...'

An overheated Oliver, his head halfway into the opened-up, steaming chest freezer says, 'I can never hear a bloody thing anyone's saying on our mobile, so what's the point of a deaf old fart of eighty-six having one?'

'Well, really,' a woman says as I lower the lid over Oliver.

'Quite,' I hear, and everyone forms a queue to buy a ticket from Veronica. It seems Oliver's just done all the Mr Longbottoms an enormous favour.

'Only eight pounds,' sings Veronica. 'Children under ten six-fifty. Automatic entry into the raffle.'

'Ooh, what's the prize?' asks Betty-from-the-pub.

'Well, we've got two prizes,' Veronica tells us excitedly. 'The second is a week's supply of selected items from Ted's shop...'

Appreciative murmurs make their way towards a modestly nodding Ted as Oliver stands up straight, his face all red from the cod-in-butter sauces, and says, 'First prize a day's supply?'

While I type furiously in a sun-soaked Troy Shed, Oliver spends the afternoon in a tepid bath reading *Arctic Dreams*. His mood over dinner is pleasingly upbeat and I marvel at his ability to find such a cheap form of therapy. *Anxious? Depressed? Feel you can't go on? Have a tepid bath!* He doesn't even seem to mind going to the barn dance. 'All in a good cause,' he says amnesically.

A middle-aged man with Teddy-boy hairstyle, fringed shirt and pointy boots, and an accent somewhere between Little Rock and Solihull, gives us instructions for the first dance as we stand in two straight lines, myself opposite Frank and his pacemaker. 'Then four to the right ... clap twice ... form an arch ... first couple ... under ... figure of eight ... left kick ... on the spot ... next partner and start again. OK, got that guys and gals?'

'Yeeesss,' we all call out, but of course we haven't. Next to me, Jean Crowbar, the only person with a handbag on their arm, offers me her bony hand while our MC fiddles with his little cassette player. To my right, with a, 'Mind if I squeeze in here?' appears Ted. He takes my other hand and gives it the subtlest of caresses with his big hairy shopkeeper's thumb.

The music strikes up and within seconds it's obvious that I'm the only one who hadn't been listening. As everyone skips, twirls and figure-of-eights like they've got a barn dancing degree, I find myself repeatedly bouncing off large-chested women. 'Oops, sorry!' I shout several dozen times before the interminable music ends with a lengthy accordian chord and a cheer from my fellow dancers – none of them, I notice, facing the way I am.

'Come and dance,' I say to Oliver's back. 'It's great fun.' He turns around, thus revealing the two young women he's had pinned to the wall. They throw me a grateful look and take the opportunity to sidle off.

'Really? he asks, pointing to my eyes. 'Why have you been crying then?'

'Stubbed my toe.' I don't add 'on Frank's shin'.

I notice he's looking hot and bothered again – could be the heat, could be the girls – as I steer him on to the dance floor, place him opposite me and tell him to listen *very carefully* to the instructions.

'OK, OK,' he snaps. 'It's hardly quantum mechanics.'

Ha, ha, you wait.

When the acned, six-foot-three, shaved-headed, sixteen-year-old Jason Hogg, well-known bus-shelter trasher and torturer of small children, takes hold of his hand, Oliver stares disbelievingly at me, wide-eyed, mouthing 'Help!' and paying not a jot of attention to what Mr Fringed Shirt is telling us. The music starts up and it's nice this time not to be bottom of the class. When the ordeal's over, and Oliver begins inching towards the bar, I grab his arm, turn him round and say, 'Come on. It's easier the second time.'

'Oh, I don't know, Roo. It just doesn't feel right to be holding hands with Ted.'

I know what he means. 'Go on,' I urge again. I need Oliver on the floor to make me look good. 'It's excellent exercise.' I watch Frank limp past and mentally take that back.

This time we both listen carefully. 'Four to the left ... blah blah ... form an arch ... blah ... four claps ... blah ... figure of eight ... and change partners.' Oliver's been nudged down the line and I find my first partner is now the vicar.

Off we go, and hey, I'm remembering it. I swivel the vicar round and clap my four claps at the same time as everyone else. That's very satisfying.

'And CHANGE PARTNERS!' shouts the man on stage.

'Oh, wotcha, Mum,' says Poppy, linking her arm with mine.

'Poppy! Didn't know you were here.

Where are Dan and Grace?'

'At home. I came with–'

'And CHANGE PARTNERS!'

'Good evening, Mrs Grant.'

'Benny!' I cry as we skip our obligatory circle, then turn and do it the other way. 'Is Josh here?'

He nods towards the bar, where Josh is sipping from two pints in his 'Take me to your dealer' alien-with-spliff-in-mouth T-shirt. I wave at him and consequently mess up my four claps.

'And CHANGE PARTNERS!'

'This is fun, isn't it?' shouts Oliver while we spin round like old hands. He gives a hearty laugh and I wonder if there was ever a person so up and down.

'And CHANGE PARTNERS!'

I smell that nice cologne first. Then follow the arm that's hooked itself through mine ... all the way up to Hamish's face.

'I was hoping to find you in a cute little gingham dress,' he says with a grin.

I scratch around for a witty retort à la Jane Austen heroine gliding around effortlessly at a ball and subtly flirting with her suitor. 'Bu– wha–' I manage.

'Happened to be passing through. Saw the poster. Couldn't resist.'

'And CHANGE PARTNERS!'

Don't want to.

Hamish moves off to partner Tina – who is wearing gingham and not much of it I'm alarmed to see – and I get Veronica.

'Do you think we could get that dashing friend of yours to pick the raffle tickets?' she puffs. Her eyes are fixed on Hamish's rear as we go through the motions. So are mine, come to think of it.

We're all pleased that the extensive and impoverished Granger family have won Ted's hamper – custard creams, tinned carrots, Day-Glo lemon squash – and clap as vigorously as the stifling heat will allow.

Veronica, as predatory as I've ever seen anyone in beige pleats, strokes Hamish's upper arm as she builds up the excitement for us. 'And *now*... for the winner of the first prize. This *terribly* useful chain saw, donated by Brownlow's Garden Centre.'

I look over to where Norman Potts is holding his raffle ticket at arm's length to read it and say, 'Oh please, God, no.'

Veronica holds the Tupperware box level with Hamish's nose, and he dips in, takes a ticket and unfolds it. 'Number one four six,' he announces beautifully.

'Yeah!' screams Tina, jumping on the spot and punching the air.

Everyone claps and cheers while Maximilian – great big smile, eyes the size of golf balls – runs over to their large boxed prize, picks it up and somehow staggers from the hall with it.

'Ha ha ha,' we all go as Tina chases after him. Then an eerie silence falls as everyone thinks of another village they could move to.

Bedtime journal entry: *Dear God. Please promise You'll make my children slip me a lethal dose of something before I become as old, curmudgeonly and completely off-message as Lottie Hardwick –yesterday dragged swearing and brandishing coal tongs to an old people home. Having discovered on my 'Would you like to subscribe to* Grapevine *and save four pounds a year?' round that the said lady's kitchen contained only a packet of stale ginger nuts and what could once have been corned beef, I took it upon myself to sustain her. At first things were quite jolly when I turned up with plates of hot food and freshly laundered bedding. 'I'm eighty-two, you know,' she'd announce each time. 'Never!' I'd say back while she did a bit of wobbly charleston, and we'd have a good old chuckle. But soon it became, 'Call that mutton stew?' when I'd placed a dish of gammon, green beans and buttered new potatoes on her Silver Jubilee place mat. 'You don't know mutton stew from your arse.' She'd push the food away and I'd go home and cry, partly through hurt feelings, but mostly because old age is just so demeaning. Oliver, on the other hand, thinks it's a luxury we've all got to look forward to – being as obnoxious as we please without fear of violent retaliation. I refrained from pointing out that life for him in his dotage won't be that different.*

Can't sleep. I glance at the clock for the hundredth time – 2.25 a.m. – put the light on and heave my journal back on to the bed.
   Have I got enough food for tomorrow's lunch? Will Claudia notice cauliflower florets, parsnips, and indeed roast potatoes, are frozen? Aga or cooker? Cooker, I think, as long-term and pervasive heat from Aga might kill Oliver.

3.56a.m., switching light back on. *How would anyone happen to find himself 'passing through' Upper Muckhill?* I write with floppy wrist, heavy eyelids and a battalion of butterflies in my tummy. *And so often?*

I take in the people around our extended

dining table, one by one. Poppy, Dan, Little Grace, Dad, Josh, lovely Benny, Tim, *Claudia*, Oliver, me. Then I go round again. Muckhill, Muckhill, Muckhill, Muckhill, Muckhill, Muckhill, London, London, Muckhill, Muckhill. And now there'll be Hamish too, of course. How has this come to pass, I wonder. I wouldn't have thought Oliver and I had such tremendously magnetic personalities. Maybe Upper Muckhill's on an irresistible ley line, or something.

'There's plenty more gravy,' I tell everyone except Claudia, who's picking at the broccoli, cauliflower and green bean medley in front of her.

'The *what* diet?' I heard Oliver ask, the first time Tim was planning to bring her to lunch. He put his hand over the receiver. 'Tim must be going out with a bloody horse,' he whispered to me. 'Seems she's on a hay diet.' Then back into the phone, 'Not sure they sell that at Tesco's, Tim. Could be a bit tricky. What?... Oh, I see. Right. And what happens if she *does* mix protein and carbohydrates? The end of life as we know it?... No, no, I'm not being facetious... What? Oh, OK... Roo, he wants to talk to you.'

'*Anyway*,' Claudia's now telling us. 'I got myself zero-balanced and the headaches

325

cleared up immediately.'

'Zero-balanced?' asks Dan, helping him-self to more chicken. 'Sounds like our bank account, doesn't it, Pops?'

We all laugh at Dan's joke, except Poppy that is, who shoots an anxious and embar-rassed look at Benny.

Dad, who's on his third glass of wine despite being practically teetotal, winks at Claudia. 'You know what they say's the best cure for a headache, don't you?'

'More gravy, Dad?' I almost shout.

'No, Ken,' says Claudia. 'I don't know.'

'Dad, you couldn't just fill the gravy boat again, as you're nearest?'

'Well, lass, maybe you're not getting enough rumpy– *Ouch!* Was that you, Ruby?' He rubs his shin, then gets up with the gravy boat and hobbles to the kitchen. When he returns, he's holding the mobile out to me. 'Call for you.'

I take it into the garden.

'Hi, it's me,' says Hamish.

'Hello.'

'I found out something interesting about Victor.'

'Hamish, I didn't get much sleep last night and now I'm in the middle of a big family lunch.'

'Ah. Sorry. How stressful on a scale of one to ten?'

'Eleven. It's Claudia, really. Oh, and Dad, who's a bit drunk. Then there's the Poppy, Benny thing. Oliver's morose. Make that twelve.'

'OK, talk to you later.'

'It was only a little bit, darling,' I hear Tim saying when I go back in.

Claudia's peering at her meal in the manner of one who's just discovered a small colony of rats in it. 'No, no, I couldn't possibly eat it now.'

'Grace threw her spoon and it landed on Claudia's plate,' explains Poppy. *Naughty Grace.*'

'Let me get you some more,' I offer, snatching the plate away.

'No, please don't. I do tend, on the whole, to avoid non-organic vegetables. I thought Tim might have told you.'

'I believe,' says Oliver, piercing a roast potato with more force than I'd have thought necessary, 'that he mentioned it.'

We decide to go for a walk. All of us. Even Oliver. We take Ganja, but leave the young exhausting dogs behind. It takes us a while to get going as Claudia has to cover herself in something homeopathic and gather together spring water, Rescue Remedy and a working umbrella. But we eventually slip Grace into the contraption on Dan's back and set off in the heat, myself in front and Claudia at the rear under a large black brolly.

I consider what an odd bunch we must look to passers by: Poppy in one of her creative, charity shop ensembles, Dad ramrod straight in vest and khaki shorts, Tim in trouser creases you could slice bread with in an emergency, and Benny with his beaded hair, now kindly holding the umbrella above Claudia. Luckily there's nobody around to watch slack-jawed as we pass; we being the only ones mad enough to take an afternoon hike in a late-July scorcher.

'*Don't* pull Daddy's *hair*,' I hear Dan tell Grace in an uncharacteristically firm tone. What hair, I wonder. 'Pops, can you stop her doing that?' he adds, but Poppy has slowed her pace enough to be sharing the shade of the umbrella. How keen she must be on Benny to choose to walk with Claudia.

Oliver's just saying 'Jesus,' over and over as he heaves himself up the incline we've encountered, occasionally stopping to lean on Ganja. 'Jes*us*.' He's certainly very flushed.

'Mum, where was it we picked those magic mushrooms?' calls out Josh.

Tim gives me a terrific-mother-you-are look, while I turn the same colour as Oliver and frown and shake my head rapidly at Josh.

'It was just over this hill, wasn't it?'

Shut up, Josh.

Dan says, 'Yeah, only it's too dry for them now.'

'Too dry for what?' asks Dad, who's been treating us to a vibrato whistling of something unrecognisable, but possibly an old Ken Dodd song.

'Cowslips,' I say, and everyone walks on in silence.

After twenty minutes or so we find ourselves veering towards a welcome clump of trees at the top of a hill, scattering the small flock of sheep who've probably been shading themselves there since early June. Oliver arrives first, falling face down and lying so still that when we reach him a certain amount of concern ripples through the parry. We gather round him. Claudia's reluctant to hand over the last of her water, so Poppy pulls Grace's beaker from a pocket, Dad rolls Oliver on to his back and I insert the much-chewed spout between his parched lips and tip Ribena into his mouth. Grace screams possessively and bashes her father's head.

'You can have it back in a minute, love,' chuckles Dad. 'After we've saved your granddad's life.'

Oliver splutters, pushes the beaker aside and sits himself up, wiping the juice from his face. He isn't looking too happy. Hair wild and damp, chin set at pissed-off position. 'I am *not*,' he says measuredly but with some volume to Dad, 'her bloody *grand*father.' At this Grace screams louder, until the beaker is passed along and popped in her mouth.

'I *said* I didn't want to come to this sodding lunch,' we hear Claudia whisper to Tim in the ensuing silence. She tilts her head back and drops something from a pipette under her tongue.

'We didn't bloody well want you to come either,' says Oliver, now on some kind of delirious roll. I look around for something to gag him with. Perhaps one of Poppy's strange accessories. But she's not there, and neither is Benny. Dan seems not to have noticed as he and Josh are rolling a cigarette and heading round the back of a tree.

'Hey, isn't that Barbara?' asks Dad, shielding his eyes and staring into the middle distance where a lone woman is walking a dog. 'Barbara!' he calls out with a wave and a beckoning arm.

When she gets to us, she sits herself so close to Dad that she may as well have gone for his lap. 'Glorious day, isn't it, Ken? Hello, Ruby, Oliver.'

'Hi,' I say for both of us.

'I'm a bit of a widow this weekend,' she tells Dad with an exaggerated sigh and a glint in her eye. 'Gordon's at a weekend convention of the geranium and pelargonium society.'

Oliver snorts. 'So plants are forming their own societies now? Ingenious little buggers, aren't they?'

Barbara laughs, not realising the extent of Oliver's sunstroke. The rest of us stay quiet so as not to encourage him.

Dad cups his hands around his mouth. 'Are you off then, Tim?'

What? I turn to see Tim and Claudia halfway down the hill, brolly aloft. I jump up and run down to them and arrive panting. 'I'm sorry, Claudia. It's just that Oliver isn't very good in heat.'

She chooses not to respond and instead stares intently at a point above my head. Tim, to his credit, gives me a sympathetic look and pecks my cheek. 'Got to get back to London. No need to see us off.'

'OK. Well ... sorry again, Claudia.'

She's obviously sent me to Coventry, and perhaps Tim too, so I return his sympathetic look and pat his arm. 'Thanks for coming.'

Back at base camp, I find Poppy and Benny returned from their stroll, Dad entertaining Barbara, Oliver almost asleep, and Barbara's dog, Winston, chewing determinedly on Grace's plastic beaker. I flop on my back and stare at the branches and leaves above, suddenly feeling rather calm and at peace with the world; eyes closing, head trying not to think of the devastation in the kitchen.

I conjure up Lydia Wildgoose, now on the trail of her elusive ventriloquist, wandering around the house she's cheekily let herself into with a picklock. How would it look, I wonder. Mock pine and Artex à la Marjorie Bradshaw? Wall-to-wall muck, as in Josh's place? No. Neat as a pin, I think. Lydia pads over polished floors, rifles through a bureau, a letter rack and a couple of kitchen drawers. Nothing. Then into the garden, where – shock, horror – she encounters the owner reclining on a sun lounger. He's slim but muscular and frightfully good-looking – thirty-five, perhaps? – and he's smoking a joint. Yes, definitely smoking a joint. The sweet, familiar odour reaches Lydia's nostrils. Mm, well at least her suspect will be nicely chilled. 'Ooo, er,' Lydia hears someone saying in the background. 'What's that funny smell, Ken?'

'Search me,' says Dad. 'Ruby?'

'Mm?' I sit up and rub my eyes and register the smell of dope wafting our way from behind a tree.

'*Ganja!*' says Poppy.

Barbara's nose twitches. 'So it is.'

'Ganja! Leave Winston alone! *Bad* dog.'

We hear Grace gurgling and giggling behind the tree, and Barbara says quietly to Dad, 'If it was my great-granddaughter passively inhaling drugs, I'd be down on those kids like a ton of bricks.'

Dad's on his feet in an instant. 'Drugs? Drugs? They want bloody horse whipping, those lads.'

'No, Dad,' I tell him. '*I'll* have a word with them.'

I look to Oliver for support but he's

quietly snoring, so hoist myself up again just as the mobile begins its annoying little tune in my pocket. I wonder if it might be Tim from the house, but it's Hamish with a, 'Hi, it's me again.'

'Oh, fuck off!' I hear myself saying, than slap a hand over my mouth in horror.

Hamish gives a quiet, 'OK,' and I look up to see all eyes on me.

'Replacement windows,' I explain.

AUGUST

I'm in Troy Shed e-mailing an apology to Hamish, and Oliver's in his office e-mailing one to Tim and Claudia. Neither of us is feeling brave enough to use the phone. Grace, now crawling, has decided that the contents of my bottom shelf should be chewed, ripped, crumpled out of recognition then scattered willy-nilly across the floor. Ah well, at least it's keeping her happy while her mum's on a three-day 'Back to Study' course and Dan's creating a French farmhouse kitchen in Little Crompton.

I click on Send and Receive, only to find that my e-mail has crossed with one from Hamish. **Sorry, Ruby,** I read. **Bad timing on my part. Lots to tell you. H.**

Two other new messages await me, both from Muckhillites, and both, I'd wager my house, nasty in tone. How foolhardy I'd been to set up the *Grapevine* 'Best Kept Front Gardens Awards' this summer. Judged by the manager of Brownlow's Garden Centre three weeks ago, it has led to covert attacks on hanging baskets and former lifelong friends not speaking. Not to

mention the venom directed at my computer and the boycotting of July's edition
boasting photos of all the winners. I delete
both messages without reading them.

'No, Grace, not the thesaurus.' I rush over
and grab it from her cruel little fingers.
'Come on, let's give you to Oliver for a
while.'

'No, sorry,' says Oliver. 'Got to get this
finished by the end of the week.'

I tell him it's only Tuesday and plead with
him. 'I've got an article to write and it's just
impossible.'

'Where's your dad?' he asks.

'Replacing Barbara's washer.'

'Still?'

I nod. He left at ten this morning, leaving
a trail of Old Spice and saying he thought it
was going to be a bit of a tricky blighter so
he'd probably be gone a while.

Oliver pushes his chair on to the landing.
'Oh, come on then, Gracelet.' He takes her
from me, knowing he's got a lot of making-
up to do for last Sunday's behaviour. 'Let's
go and find some ducks to feed or something.'

We get together the paraphernalia Grace
needs to venture anywhere, throw it into the

Range Rover and belt her into the child seat we've now got permanently fitted for just such occasions. I hand Oliver half a loaf of bread for the ducks and tell him to take his time, then turn to Grace. 'Bye-bye,' I say with a comical wave and a sudden lightness of spirit. 'Bye-bye.'

I could work, or I could stroll down to Bankside Cottage and see how the website's coming along. I go for the latter and arrive to find someone's cat chewing at ancient lasagne on Josh's front path. The front door's ajar and Josh is slumped over his computer in the living room, dead to the world, while a smoke alarm is beeping shrilly in the depths of the kitchen. I sniff and can't smell anything, but as I make my way towards the kitchen, have to hold an arm across my face against the acrid fog suddenly swirling my way. First I turn the cooker off, then locate the alarm under a pile of mildewy clothes piled on the work surface. I cough my way back to the front door, open it wide and kneel down next to the cat. Must go and save my son from asphyxia, I think, but then hear him cursing. He appears at the door in an oven mitt with a roasting tin full of charcoal. 'Those sausages were the last of the food. Fuck!'

I take him home for a bacon sandwich –
well, three in the end, which he washes
down with a pint or so of milk. 'Benny was
supposed to shop this week, only he's pissed
off to town for three days.'

Three days? My stomach does a little
lurch. 'Why?'

'Dunno.'

'Look, Josh, I'm going to have to get back
to work. I just wondered how the website's
coming along.'

'Good, yeah. Got the banners organised
but I'm gonna need some metatags off you.'
He spends some time translating, then says,
'No chance of some money up front, is
there? Fuckin broke at the moment and the
rent's due.'

'I suppose so. You will finish it, though,
won't you?'

'Yeah, yeah.'

I get my cheque book out.

'Gotta be cash really. I'm overdrawn on
my overdraft, you see.'

'Right.' I open my purse. 'Twenty OK?'

He pulls a face. 'Any chance of a hundred?' he asks, whipping the note from me.

'But you only quoted fifty pounds, Josh.'

'Well, a lend then. This geezer's still got to pay us for finding his brother on the Web. You'll get it back Friday.'

Which one, I wonder.

In Troy Shed I find the mobile ringing. It's Hamish wanting to meet for afternoon tea. 'Usual place?' he suggests.

Oh, why not?

The teashop in Liddleton is quieter than usual. Hamish and I take a window table and both feel Victor's presence – or lack of it, I suppose.

Hamish shakes his head. 'I still can't believe it.'

'No.' As I stir my tea I'm aware that a large tear has splashed into it.

'Hey,' says Hamish. 'Ruby?' His hand moves across the table and lands awkwardly on mine. 'I didn't realise you'd formed such an attachment to Victor in those thirty minutes.'

I shake my head, sending another tear flying off in the direction of the next table. Luckily, it's empty. 'It's not that.'

'Well, what?' He attempts to brush away another tear, but they're gathering force. 'Hey. Here, have my serviette.'

'Thanks. It's just...'

'What?'

'Oh, I don't know. They're all ... you know ... *there*.'

'Who?'

'All of them. I mean, you move to the country for a bit of peace and independence, and you end up changing nappies and worrying about your father's moral code.' I give a quiet sob.

'Poor you.'

'Then there's the magazine. It's made me the most unpopular person in the village.'

'I'm sure it hasn't.' Hamish seems to be beside me now, on another flowery-cushioned chair. 'You know, you're even more gorgeous when you cry.' His arm has worked its way around my shoulder.

'Excuse me?'

He eases me closer to him, so that my forehead is resting against his. Nice aftershave. 'You must have realised I'm crazy about you?'

'I'm not sure I have,' I say hoarsely, and wave at Grace through the window.

Grace! I blink away the tears and look again at her bobbing along on Oliver's back. Oh no. I quickly turn my head away and Hamish seems to take this as a cue for a kiss. A rather nice kiss actually, and one I might be enjoying more were I not aware that my car is parked ten paces up the street. 'I've got to go,' I say, when he's finished. 'Emergency. Stay in the café for another ten minutes.' I grab my bag and leave him understandably bewildered.

'Hey, fancy seeing you two here!' I say when I've caught up.

'Roo?'

'Had to come out for an ink cartridge.'

'Right.' He's giving me the oddest of looks. I point across the road. 'From Burridges.'

'Uh-huh.'

'See you back at home then?'

'OK.'

I feel I ought to buy one now, so cross to the shop where I'm met with equally strange looks. Back in the car, I catch sight of my ghoulish, mascara-streaked face in the rear-view mirror. I really think Oliver might have told me.

Thought, I write later in a rare, tranquil moment, *I wonder how Oliver and I always fail to organise ourselves a lovely, lazy summer holiday in a picturesque foreign spot? Possibly because Oliver says he won't go anywhere he might have to look at ageing European men in thonged swimwear. He also finds the planning stage way too stressful and effort-requiring – even if it's me that's making the effort – all that phoning, phoning again, looking up on the Internet to see if there's anything better, deciding where you're going, then losing sleep because you think you've made the wrong choice. That's before you get round to the buying of shorts, T-shirts, etc., plus sundry items you feel compelled to take on holiday but have never in your life found use for – dry shampoo, a nightie.*

But mostly it's the prospect of all that heat that bothers Oliver. When I broached the subject of having a break somewhere soon last week, he said no, no, it was out of the question as Veronica's keeping his passport in their safe until the function room plans are finished. He shrugged and sighed and tried to look gutted about it, but I suspect it was his idea.

'We're using a system of proportional representation,' says Veronica. She hands me one of those tiny pens Argos go in for, and a slip with '1st, 2nd, 3rd' written on it, then points to the far wall of the hall where thirty-odd photographs of hopefuls are pinned. 'Choose your favourite three and pop the slip into this box on your way out.

Hello, Pam. We're using a system of proportional representation...'

As I wander down the room, I write 'Oliver Jeffries' against '1st', just in case I'm tempted by another when I get there. All candidates were asked to submit a recent photo of themselves, and I spot Oliver's immediately – so far from recent that he's in a college scarf. A swathe of thick blond hair flops over one eye and a couple of textbooks are tucked under a cricket-sweatered arm. It's very *University Challenge* – 'Hello, I'm Oliver Jeffries from Upper Muckhill, and I'm reading *Brideshead Revisited*' – and about as far from beefcake as you can get, especially compared to Darren Eastwood shampooing his car in vest and 501s in the next photograph.

OK, second choice, second choice. I suppose it'll have to be Dad. The last thing I want to see all over the village for an entire month is my father in the altogether, but I'd hate to see him get no votes. 'Ken Grant' I write next to '2nd'. Luckily, Dan was forbidden by Poppy to enter – something about a mole – and Josh has probably been put off by all the work involved: finding a photograph, walking down to the village hall.

Several women are gathered at the far end of the wall, chatting excitedly. I make my way slowly past the Bobs and Daves and Petes, almost all with heads cocked and hands on hips, I notice, and hear Rose Jessop – seventy-eight if she's a day – whispering, 'Well, you know what they say about coloured chaps, don't you?' There are one or two giggles, then the little group goes quiet while we all write down 'Benny Fitzharris'.

'Oh hi, Mum,' says Poppy, emerging from the middle of the group and quickly smacking her slip of paper face down against her chest.

'Hi,' I say, kissing her cheek. 'How was your course? Useful?'

Her eyes grow wide and she colours up. 'Um, great, yeah.'

'Good.' I lean forward and peer at the photo of Benny. 'He looks fantastic, doesn't he?'

Poppy blushes even more and I'm beginning to feel cruel. She glances over at the picture and catches her breath at the sight of him. 'Alright, I suppose,' she says, suddenly all matter-of-fact and looking everywhere but at me. 'If you like that kind of thing.'

I lunch with an edgy Oliver who asks several times when the polling ends. 'Eight o'clock,' I say again. Then, 'Why?'

'Not sure I chose the best photo.'

'It's fine. You look very ... erudite.'

'Only ... I found this one.' He hands me a photograph I've never seen before, of an Oliver I can't say I've seen before either. Very slim, tanned and laughing, with shades perched sexily on his head and what looks like Greece in the background. The photo's been torn in half.

'Paula,' he explains.

'Ah.' I make a mental note to check all the bins later. 'It's very nice. Hang on, let's just neaten it up.'

Oliver passes me the scissors and with a few careful snips we've got a strangely narrow, but nevertheless attractive photograph of Oliver.

'Back in a tick,' I tell him, and hurry to the village hall, where, when nobody's looking because they're gathered around Benny's photo, I take down Swotty Oliver and pin up Taverna Man.

At four o'clock the mobile rings in Troy Cottage. 'It was totally out of order of me,' says Hamish, without even a 'hello', 'you

347

being married and upset and in public.' I get the feeling that he's rehearsed this but it's coming out all wrong.

I smile into the receiver. 'Don't worry about it.' Then there's a silence. 'Hamish?'

'I really want to see you.'

'I know.'

Bloody Barbara's at the kitchen table again. 'Oh, ha ha ha,' she's going at something Dad's just said. I charge, frosty-faced, straight for the kettle, and take it to the sink where it's evident no one's bothered to wash up the breakfast things.

Dad tears his attention away from Barbara. 'Making a pot, Ruby?'

'*Yes.*' I make as much noise as I can filling the dishwasher. It seems to do the trick. 'We'll be in the living room,' he yells to me.

'*Right.*'

After pouring myself a cup, I take a tray of tea things through to them and plonk it down so hard on the coffee table that nearby Ganja is startled from sleep and continues to bark until I've left the room and slammed the door.

In the kitchen I deep breathe for a while and sip tea. I'm just thinking I'll get back to work when Poppy walks in with babe and a bag of disposable nappies. 'Mu-uu-umm?' she asks. 'I don't suppose you'd–'

'No, I bloody *wouldn't*,' I tell her, and we all watch my mug fly shoulder height across the room until it drops and shatters on the Aga. Oh dear, tea everywhere.

Dad charges in. 'What the heck!'

Behind him, possibly superglued, is Barbara. 'Ruby?'

'No, no, just stay where you are,' I say with a maniacal laugh. '*I'll* clear it up. More tea, Dad? Barbara? A couple of days' free childminding, Poppy? Tell you what, I'll just lie down here by the door, shall I?' I surprise myself by doing just that. 'Come on then, wipe your feet on me. All at the same time if you want.'

Poppy jigs Grace – now with quivering bottom lip – up and down. 'Mum?'

I open my mouth to say something, but change my mind and slowly haul myself up and make as dignified an exit as I can.

Hamish is surprised to see me, blushing slightly as I wave and order myself a coffee. When he's finished with a customer he comes over. 'Are you alright?'

I stir my cup and look up at him. 'I think I'm turning into Basil Fawlty.'

'Oh.' He sits down. 'That's quite serious.'

'Yeah.'

'Want to talk about it?'

I nod. 'But aren't you busy?'

'Lucy can cope.' We both look over at the natural blonde, leggy young woman who replaced Josh. She's guiding a bespectacled middle-aged man with a loud voice towards the travel section. She's poised and pleasant and stunningly beautiful, and I think I hate her. 'She's fantastic,' he adds unnecessarily.

We're quiet for a while. My head's full of the irritations I want to spill out, but as I mentally go through them they suddenly seem minor and hardly worth voicing.

'How's Josh?' he asks.

'Hard up and a danger to himself.' I tell him about the mini fire.

'Poppy?'

'Thinks I'm running a free crèche.'

'Uh-huh. And your father?'

'Taking root and seeing a married woman.'

'OK. Oliver?'

'Alienating absolutely everyone.'

'Well, that's nothing new.'

'No.'

'And your novel?'

'I spent the whole of yesterday writing about footcare for the *Liddleton Echo*.'

He laughs and leans across the table and says, 'I adore you, you know.'

'How could you?' I whisper back.

'It's easy.' He tucks some strands of hair behind my ear. 'Come away with me? A weekend? Anything?'

'Don't be silly, Hamish. I mean, who'd walk the meals and cook the dogs?'

He cups one of my hands in both of his and strokes my thumb.

'Hamish, I could do with some help!' calls out Lucy.

'Ah,' he says, after looking from me to her and back to me. He gestures towards her with his head. 'Touch of the green-eyed monster, I think.'

'Really?' Lucy's beautiful mouth has become all pinched and ugly, I notice with glee. 'Is she sweet on you?'

'A bit.' He stands and holds out his hand. 'Come here.'

I follow him through to a tiny windowless office. Hamish shuts the door behind us and Lucy slams the till drawer shut.

Oliver came eleventh. Consequently, when he's not strutting around singing, 'Do Ya Think I'm Sexy?' he's up in the bedroom on his weights machine; a black, ceiling-height, monstrosity of a thing which recently had me screaming in the night when I woke to see my husband dangling from a set of gallows. It turned out he was beside me in a deep, exercise-induced sleep and only his towelling robe hung from the top bar of the apparatus.

Veronica, quite wisely, didn't go in for the Eurovision-style results display, so we'll never know if Dad only got *'deux points'* (mine and Barbara's). What we do know is that Benny managed to poll 652 – far more votes than there are women in the village, but the result, I guess, of Veronica's PR system.

Decision, I write while Oliver goes, 'Aaarggh,' above me, and now and then lets the weights thump down, causing the ancient ceiling over my head to shudder. *Shall I really throw myself into rural life and submit something to the Upper Muckhill Show in September? But what? So many inviting categories to choose from – Three Onions, A Victoria Sponge (recipe given), Four Courgettes, Chrysanthemums. I'm slightly puzzled by the 'Bucket of Compost' category. I mean, how will they judge it? With a teaspoon each? – Mm, a little heavy on the cabbage leaves, wouldn't you say?' And how will they know they're not awarding the 'First' rosette to something that was in B&Q the day before?*

I stop for a while and stretch and listen to Oliver, but then Hamish pops into my head, causing me to quietly gasp, so I hurriedly pick up the pen again. *Can there be anything more competitive than a group of people thrown together in the English countryside? If they're not vying to be May Queen, best quiz team, best float, best-kept garden or naked pin-up, then they're trying desperately to produce a better bucket of muck than their neighbour.*

'Aaarrrggghhh.'

I wonder–

'Aaarrrggghhh. Roo!'

Oh Lord. I leap from my chair – 'What?' – and take the stairs two at a time.

'Back,' he rasps, flat out on the narrow bench, one hand beneath him. 'Can't move.'

At the hospital they give him industrial-strength painkillers and a strange corset affair to which Oliver says, 'Over my dead body.' It's rather unfortunate that the nurse who eventually leads us to a bed and takes down details is our very own Penny Baker, who would come second only to Jean Crowbar should Upper Muckhill decide to run a Best Gossip competition. 'And how did you manage to do this then?' she asked.

As I drive us back into the village, people are throwing Oliver the odd knowing glance, and I begin to sense Penny has already been on the blower. This is confirmed when a tasteful card awaiting Oliver on the doormat wishes him a speedy recovery, 'from Veronica and Frank. PS. Hope you didn't have to "weight" too long at Casualty!'

'Oh, the humiliation,' he says as I lower him on to the sofa.

Dad's chuckling at something in the *Liddleton Echo* while Oliver gingerly stretches out. 'I'm absolutely famished, Roo. Must be the tablets.'

'Right.' I suddenly foresee weeks of slavery ahead of me and sigh. 'I'll make a sandwich or something.'

Dad puts his paper down. 'Best let me do it, love. You know what a crazed, homicidal lunatic you turn into in that kitchen. Ham all right, Oliver?'

'Lovely.'

Dad shuffles off and firmly shuts the door behind him.

Oliver groans. 'I'll be a figure of fun in the village.'

'No you won't,' I say, sitting beside him and patting his hand reassuringly while we listen to Dad laughing uncontrollably in the kitchen.

We lapse into silence for a while. 'Multiplex given go-ahead', I read on the front of the newspaper flung aside by Dad. I twist my head to see the smaller headline at the bottom of the page. 'Estate agent dies'.

Oliver gives a little groan. 'I'll have to give up my calendar slot. I mean, I can hardly pose with a grimace and a hand in the small of my back.'

I surreptitiously inch the newspaper towards me. 'They can just do a horizontal shot,' I tell him. 'It'll be very provocative, I'm sure.'

Local estate agent Miles Fletcher-Maycock – *Hamish's estate agent!* – was found dead at his Liddleton home yesterday evening. When Mr Fletcher-Maycock, 31, failed to turn up for work for two days in a row at Barker Brown's Liddleton branch and could not be contacted via his mobile phone, a colleague broke into the house in Kestrel Avenue, where Mr Fletcher-Maycock lived alone, and found him floating in his pond. A police spokesman said they believe his death had been the result of an unfortunate accident with the pond's pump.

'Isn't it, Roo?'

Was Oliver still in the room? I'd quite forgotten. 'Yes, it is,' I say, while I speed-read the rest.

The article gives a potted biography and one or two details of family in Stratford-upon-Avon. I leap from the sofa, causing Oliver to yelp. 'Sorry. Got to make a quick call.'

After bounding over to Troy Shed, I ring Hamish on his mobile.

'Have you heard about Miles Fletcher-Maycock?'

'Who?'

'Your estate agent.'

'Oh yeah? Been ticked off by the Office of Fair Trading, has he?'

'No, worse. *Much* worse.'

'Not...'

'Mm.'

'In the bath?'

'Pond. Something to do with the pump.'

'Bit of a strange coincidence, wouldn't you say?'

'Well...'

'See you in our pub in half an hour?'

I think of Oliver. 'Make that an hour.'

'So, that's two local estate agents involved in water and electricity fatal accidents.'

'Mm,' I say, and throw a twenty. 'Yes!'

Hamish pulls the darts out of the board and chalks up my score. 'You're getting too good at this game.'

'I had an excellent teacher,' I tell him, and flash back to Hamish with his chest against my back, hand over mine, slightly minty breath in my ear as we both aimed a dart. 'OK ... short, sharp thrust,' he whispered, and I almost fainted.

Game over, we sit down with our half-pints. Hamish pulls out a pad and pen. 'OK,' he says. 'I'll make a few enquiries about this ... what's his name ... Fletcher-May...?'

'Cock,' I tell him, and wonder if he did that deliberately.

I've had a week of serfdom now. 'Bit more to the left,' Oliver's telling me. Apparently the light from the window is shining on *Quincy*. It's just after two p.m.

I turn the TV a couple more degrees. 'That OK?'

'No, right a bit now... Yep, that's it.'

'Anything else, now I'm here?'

'A cup of coffee and a cheese roll would be nice.'

'*OK.*'

'Did you know,' he calls out while I'm buttering the bread, 'that your dad's let his flat in Spain for the winter?'

'What!' I stride back into the living room with the butter knife.

'Heard him on the phone.'

I flop in an armchair and digest the information. I suppose he could be planning to elope with Barbara and start a new incognito life in a Scottish croft. On the other hand, he could just be planning to live out his days here and we'll be constantly tripping over them both.

'Roo?'

'Mm?'

'Sandwich?'

'Oh, right.'

The phone rings. 'Don't answer it!' snaps Oliver. 'It might be Veronica again about the plans.'

'Oh, don't be silly,' I say, and pick it up. 'Hello?'

'It's Veronica.'

'Hi, Veronica.' Actually, she doesn't sound too friendly.

'May I speak to Oliver?'

'He's just resting at the moment.'

'Perhaps you could take a message?'

'Of course.'

'Tell him he's fired.'

'Will do.'

She hangs up.

'Ah,' he says wearily when I tell him, and then, 'Don't suppose you'd nip round and get my passport back, would you?'

The phone rings again. 'I forgot to mention,' says Veronica, 'that we're having a calendar meeting tomorrow in the village hall at eight. Melanie Parsons will be giving tips on glamour modelling. Perhaps your husband could drag himself along. Goodbye.'

'You know,' says Oliver, after I've passed on the news. He sits himself up straight and prods at his lower back, 'I've noticed a definite improvement the last couple of days.'

I hear a commotion in the kitchen and find Josh has let himself in, as have a large bulging rucksack, several pairs of trainers and a computer. 'Alright?' he says, pulling his head out of the fridge, then sticking it back in. 'Fuckin famished.'

'What...?' I ask, pointing to his things.

He stands up with three eggs, a tub of cherry tomatoes and a pack of bacon in his arms. 'Yeah, right,' he says, kicking the fridge door shut behind him. 'Had a bust-up with Benny over the phone bill. Tight-fisted git. It's alright for him with his monthly allowance.'

He opens four cupboards before he finds the frying pan, then picks up the bottle of extra-special, extra-virgin olive oil I paid too much for and says, 'Hey, nice one.'

I rush over and grab it and hand him the Spry. 'So where are you going to go?'

'What?'

'You know, to live?'

'Oh, right. Wondered if I could crash here for a while?'

'But we haven't got any spare rooms, Josh. And Oliver's permanently on the sofa.'

He cracks the eggs into the pan, says, 'Fuck, broke one,' then points to a large bundle under the table. 'No prob. Got a tent.'

I put the butter knife down before I throw it and walk calmly from the house and over to Troy Shed, where I get Lydia Wildgoose up on screen, and with no premeditation begin Chapter Three.

Lydia woke at eight thirty, and before opening her eyes, slowly extended an arm to the other side of her double bed and patted tentatively. Ah good, no one there, and a Sunday to boot. Heaven. She lay for a while planning just how she'd indulge herself. Coffee and croissant, an aromatic bath, a stroll down to the shop for a newspaper. She might buy herself some flowers, do a little light housework (though hardly necessary in her spotless, open-plan apartment), rustle up a small artichoke salad for lunch, watch an afternoon movie, then spend the evening calling the more interesting of her friends for the latest gossip. 'Mm,' she said, before stretching, yawning, rolling over and going back to sleep.

I read through it with narrowed eyes, wondering how many other writers have grown to loathe their central character. Maybe I should kill her off, I'm thinking, and replace her with someone I could warm to. A full-time secondary school teacher called Wendy, perhaps, with a migraine problem, four adolescent children and an irascible live-in mother. She'd have a semi-absent husband – on the premises, but not really there – a guinea pig the kids have lost interest in and an old Fiesta with a clutch problem. Might be hard to weave the sex in, though. I plough on.

Lydia woke again, blinked slowly, picked up the bedside phone and pressed one key. 'Hi,' she said with a husky chuckle into the mouthpiece. She moved the soft cotton sheet to one side, spread open her long, tanned legs and caressed a silky thigh. 'How would you like breakfast in bed, sweetie?'

SEPTEMBER

Still hot. When searching for more light, sleeveless clothes in town this morning, I could find only jumpers, coats, boots and shimmering Christmas partywear. Why do the retailing powers that be insist that winter starts in July and summer round about Pancake Day? Most of the shops had end-of-season sale rails: size 18 shorts, lime-green T-shirts, things with tassels. Even if you do find something you think quite nice and slashed to one pound fifty, you can't possibly buy it, knowing it's been rejected by every other woman in the city.

So desperate was I for something different to wear that, back at home, I dusted down an old Laura Ashley dress. I'm swanning around the house in it now, feeling like Nanette Newman in *Stepford Wives*. Which is good in a way – the living room is gleaming with Pledge and the cushions have never been treated to such a plumping – but I decide to go upstairs and change before I find myself gliding over to the new couple in Marjorie Bradshaw's place with a fixed smile and a steaming casserole.

'That would be topless, would it, ha ha ha,' I hear Oliver say quietly through his slightly open door.

Topless? He's probably talking about an extension or something.

'Obviously you can't come here.'

Must be talking to a client who hasn't got a car.

'I've got some oil if you– Mm, I *bet* you have.'

Engine oil? I head for the bedroom to change into something more butch.

Saturday morning, and two people are pouring into the village hall for the Upper Muckhill Show – well, three if you count me, clutching my pen and pad to do a write-up. Inside we find half a dozen others gathered around exhibits and talking in hushed tones. It's hard to know what they can be finding to say about a plate of shallots or a quiche Lorraine they're not allowed to try, so I manoeuvre myself to within earshot of Jean Crowbar and her friend.

'They say he's got debts coming out his ears.'

'And another kid over in Crompton.'

They both shake their heads in despair.

'Grows a lovely marrow, though, don't he?'

'Oh, yes.'

For some reason I'm writing all this down.

A child begins wailing in the corner. I go over and find it's Maximilian. 'But you got third prize, Maxi,' Tina's telling him. 'That's ever so good.'

'I want first,' he says between sobs. I can't help feeling this isn't normal behaviour for an eight-year-old.

The children of the village were invited to create a 'garden on a plate'. I take a look. First prize went to a veritable Hanging Gardens of Babylon by four-year-old Gemma Knight, who obviously had someone with RA after their name helping her. Second is what you'd expect: Playdoh flowers, a mirror for a pond. Maximilian's is something of a Gulf War scene, made up of sand and toy soldiers in various stages of death.

'Hey, it's great,' I tell him. 'Just like your garden.'

Tina takes umbrage at this, and while Maximilian is tipping his exhibit on to the table in a fit of pique, I try to explain that I meant just the sandpit. She yanks her son away and I make a note not to let her near my hair for a while.

I jot down the names of all the winners and hurry to the church to see the flower categories. Life really doesn't get much more exciting than this.

'Well,' I hear Veronica telling Angela, our local bobby's wife, 'the other judges and I thought it was original, vibrant and refreshingly unstudied.'

'Mm,' says Angela in agreement, finger on chin. She leans forward and peers. 'And this leaf is so unusual.'

I look through the space that's formed between them and see an arrangement of enormous peonies similar to those Dad has produced in our garden this year, several bits of honesty, just like the ones under our front window, and, in a nice contrast to the red and cream, the odd bit of cannabis plant.

My eyes drop to the two labels at the base of my best vase. 'First Prize' announces one. 'Josh Grant and Dan Palmer' says the other.

Veronica nods knowingly and cocks her head at Angela. 'Part of the fern family.'

I go home and knock on the tent. 'Josh?'

There's a groan and clonk before he appears at the flap, rubbing his head and cursing the gaslamp.

'Well, you and Dan got first prize for your

flower arrangement.' I look over to where the peonies used to be. 'Congratulations.'

'Hey,' he says, emerging from the tent with a litre bottle of Coke. 'Did you notice–'

'Yes.'

'Me and Dan had this bet on, yeah? I said Upper Muckhill's a cool, spliff-tolerant place and Dan reckoned we'd have village vigilantes after us with big fuckin guns. Ha! Looks like I won twenty quid.'

'Well, actually,' I tell him, 'I don't think they recog–'

'I'd better go and get our weed back, though,' he says, suddenly looking worried. 'Worth a bit, that is.' He reaches into the tent for a canvas bag, then sprints across the garden in bare feet and ripped shorts.

I hunt around for Oliver, but he's nowhere to be found. Dad tells me a taxi came for him.

'A what? Why? Where's he gone?'

'Search me.'

'He's been behaving oddly lately, don't you think?'

'No odder than others round here.'

Josh bursts through the door. 'Some fucker's only gone and nicked it.'

'Language, son,' says Dad, rather pointlessly.

Up in Oliver's office, I flick through his page-a-day diary to today's date. 'MP' is the only entry. Member of Parliament, Military Police or Melanie Parsons, I wonder. I deduce it's the last one, as there's a photo of the said MP pinned to the top right corner of Oliver's drawing board. She's wearing a large gold crucifix – that's all – and has a mobile number scrawled across her navel.

I pick up the phone and dial. It rings for a while. 'Hello, Melanie Parsons,' she eventually sings in a lovely Essex brogue.

'Could I speak to Oliver, please?'

'Just one moment.'

I hear muffled voices before Oliver gives a tentative, 'Hello?'

'Hi.'

'Roo. Hi,' he says, far too cheerfully.

'What are you doing?'

'Having a bit of back treatment. Didn't I tell you? Melanie's a masseuse.'

'Is it helping?'

'Yes, yes. Definitely.'

'Oh good. See you later, then.'

'Right.'

I lean back in Oliver's nice comfy office chair and listen to an altercation between Dad and Josh in the kitchen. I sigh, close my eyes and conjure up Lydia Wildgoose. I decide that the man she's suspected of withholding information – tall, dark-haired, southern European hue – has agreed to meet her in the bar of the hotel he's staying at.

'You look a little tense,' he told her over their cocktails.

'Mm,' said Lydia, rubbing at the back of her neck. 'I am rather.'

He stretched out an arm and gently pummelled the area between her shoulder and neck. 'I give a mean massage, you know.'

'Oh, really?' She crossed her legs with a quiet swish of silk and nylon.

'Want me to show you?' asked Hamish.

Hamish?

I hear someone taking the stairs two at a time. 'Phone call, Mum.' Josh hands me the mobile.

'Oh hi,' I say into it. 'I was just thinking about you.'

'I'm always thinking about you.'

'Hang on. Thanks, Josh,' I say pointedly. He's hovering in the doorway, afraid to go downstairs, no doubt. 'Bye.'

'Oh yeah, right.'

I hear him bound down the stairs and slip out the front door.

'Still there?' I ask Hamish.

'Of course. Listen ... I, um ... I was just wondering if you'd like a trip to Stratford on Sunday? Have a quick chat with the Fletcher-Maycocks.'

My stomach does a little flip. Better act cool, though. 'Sunday,' I say, almost yawning. 'Could be tricky.'

'Go on.'

'Oh, OK.'

Oliver arrives home at seven forty-five. I hear the taxi idling for a long time, so go and investigate and find that a not-too-tall, middle-aged cabbie has Oliver half flopped over one of his shoulders and is inching his way up the path. I rush over to help. 'Oliver? What happened?'

He puffs hard as he tries to take some of the weight on his own feet. 'Bit of a relapse.'

We lower him on to the sofa. I pay the taxi driver, thank him profusely and pour Oliver a whisky. I can't help noticing he's wearing a lilac chiffon scarf and enquire as to why.

'Ah. Got a bit chilly after the massage. Borrowed this from Melanie.'

'It's very fetching.'

Oliver stretches out. 'Couldn't get me a duvet, could you, Roo? Think it's best if I sleep here tonight.'

I look at my watch and sigh. Five to eight.

With a large glass of wine and a couple of candles, I make my way over to Troy Shed where, enveloped in the aroma of next-door's barbecuing steaks, I write up Lydia's massage scene. In an inspired moment I make the man blond, so as to keep Hamish out of the picture. Seems to work. I'm clicking on 'save' when a couple of knocks and a high-volume 'Anyone in there?' make me jump out of my skin and look around for the nearest weapon. 'HELLO?' shouts Norman.

I relax and go to the door. 'Care to join us?' he asks.

It's one of those disorientating Indian summer evenings. Warm and sultry, but getting dark by eight. Perfect for a cosy barbecue. 'Love to. Thanks. I'll just get some vegebangers from the freezer.'

'Got plenty of meat. Come on.'

'Well, let me bring a bottle of wine, anyway,' I add, suddenly realising that what I want is a juicy, medium-rare steak.

In the kitchen I choose a relatively cheap bottle of red, just in case there are a hundred and fifty people there ready to pounce on it, then go and check on Oliver. He's fast asleep, the remote in his hand, the duvet kicked off and the lilac chiffon scarf half way towards the floor. On his exposed neck is a mottled purple mark, the size of a ten pence piece and similar in shape to the Isle of Wight. Melanie Parsons obviously ascribes to the brutal school of massage, I decide, then take myself off to the party, which I suspect will be me, Norman, Trevor and a couple of tethered goats.

Due to unexpected hold-ups, such as emergency work on the village hall wiring and Jean Crowbar winning a fortnight on Lake Lucerne in a Swiss roll competition, the Upper Muckhill Players are putting on a 'Late Summer Production' of *Abigail's Party*. First night tonight. I leave Oliver on the sofa in the polo-neck jumper he's sweltered in for the past three days, and – having failed to wangle a 'press' pass from Veronica – join the queue to fork out seven pounds for a ticket.

I can't help thinking, as I switch from foot to foot behind the scruffy, bickering Granger family, that, were I another person, living in a different place with a dynamic partner and a heftily improved income, I might be doing something more exciting with my Saturday night. But I shake these thoughts away. Who knows, maybe Jean Crowbar's Abigail will move me to tears.

'I notice my letter didn't get into the August *Grapevine*,' says a voice behind me. This happens all the time.

'Can't fit them all in,' I say jollily to a fifty-something man in a blazer, whose name I know not, but probably should. Beyond him, further down the queue, I see Dad and Barbara surreptitiously canoodling. They're such an embarrassment. 'What was it about?' I ask.

'The Little Crompton Scrabble Club.'

'Ah, yes.'

He tells me about it as we shuffle forward, and I remain as animated and interested-looking as one can when it comes to Scrabble until we reach the door. 'You have to realise clubs like ours are the mainstay of a rural community,' he continues, while I hand Frank a tenner.

'I'm sure they are. I'll try and squeeze it into the next issue, but I can't promise anything.' I take my change and ticket and hurriedly move off.

'You publish far too many letters of

complaint, if you ask me,' Mr Blazer calls after me in a somewhat less friendly manner. 'And as for those stupid bloody poems...'

I'm not sure anyone did ask him.

'Oh, good, there you are Mrs ... er...' says Dan as he hands me Grace and a small drawstring bag. 'Pops says hope you don't mind, only she's got to write this pre-course essay.' He kisses Grace's head and rushes off to the orchestra pit.

I look around for a seat while Grace eats my handbag strap. The place is filling up fast but I eventually spot an empty place next to Josh and Benny, now best of friends again.

'Is anyone sitting here?' I ask, at which Josh says, 'You know you really ought to get your eyes tested, Mum,' and both he and Benny begin giggling uncontrollably, arms wrapped around their stomachs. I guess they've been at the wacky. Not a bad idea in the circumstances.

The play begins. We're very near the back and Jean isn't projecting too well. Grace is growing more bored and fractious by the minute, trying to screw my nose off, pulling the hair of the extremely patient woman in front. I rummage in the bag and find her beaker, which quietens her down for a while and leaves me only having to put up with Josh and Benny tittering behind their hands and constantly tapping their size-twelve feet.

We struggle through an hour and a quarter to the interval, by which time Jean *has* moved me to tears and I decide Grace should go home.

'You're quite a little vixen, Mel,' I hear Oliver say when I enter the house an hour later, Poppy having got me to proofread her essay while I was there.

I slam the door shut and call out, 'Hi.'

There's a mumble and the clonk of the phone before he limps into the kitchen and says, 'Have a good evening?'

'I've had better.'

Oliver trundles off and I take my journal over to a gloriously quiet Troy Shed, where I chew on a pen for a while and try to think of anything but Stratford-upon-Avon.

DIY stores/garden centres, I eventually write for want of a more gripping subject, *must employ people especially to think up new titles for their ever-expanding range of goods. On a recent shopping trip to Brownlow's DIY and*

Garden Centre – now roughly the size of Luxembourg – with my insatiable father, I had trouble distinguishing between a 'Fence and Shed Brush', an 'Exterior Wall Brush' and a 'Pebbledash Brush'. To my inexpert eye they were the same brush. Similarly, 'Shed Roof Felt' looked suspiciously like 'Aviary Roof Felt' and 'Kennel and Hutch Roof Felt'. The we-saw-you-coming prize though goes to 'Garden Furniture Cleaner' which comes in the ubiquitous household spray bottle, and no doubt gets put in the cupboard under the sink next to 'Garden Ornament Cleaner'.

I put the journal down, do a bit more pen chewing and think of ways I can bottle out of tomorrow's trip. Car not working? Desperately ill aunt? A painful sty or unsightly rash? I cross those last two out. 'Look, I'm sorry, Hamish. If I don't defrost the freezer today, we'll be living on an iceberg.' Terrible. 'My brother and his fiancée have just turned up.' No, don't want to tempt fate.

Hmm, back to the journal. *Am becoming more and more concerned about possible intellectual gulf between Poppy and Dan. While returning Grace this evening couldn't help noticing their flat is littered with a combination of literary novels, economics books and several editions of the* Financial Times *(presumably Poppy's), and piles of* Loaded *and* What Car? *magazines (presumably not). As I sat there I hoped I was wrong, and that Poppy could tell me all the specs of the newest Toyota model, and Dan would choose John Maynard Keynes as his specialist subject on* Mastermind. *However, when Dan popped home during the interval and said he thought Abigail's was the most boring party he'd ever come across and couldn't see the point of making a panto out of it, I heard Poppy sigh heavily before she said, 'Play, Dan. It's a play.'*

One p.m. and I'm about to set off for my Liddleton rendezvous. 'Interview in Stratford,' I tell Oliver.

'Really,' he asks, with a quick glance at his watch. 'Think I'll just take it easy.'

'Back not too good?'

'No.'

'Planning any more sessions with Melanie?'

'Good Lord, no.'

'Do you want to drive or map read?' asks Hamish. 'There's a picturesque cross-country route we could take.'

My palms are damp, my vision's blurred

and my stomach's doing somersaults. Better navigate. I lock my car in Liddleton market square and head for his.

'Choose a CD,' he says, once we've got going.

I look through them. Handel, John Lee Hooker, John Williams, John Coltrane, Bach, Ella Fitzgerald, *Best of Kenny Rogers...* 'Kenny Rogers!' I say. 'Did you get that for–'

'Yep,' he says with a grin.

I slip it in the player and we listen to Kenny crooning until we're halfway to Stratford. I'm not sure it's Hamish's cup of tea, but it does relax me, until that is, 'Ruby Don't Take Your Love to Town' comes on and I have a guilt pang and quickly skip to the next track.

I watch the lovely scenery go by, thinking, well, this isn't so bad. Hamish hasn't declared undying love and lured me into a Warwickshire copse. I expect I'll be home by seven. Might make Oliver a special dinner, what with his back and everything.

'Here we are,' I hear Hamish say, as the engine's switched off.

'Mm?' I groan with a start, then pull myself up from asleep position. Asleep! 'That was quick.'

He laughs. 'Thanks for navigating.' He hands the map to me from his lap.

'Sorry.'

Just as we're getting out the car, my mobile rings. 'Hello,' I say groggily.

'It's Oliver.'

'Oh, hi.'

'Where are you?' he asks.

'Um, just arrived in Stratford.'

'Are you sure?'

I glance around. It looks like Stratford. I'm outside a half-timbered building with a 'Hamlet Guesthouse' sign. 'Yes. Why?'

'Oh ... er... well, nothing. See you later then.'

'Yep. Bye.'

Odd.

Hamish and I are sitting on a mink-coloured, two-seater sofa interviewing Mr Fletcher-Maycock, father of Miles. He looks absolutely lovely, I suddenly notice, in different shades of blue, and smells of something musky and expensive. Hamish, that is. Geoffrey Fletcher-Maycock, on the other hand, is the same colour as his wing-backed armchair – ashen complexion and all done up in beige – and looks as though he might smell of coal tar soap. 'G and T?'

he asks us.

'I'm afraid I'm driving,' says Hamish with a no-thank-you hand gesture.

'Good Lord, after coming all this way? Won't hear of it,' barks Geoffrey, hauling himself out of the chair and making his way to an array of bottles and decanters. 'Had a couple of cancellations and Chef's promising to excel himself with a grouse dish. You must stay the night.'

'That's very kind!'/'We couldn't possibly!' cry Hamish and I respectively.

Geoffrey casts a glance at my wedding ring. 'I'll have young Rachel prepare the Ophelia Room.'

'Actually, we're not–'

'Glorious view of the lake it's got.' He hands me a colossal gin and tonic.

'I'm sorry, do you think I could have something else?' I ask. 'Only gin makes me suicidal.'

'Ha! Well, we can't have that in the Ophelia Room, now can we?' He winks at Hamish. 'Keep her away from the lake, eh?'

We all go quiet for a while and picture poor Miles in the pond.

After a stroll round the lake – more of a large pond really – we dine with our hosts.

'So what you're saying,' whispers Mary Fletcher-Maycock, a petite, elegant woman, who's obviously been crying a lot, 'is that two ... um ... two local ... um–'

'Damn it, Mary, say it. *Estate agents.* Our son was an *estate agent.*' Geoffrey knocks back some Margaux and plonks his glass down on the dinner table. The rest of us jump.

'We were so hoping he'd go on the stage,' explains a shaky Mary. 'He was such a wonderful Hamlet in the sixth form.'

'Really?' I say. 'So was my husband.'

'Were you?' Mary asks Hamish.

'So they told me,' he says, quick as a flash, then adds a modest shrug.

'Anyway...' Mary continues, then seems to forget what she was about to say and stares thoughtfully through teary eyes at her untouched food.

Actually, mine's untouched too, but for a different reason. The Ophelia Room.

No amount of fine wine seems to dull my anxiety, or stop me fretting about karma. But hell, it's only fifty-five miles from Stratford-upon-Avon to Upper Muckhill. I'll get a taxi.

'And you say the police don't want to know?' asks Geoffrey. Hamish shakes his head. 'Uh-uh.'

'Have you really been to the police?' I ask
Hamish when the Fletcher-Maycocks have
gone to circulate amongst their other guests.
   'Hardly,' he says with an adoring smile
and a gentle touch of my upper arm. He
points to my plate. 'Aren't you going to eat
that?'
   'No.'
'I'm not sure you should be drinking on
an empty stomach, Ruby.' He lifts my dress
strap back into place, briefly stroking my
shoulder with the back of a finger. 'You
might do something you regret.'
   'I was thinking maybe I'd get a taxi home.'
   'Oh yes?'
I dab my mouth with the napkin, even
though I've eaten nothing, and excuse
myself.

'What do you mean, he's out again?' I ask
Dad from my phone in the ladies. 'He's
supposed to be mobilely challenged.'
   'Meeting some chap called Mel, I believe.'
   'Right.'
I explain that I might be stuck in Stratford
for the night, and he says, 'Oh, aye?' and
that he'd better go as he and Barbara are in

the middle of gin rummy.

'Well, money's no object,' I hear Geoffrey Fletcher-Maycock tell Hamish as I slide back into my seat. He puts a convoluted signature on a cheque, then hands it over. 'That should cover a week, shouldn't it?'

I hear Hamish swallow. 'I'd imagine so,' he says, taking it rather gingerly from Geoffrey's hand and pulling his wallet from a pocket.

'Report back in a week or so, and let me know what the damage is then, eh?'

'Will do.'

'Better go and chat up the Yanks,' says Geoffrey, rising from his seat and nodding towards a group of jolly octogenarians. 'Tell them Shakespeare was thought to have written the "To be..." soliloquy in that very corner.'

'Really?' Hamish and I ask.

Geoffrey winks exaggeratedly at us and tucks his chair under the table. 'Ah, almost forgot,' he says, turning back and foraging in his jacket pocket. 'Here, catch.'

A large object is suddenly hurtling towards us. My left hand shoots up and plucks it from the air, impressing Hamish enormously, I can tell.

'Spent years playing two-ball against a wall,' I explain, and put the key down on the table. A large plastic disc the size of a coaster tells us we're in Room 23, and Miss T. Ree's ethereal voice all of a sudden floats back to me. *The number twenty-three will open doors.*

We both casually ignore it.

'You can't possibly keep that cheque,' I tell Hamish.

He moves closer. 'I know.'

'Did you ever think Victor's death was murder?'

'Not for a moment.' He takes my hand in his and begins kissing each fingertip. I didn't know that happened in real life.

'It's funny, isn't it?' I say to Hamish, trying to think of something harmless and neutral to talk about while he works his way round my digits.

'Mm?'

'How... um ... how people don't really wink any more. You know, like Geoffrey just did. Not unless they're over seventy or Anne Robinson. Why is that?'

Hamish stops and tops up my glass. 'Well... I suppose if you're not careful it could be construed as sexual harassment.'

I ponder for a while on how one might

wink carefully.

'You know...' I start again, with no idea of where my sentence might be going. *Twenty-three. Is this what she meant?* 'I ... er ... I really think Mel Gibson was the best Hamlet I've ever seen. I mean, forget Laurence Olivier hamming it up with all that oedipal stuff.'

'Ruby.'

'Mm?'

'Shut up.'

He takes my chin in the crook of his finger and turns my face towards his. 'I don't know about you,' he says after a warm soft kiss, 'but I'm bushed.'

On waking to bright sunshine I do a Lydia, tentatively feeling the other side of the bed.

Damn.

I spend some time examining the trail of clothes leading to the door, carefully working out which are mine, before sliding from the bed, silently picking them all up and tiptoeing to the ensuite bathroom – a room I decide I hate, as everywhere I turn there's a woman in a mirror giving me a disgusted, how-could-you look. I step into the shower to get away from her.

No matter how hard I try I can't shower quietly, and before I know it Hamish is sliding back the Perspex door and joining me with a 'Morning, gorgeous' and a pleasing nuzzle of my neck.

Ah well, in for a penny.

Monday evening journal entry.

Everything a bit strained on Troy Cottage front. Lunchtime (and only) conversation with spouse:

Oliver: Why was your car parked in Liddleton market place yesterday?

Me (thinking quickly but not that cleverly): I caught the train.

Oliver: Ah, so the railway's reached Liddleton at last. Not bad after two hundred years.

Me: I mean bus.

Bit of a silence.

Me: What were you doing in Liddleton anyway?

Oliver: Went for a drink with Mel. Um, Melvin. Doing a bit of business together. Don't suppose you remember him.

Me: No, no, I remember. Big blonde hair and breast implants.

Oliver (looking shocked): She's got implants?

Me: It's obvious, Oliver.

Longer silence while colour fades from Oliver's cheeks and we pretend to read our newspapers.

Dad (entering room): Anyone brewing up?

DECEMBER

'Settled in then?' asks Ali in the corner shop.

'Yes, thanks, it's great.'

No one visits, but I don't tell her that. And besides, I rather like it. Actually, it's not true to say no one comes. Josh has popped in a few times when he's been in town. Hamish visits when I let him. Oliver often rolls up too. We've managed to stay friends, as they say. In fact, he even comes round and pours his troubles out. Since his flingette with Melvin, as I call her, Oliver's gone through quite a number of young women of a similar ilk. Told me he hates the idea of going out with people who've never heard of Led Zeppelin, it's just that they've got these lovely bouncy titties. 'Almost as nice as yours,' he added considerately.

'Better get back to work,' I tell Ali.

'Huh, call that work?'

'It's harder than you think.'

'I bet it is,' she says with a throaty laugh and a nudge that sends my packet of basmati rice flying.

I let myself into my flat and hear the phone ringing, but don't get to it in time.

'Hello, lass,' says Dad's message. 'Just ringing about Christmas again.'

Oh hell. How can I tell him I can't really face it? That I'd just like to be on my own, preferably in some tropical spot with dusky young men fanning me.

'Barbara's now making the cake,' he continues. I hear a 'Yoo hoo,' in the background. 'And young Josh has gone off to fetch a tree.'

Dad's certainly knocked Josh into shape. Last thing I heard he was decorating Troy Cottage in lieu of rent.

'We've invited Oliver. Says he'll bunk down in the shed with Josh.'

'Unless Ruby wants to bunk down with him?' shouts Barbara.

Oliver or Josh?

'Ta-da, then love. Let us know.'

Right, back to work. I get Lydia back up on screen. Where was I? Oh yes, trying to think of another word for a man's member. I've exhausted the thesaurus and turn instead to my pile of well-thumbed erotic novels. Shaft? Sounds painful. One desperate author writes of her hero's throbbing lingam. I look it up in the dictionary and find it's Hindu. I'm not sure a lingam could sound anything but limp, so rule it out. Ali has no idea how difficult this business is.

I give up for a while and dwell on Christmas. It would be nice to see them all again, especially Poppy, who's been busy with her course and making another go of it with Dan after their autumn bust-up. I do miss little Grace, one in a week's time. *Send big birthday present*, I write in my diary.

I e-mail Miss T. Ree. **Should I have a family Christmas? Please reply a.s.a.p., Ruby**. I try not to do this too often, but she was spot on with the number twenty-three business. Not only did it open the door to the Ophelia Room, but at breakfast the next day, when Hamish indiscreetly brought up my raunchy private detective at our shared table, it turned out one girl's cousin's best friend worked at Libido Books and that was just the kind of thing they wanted.

Actually, it wasn't exactly what they wanted – 'Fab,' wrote editor Jonty Phillips after receiving my manuscript. 'Just thin the plot and up the ante. Remember sex, sex, sex!'

This I did in a week, and they liked it. Now they want another eighty thousand words. I've only written three – thousand, that is – and have already used up all my euphemisms.

'…his manhood…' I type in with a sigh.

After an hour or so, I check for incoming e-mails. There's one from Miss Ree. **Yuletide will see you fulfill** (sic) **a long-held desire,** she tells me.

Hey, perfect. I get my script up on screen, delete 'manhood' and type in 'long-held desire'.

Around six I shut down the computer, stretch and think mm, long bubbly soak. I go to the bathroom, turn on the taps, pour various liquids and oils in and strip off. I then pad naked through to my lovely living room – switching on the light and admiring my new-found tidiness on the way – grab a glass of wine and flip through the CDs for something nice to listen to. I pause at After History's demo CD – no, another time maybe – and decide on the Eagles.

I'm leaning back in the warm, silky water, sipping at wine and humming along to 'Peaceful Easy Feeling' when Hamish comes to mind. Inevitable really. I sigh contentedly, thinking about last weekend when he was up from Brighton and we got swept away on the passion front. Totally knackering, but it gave me some fresh material. Hamish is opening another café/bookshop and flits between the two cities. Sometimes I'm just too busy to see him when he's in town, and then sometimes I'm not. A good arrangement as far as I'm concerned, and when he asks for a key I say, 'Yeah, yeah, I'll get one cut for you,' fingers crossed behind my back.

I lower my head back into the water, close my eyes and think about whether to have a pizza or an Indian delivered. I haven't cooked in weeks. Not cooking gives you so many more hours in a day to ... well, do things other than cook. Hamish tends to feed me when he's here. Last weekend he did his version of the Naked Chef. That was nice.

My ears emerge from the frothy water to the sound of an insistent doorbell. Oliver, I bet. Perhaps he'll nip down the road for a takeaway. I heave myself up, wrap things in towels and mutter, 'Alright, alright,' at the repetitive buzz.

At the big bay window of my first-floor flat, I pull the curtain to one side, and with a little craning of the neck see not Oliver, but Poppy, standing in the dark by the door, hand-in-hand with Grace. Behind them on the pavement are two suitcases, a rucksack, a little sit-on rabbit vehicle and a dog.

Possibly Ganja. It's hard to tell through the rain now pelting the windowpane. Someone is pulling away in a hire van.

I stop breathing, just in case they can hear me, then slowly inch the curtain back into place, pulling a face as I do so. But it's too late.

'Hi, Mum!' calls Poppy.

Three wet heads are now looking up at me. Poppy waves. Grace begins jumping on the spot with excitement. The dog barks.

The publishers hope that this book has given you enjoyable reading. Large Print Books are especially designed to be as easy to see and hold as possible. If you wish a complete list of our books please ask at your local library or write directly to:

Magna Large Print Books
Magna House, Long Preston,
Skipton, North Yorkshire.
BD23 4ND

This Large Print Book, for people
who cannot read normal print,
is published under the auspices of

THE ULVERSCROFT FOUNDATION

... we hope you have enjoyed this book.
Please think for a moment about those
who have worse eyesight than you ...
and are unable to even read or enjoy
Large Print without great difficulty.

You can help them by sending a
donation, large or small, to:

**The Ulverscroft Foundation,
1, The Green, Bradgate Road,
Anstey, Leicestershire, LE7 7FU,
England.**
or request a copy of our brochure for
more details.

The Foundation will use all donations
to assist those people who are visually
impaired and need special attention
with medical research, diagnosis
and treatment.

Thank you very much for your help.